My Husband's Wife

Amanda Prowse has always loved crafting short stories and scribbling notes for potential books. Her first novel, *Poppy Day*, was self-published in October 2011. Her novels *What Have I Done?* and *Perfect Daughter* have been number one bestsellers.

Amanda lives in Bristol with her husband and their two sons. She has now published ten novels and six short stories.

www.amandaprowse.org

Also by
Amanda Prowse

Novels

Poppy Day
What Have I Done?
Clover's Child
A Little Love
Will You Remember Me?
Christmas For One
A Mother's Story
Perfect Daughter
The Christmas Cafe
Another Love

Short Stories

Something Quite Beautiful
The Game
A Christmas Wish
Ten Pound Ticket
Imogen's Baby
Miss Potterton's Birthday Tea

Amanda
Prowse

My Husband's Wife

HEAD
of ZEUS

First published in the UK in 2016 by Head of Zeus Ltd.

9 7 5 3 1 2 4 6 8

A catalogue record for this book is available from
the British Library.

ISBN (HB) 9781784977764
ISBN (XTPB) 9781784977771
ISBN (E) 9781784977153

Typeset by Adrian McLaughlin

Printed and bound in Germany
by GGP Media GmbH, Pössneck

Head of Zeus Ltd
Clerkenwell House
45–47 Clerkenwell Green
London EC1R 0HT

WWW.HEADOFZEUS.COM

I am my husband's wife, a role I cherish, every single day. This book is for my Simeon who encourages me to follow my dreams, who loves me unconditionally and who has taught me that the real world is what happens behind our front door, everything else is just pretend. I love you Mr P, my soulmate. X

Prologue

Rosie always laid three places at the dinner table.

Mum, Dad and herself.

Three knives, three forks and three wipe-clean placemats with scenes of Venice printed on them.

Every evening after school, she ate her tea with pictures of the Grand Canal, St Mark's Square and the Bridge of Sighs lurking beneath her plate. She had a hankering to visit these places despite having no idea where they were. They looked mighty impressive, even with an escaped baked bean sitting astride a gondola or a blob of ketchup in the middle of the grand basilica.

Her dad never mentioned their eating arrangements. He simply smiled, handed her her plate and gave the same mono-tone instruction that she sounded in her head with precision as he spoke it. *'Mind out, the plate's hot.'*

She would wait until he went back into the kitchen to

fetch the gravy or the glasses of weak orange squash that accompanied their evening meal and then she'd touch her finger to the edge of the china. It felt daring and illegal and was about the closest she got to misbehaving. The temperature was only ever warm at best.

The first time her friend Kev came home for tea, he hadn't been invited as such, he just happened to be sitting in front of their TV when her dad popped the macaroni cheese under the grill to bubble. It felt rude not to invite him to stay. Rosie set the table with four places to accommodate their guest.

Kev smiled as he took his seat and looked up at her. 'You've set four places,' he pointed out, as if she had done so in error.

Rosie felt panic flutter in her throat, unwilling to admit that she always laid a place for the mum she had never known, let alone eaten with. She liked Kev, but she didn't know if she could trust him to keep this secret. Recounted out loud, it might make her seem weird, and at school weird was poison; it isolated and alienated you. Like all her classmates, Rosie feared weird.

She was trying to think what to say, how to explain, when her dad walked in carrying two plates heaped with golden-crusted macaroni cheese and slices of ham.

'Four places set, Rosie?' He looked at Kev and tutted. 'She never was very good with numbers. Mind out, the plate's hot.'

Her dad gave her an almost imperceptible wink and Rosie felt a rush of love for him that was new and overwhelming.

It made her forgive him a little, for having driven her mum away in the first place.

One

Having lived in the small seaside town of Woolacombe her whole life, it was hard for Rosie Tipcott to see it the way visitors saw it. Where tourists might rave about the surfing, linger for hours in the famous sand dunes or spend every afternoon on the crazy-golf course, Rosie was often preoccupied with what to make for tea, how many shifts she'd get that week or whether she'd remembered to switch off the iron.

There was of course the odd day when she would take a moment from her chores to sit on her favourite bench up on the Esplanade and look out at the big, big sea foaming against the deserted beach at Barricane. Or when her eyes were drawn to the dazzling red sunset, as beautiful as any on earth. Either could stop her in her tracks and quite take her breath away. But what she really loved about the North Devon town was that it was home, the place where she lived in a quiet backstreet with her beloved husband and daughters.

was not a day for taking time out to appreciate lacombe's charms. In the cramped cloakroom under the stairs of their stone-built terrace in Arlington Road, Rosie peered at the peach-coloured hand towel that she had just lobbed over the little wooden shelf so as to hide it from view. She took her time, washing her hands and then drying them by flicking the droplets into the sink and finishing them off on her jeans so she didn't have to move the towel. Her stomach leapt in anticipation and she closed her eyes to quell the excitement. She then applied a squirt of hand cream that she massaged into the gaps between her fingers, sniffing the intoxicating scent of jasmine as she did so. This was one of her small joys, a little luxury, courtesy of Auntie Mags last Christmas.

'Mum?'

'What, love?' Rosie let her head hang on her chest. All she wanted was five minutes! She'd even laid the foundations so she could disappear for that small window of time, asking if either of the girls needed a drink or the loo. They had both shaken their heads and she had mistakenly thought she was safe.

'Leona's got my rubber!' Her daughter's Devonian accent turned the last syllable into the longest.

Rosie sighed; having to referee between her daughters was a constant. When her day was going well, it was amusing, the things they found to squabble about. But when she was tired, it was draining.

'I'll be out in a minute, but tell her to give it you back.'

'She can't!'

'For goodness' sake, Naomi, I'll be out in a sec! Can you just give me one minute please!'

'It's my favourite one. You know, the one that came in that set from Nan that looks like a little poo with a face on it.'

Sweet Jesus! 'Just ask your sister nicely to give it back to you, please, love. Just give me one second! I'll be out in a mo.'

Her daughter started knocking on the door in a slow rhythmic beat, as if her blathering through it wasn't irritating enough.

'I can't! She put it up her nose and now she can't get it out.'

Rosie closed her eyes as her eldest kicked the door, making the bottom flex.

'Don't kick the door!' As so often with the kids, she found herself shouting.

'But she's got my little poo rubber stuck up her nose and I need it!' Naomi shouted back.

Rosie grabbed the fringed hand towel that had been hiding her pregnancy test and stared at the little clear windowpane. Only one blue line. Negative. *Bugger it.* There was no time to properly consider her disappointment, the quake of regret in her gut. That would have to wait until the great rubber-up-the-nose debacle had been resolved.

Wrapping the white plastic spatula in a wad of loo roll, she shoved it into her bra and pulled her sweatshirt down sharply to hide it. She'd throw it in the bin later when the girls weren't around. But even wrapped in loo roll, hidden inside an old cereal box and with gravy scraped on it, there was still no guarantee that they wouldn't go foraging.

She pictured the early morning the previous year when she'd woken to the sound of her girls' laughter. Happy that they were playing nicely, she'd taken her time, coming to leisurely, finding her slippers and checking for chin hairs in the magnifying mirror she kept in her make-up bag by the side of the bed. She also checked before she went to sleep but knew that, unlike regular hairs, they could sprout overnight and take hold. It was only when she crept out onto the landing that she saw the kids peeling condoms from their fine foil wrappers, stretching them to their full length and flinging them down the stairs with a pencil.

'Aaaaagh!' she screeched, her hands outstretched, carefully trying to find the right words that would neither alarm nor interest the kids too much.

'Where... where did you find those?' she asked tentatively.

'They were just in the bathroom.'

'*Just* in the bathroom?' She couldn't believe her husband, Phil, could be that careless.

'Yes,' Naomi confirmed. 'In the bathroom. In the cabinet. In Dad's washbag. In the side pocket. Wrapped in a flannel...'

Rosie smiled at the memory of how she'd gingerly scooped up the slippery, rubbery nest from the bottom of the stairs and begun offering breakfast options, as if her hands weren't full of discarded prophylactics. 'Who wants what? We've got waffles, cereal, toast...'

Opening the cloakroom door, she came face to face with Naomi, who was still in her school uniform of grey skirt, red sweatshirt, white polo shirt and black tights but had for some reason, which Rosie knew there was no point in trying to fathom, put a pair of her dad's Y-fronts on and stuffed her skirt into them, making it look like she was wearing padded sumo pants. One of her bunches had worked loose, her face was covered with purple glitter paint and she resembled... Actually, Rosie was stumped as to what her seven-year-old resembled, but the words 'nut house' and 'hedge backwards' sprang to mind.

'Right, you have my full attention. What's going on that couldn't wait for five minutes?'

'Leona asked if she could borrow my rubber and I said no and she said she was going to have it anyway and she took my pencil case and I hit her with my yoghurt spoon and then she tipped all my stuff out and I called her a shitstar and then she took my little poo rubber and shoved it up her nose.'

'Can you take a breath, please?' Rosie kept her tone low-key, having learnt that if she raised the volume or level of hysteria, the girls would follow suit. The earlier exchange of shouts concerning door-kicking being a prime example.

'I don't really know where to start with that, Naomi.' She replayed her daughter's words. 'Actually, I do. Don't hit your sister, even if it's only with a yoghurt spoon. In fact, don't hit anyone, ever, with anything. And don't say shitstar, ever, to anyone.'

Naomi twisted her mouth and considered this. 'What if

7

it's someone's name and I have to ask them a question?' Her daughter stared at her, unsmiling.

Rosie shook her head. 'How do you mean?'

'Supposing I was a teacher and I had a girl in my class and her name was, say, Naomi Shitstar, and I had to do the register and I had to call her name out, could I say it then, like, "Naomi Shitstar? Has anyone seen Naomi Shitstar?"' She added a grown-up voice for full effect.

Rosie felt her laughter wanting to erupt. She turned her lips inwards and bit down hard.

'Are you crying, Mum?'

Rosie shook her head and let out a little squeak. She took deep breaths and leant against the bannister, trying to compose herself. 'So...' She coughed and decided to change the subject. 'Leona has a little rubber that looks like a poo up her nostril?'

'What's her notstril?'

'Her nostril, her nose hole?' Rosie pointed to her own face, remembering to keep her patience.

'Up *one* of her nose holes, yes.' Naomi gave an elaborate nod.

'I know I'm going to regret this, but what does she have up her other nose hole?'

'Erm, it's a piece of my compass.' Naomi picked at a loose thread on the men's underpants she was wearing.

'Please God, not the pointy piece?' Rosie's tone was becoming more urgent.

'No, Mum, it's like a little silver bolt thingy that holds the end on.'

Rosie ran her fingers through her thick, dark, wavy hair, gathering it into a knot at the base of her neck, as was her habit. 'And why does she have this piece of compass up her nose hole?'

'Because it wouldn't fit up the other hole because she already had my poo rubber up it!' Naomi widened her eyes at having to state the obvious.

'Of course she did. Where is your sister now?'

'Under the kitchen table.' She pointed along the hallway.

'Of course she is.'

'It wasn't my fault, it wasn't anything to do with me, not really.' Naomi avoided her mum's gaze, telling Rosie all she needed to know.

The two hurried to the little kitchen. Rosie dropped to her knees and smiled at her five-year-old, who sat huddled forward between the chair legs with her arms and legs folded and a pirate patch over one eye.

'Hey, Leona.'

'Hi, Mum.'

'Naomi says you might have some things up your nose that you can't get down, is that right?'

She nodded. 'Yes.' It sounded more like 'Djes'.

'Can you come out from under the table so I can have a look?' Rosie coaxed gently.

Leona shook her head vigorously and closed her one uncovered eye. She still believed that if *she* couldn't see anyone, then no one could see *her*. She had been doing this since she was a baby, when Phil used to call her Little Ostrich.

'All right! All right!' Rosie lifted her palm. She was worried about what vigorous head-shaking might do to the small compass part and tiny eraser that were currently lodged inside her youngest daughter's head. 'I do need to have a closer look, love. I'll try and come to you.'

Rosie moved one of the four chairs from the kitchen table and poked her head into the cramped gap. Her knees hurt from contact with the cold, tiled floor and a tiny round pebble, probably delivered from the sole of a shoe, bit into her skin. It was on Phil's list of jobs to lay some lino and remove the tiles that she found quite hard to keep clean. 'Shitstar!' she muttered at the sharp pain. This was all she needed. 'Nearly there!' She kept the tone light and jovial rather than give in to the panic at the images that had started to creep into her mind. She wondered how close to your brain 'up your nose' actually was.

Wedged between two chairs, she smoothed the long fringe from her youngest daughter's face. Leona's beautiful, curly, caramel-coloured hair sat on her shoulders in waves. It was Rosie's pride and joy and caring for it one of her great pleasures. It was one of the things she had dreamt about when she was a little girl – having a mum who would wash and style her hair, brush it and fix it in a bun for parties.

It was cramped under the table and Rosie wished she was a more comfortable size twelve so that she didn't have to heft her size-sixteen bottom into the small space.

'Right, let's have a look at you.' She gently held her daughter's chin and tilted her face to the right, swallowing her horror at the unmistakeable bump that sat almost at the top of Leona's nose. A quick investigation revealed a similar shape on the other side.

'Okay, well that's all good,' she lied. 'I need you to come out, Leona, so I can have a better look in the light.' Rosie began reversing out, only to find Naomi blocking her exit from under the table.

'Did you get them out, Mum? Can I have my rubber back?' she asked.

'Not yet, darling, but we will. It's all going to be fine.' She looked back at Naomi and smiled. It was this particular combination of words and actions that had proved to be the best weapons she had as a mother, a combination that could make monsters disappear from under beds, quash nervous tums before special events and even soothe pain when they were poorly.

'Shall I call Dad and tell him he needs to take us to the hospital again?' Naomi was now bouncing on the spot, delighted by the drama and the possibility of more to follow.

'No! Of course not! Don't be daft!' She squeezed Leona's hand. 'I'll have a little wiggle in the light and they will pop out, I'm sure. If you could just move out of the way, Naomi, so I can get out.'

'I know what you need, Mum, one of those beeping warnings that lorries and forklift trucks and diggers have, so you don't run anyone over!'

'Yes, thank you, love. I probably do.'

'Beeeeep! Beeeeep! Beeeeep!' Her daughter's sound effects accompanied the rather ungainly manoeuvre.

*

It was an hour ater, as the trio sat in the A&E department of North Devon District Hospital, that Phil arrived, harried and covered in plastering dust but grinning at his girls.

'How you feeling, Leo?'

'Okay.' The little girl shrugged and then yawned. It was getting late.

'The nurse said it shouldn't be too much longer and it'll be a quick solution.' Rosie turned towards her husband, twisted her index finger into a hook and mimed putting it up her nose and pulling down.

'Are they going to stick something up her nose?' Naomi leant forward in her chair, quick to comment, as her sister's eyes widened at the prospect.

'No! Well, maybe, and if they do, she won't feel a thing,' Rosie said soothingly.

'What *do* you look like?' Phil stared at his eldest, taking in her school skirt, which was crumpled into a creased mess, and her matted hair. 'You look like you've been living in a barn!'

'Leona May Tipcott?' The doctor stood in the brightly lit, rectangular room and called her name, louder than was strictly necessary, Rosie thought, considering that the only other patients waiting were an elderly man who had cut his head and a young male footballer with a dodgy looking ankle, neither of whom were likely to go by that name.

Naomi answered her dad just as loudly. 'I haven't been living in a barn, Dad. I'm all screwed up because I was wearing your pants, but Mum said I couldn't go out in public like that.'

Rosie smiled at the young medic and wondered what their little family must look like to a stranger: she in her jeans, blue Converse and sweatshirt, stressed and with the fish pie she had made for supper splattered over her front; Phil covered in plastering dust; Naomi with her sparkly purple face, wild hair and screwed-up skirt; and Leona with a pirate patch on her forehead and a bump up each nose.

'Yep, that's us!' She stood up.

Taking Leona by the hand, she smiled at her husband. 'This is nearly as embarrassing as the time we went to look at that show house and she took a dump in the bidet!'

'I remember.' He laughed.

As Rosie bent to pick up her little girl, a wad of loo roll fell out of her bra and landed on the floor, in the middle of which sat her pregnancy test.

'What's that?' Naomi yelled and jumped on it, pulling the plastic from the paper and removing the lid, before placing the soggy tip in her palm. 'Urgh!' she shouted, then held up her hand for her dad's inspection.

Rosie held her husband's eye, gave a gentle shake of her head and swallowed the desire to cry. *I wanted this baby, Phil. I wanted it so very much...*

'They're both asleep.' She sighed, grateful that it was bedtime. It had been a very long day. She popped her soft bed socks on. The cold wind seemed to rattle down the redundant chimneybreast in their bedroom and straight up under the duvet; socks were her salvation.

'Only us, Rosie, eh?' Phil pulled back the duvet and patted the space in the bed next to where he lay.

'I swear I only turned my back for a single minute to go to the loo and she had them up her nose! Why she would think that was a good idea, God only knows.' She pulled off her dressing gown and adjusted her bra; her large chest made her too self-conscious to sleep without one. She sank down onto the mattress, embarrassed, as ever, by the way it sagged under her weight.

'There's no point in trying to fathom that girl, she is a law unto herself, always has been. In fact they both are.' Phil smiled, as if this fact delighted him. 'The doctor said Leo had her own filing cabinet, she'd been there that often. I think he was only half joking.'

She laughed. 'It'll be something to put in your wedding speech.'

'Love, if I was to go through everything those two have been up to, I'd be there all night, we'd have to cancel the disco! And I hate to think what's to come – they're not even in double digits yet!'

'Oh, don't say that! We're not cancelling the disco! I think about that day, you know.'

He smiled. 'Me too. I just hope I've paid off the credit card by then, or it won't only be no disco, it'll be no dress, no sausage rolls, nothing. I'll be encouraging them to elope.'

'Don't worry, I'm going to win the lottery. That's my pension plan.' She snuggled against his warm body.

'That, my lover, is genius. Why didn't I think of that?' He chuckled.

'I can try and get more shifts at the caravans?' she said. She was willing to do anything to ease the burden on her husband, whose salary was their main income, but like many jobs where they lived, the work was seasonal.

Outsiders who owned second homes in the area often wanted refurbishments, new decks, extensions and licks of paint before the summer season, but after that things always slowed, and the winter months were the slowest of all. Phil worked with his dad, Keith, his cousin Ross and, on occasion, when he was at home, his younger brother Kevin, affectionately known to his family as 'Kev, that lazy, hippy, travelling bastard'.

Rosie was always keen to defend Kev. She knew it was said in loving jest, but Kev was far from lazy, just different. The more academic of the two boys, he had gone to university and now travelled the globe working in marine conservation. Phil liked to poke fun at his long hair and laid-back attitude, unable to understand that just because he got to sail the high seas and sit on paradisiacal beaches, he was still working. Besides, if it hadn't been for him, she wouldn't have ended up with Phil.

Kevin Tipcott had been her mate and was in her class at school. He kept an eye on her, walked her to the bus and made her roar with laughter at every opportunity;

his humour was the best weapon in his arsenal. When she was twelve, Kev had taken her back to his house for tea and introduced her to his mum, Mo, who wanted to look after and spoil the poor motherless girl. And Rosie let her, willingly, pitching up at weekends for toast and honey around the family table and sitting in front of the fire to enjoy a good old gossip.

One weekend a few years later, she was sitting at the Tipcott tea table when Phil came home on R&R and informed the family that he was leaving the army, having decided it wasn't the job for him after all. Rosie had barely heard his words but had simply stared at the man, weak kneed, as she tried to work out why her heart felt as if it had been turned inside out. A whole three years older, he seemed grown-up, sexy and able, all in one bundle. So, yes, she was keen to defend Kev; he had given her her family.

Phil sighed. Rosie's job, even if only minimum wage, was at least regular. When the weather took a turn for the worse, surfers and walkers replaced the sunseekers at the holiday park and Rosie was happy enough to clean the caravans before and after their stays. 'We're okay, but thanks for offering, love. You've got enough on your plate and I don't think more shifts are going to cut it.'

She nestled in closer. 'I think about *our* wedding day a lot, and I know when I see the girls walk up the aisle on your arm, it'll be like we've come full circle. I think they'll be my proudest days, seeing them with you, starting their own books as we write our final chapters.'

'Blimey, that's quite poetic for you! Thankfully, I don't think you have to worry about that just now. We've got a few years yet. They are only five and seven!'

'I know.' Rosie clicked off the bedside lamp, plunging the room into darkness. 'I was never that fussed about the actual day for us. I remember my mates being very excited about the frock and the setting and the invites, but I didn't feel that. I was far more interested in becoming your wife and getting on with the business of setting up our little house, cooking for you, being together. It wasn't so much about the celebration but more what came after.'

Phil placed his arm around her shoulders and pulled her towards him as he kissed the top of her scalp. She laid her head on his chest.

'I remember, and I loved you for it. I wondered if it was because your mum wasn't around and you didn't have her to share it with.'

Rosie lifted her head to try and see his face in the dark. 'It wasn't that, not really. They say you don't miss what you never had but I'm not sure I would agree. I do think that's why maybe I wanted my own little family and why I treasure you all so much.' Discussions like this were rare. Her thoughts about family inevitably led to her thinking about the plastic spatula, which had been grabbed from Naomi's hand and deposited in the nearest bin. Her periods had always been irregular and a mistimed fumble in haste without reaching for precautions meant that for weeks now she had harboured the idea that she might have conceived. And the more she thought about it, the more she was convinced it was the case, with sickness and sore boobs as further evidence.

'My test was negative,' she reminded him.

'I know. Are you disappointed?'

She nodded her cheek against his skin. 'A bit,' she lied, trying to ignore the gnaw of sadness in her gut and the ache in her arms to hold a baby, their baby, one more time. She knew it was selfish, and she had so much to feel thankful for, not least their two beautiful girls, but the ache was there just the same. 'I just know we're running out of time. And that makes me feel quite sad. As though the opportunity might pass us by.'

Their sex life was now very low-key; they were always either too tired, too busy or too can't be bothered. Rosie knew deep down that if she had a better figure, she would be more comfortable initiating things, but until that day came, she would continue to layer up and hope for undisturbed sleep. She heard her husband's deep sigh, then felt the heave and sag of a body weary of the baby discussion.

'I know it's what you want, Rosie, but everything happens for a reason.'

She listened, noting his use of 'you' and not 'we'. She knew what was coming next and lay there silently, having predicted his response with uncanny accuracy.

'I think it'd be hard to cope with a baby not only financially but space-wise as well. I mean, we're okay for money right now, but next month, who knows? We just about manage as it is. The girls share a bedroom, the box room is full of crap and we could do with another room downstairs. Imagine if we had to find somewhere for a baby and all its gubbins. It'd be miserable.'

'Or it might be the spur you need to get on with clearing out the box room. Half of it's your old army stuff and sports kit, and we could knock downstairs through like we've always wanted. And actually, Phil, I think it would be the opposite of miserable,' she whispered. 'Remember when we brought each of the girls home? I had that feeling in my stomach like I might burst, like I was too lucky.'

'It *was* wonderful, but I think with Naomi it was because we didn't know what to expect and with Leona we were still shell-shocked after Naomi.' He laughed. 'But another baby? I think that ship might have sailed. We're not getting any younger.'

'I'm thirty-six! Lots of women have babies way older than me!' she protested, louder than she intended.

'They probably do, but I bet they also have spare bedrooms, spare cash and spare minutes in the day. We don't have any of those things and I don't want the girls to go without anything—'

'Neither do I!' she interrupted, irritated that he might be suggesting otherwise.

Both were quiet, firing silent reasons and justifications out into the darkness. Their bodies were tense, but neither wanted to be the first to move to the other side of the bed and escalate the row.

It was Phil that had the final word before sleep claimed

him. 'We need to give the girls the best we can. If it had happened, then we'd have dealt with it, but it hasn't and if I'm being honest, Rosie, I'm relieved.'

She accepted his final kiss of the day and wiggled over to her side of the bed, where she buried her face in her pillow. There had been a few precious minutes earlier in the day, as she'd waited for the test results to show, when there had been the very real possibility that she was going to become a mum again, maybe even to the little boy that she longed for. And unlike her snoring husband, what she felt now was far from relief. She pictured the child that lived in her mind and felt nothing but deep sadness.

In the morning, Rosie woke bright and early, shoved the washing in the machine and prepped the packed lunches for the day.

'What's this?' Phil stood in his work trousers with the padded knees and his black sweatshirt with the name *Tipcott and Sons* embroidered on his chest and peered into his Bob the Builder lunchbox.

'It's your lunch! What do you think? I always make your lunch.' She smiled.

'Yes, love, and I appreciate it, but lunch usually consists of a sandwich, a bag of crisps and a slice of one of your cakes. But this looks like...' He screwed up his nose, '... grass.'

She laughed loudly; he still had the ability to make her laugh. And she was grateful for the jovial atmosphere that morning. The pregnancy test and their subsequent discussion was forgotten about, for now.

'For God's sake, Phil, it's salad, with shredded kale and all sorts of lovely things in a sesame and soy sauce dressing.'

'Oh no! We're not on a health kick again, are we?' He snapped the lid shut. 'Better ring my mum and tell her to make Dad double!'

'Don't you dare! Yes, we are on a health kick. And we shall do it together. My magazine says we are twice as likely to succeed if we do this together.'

'But I don't want to succeed. I want to eat my sandwiches at lunchtime and a bit of your cake!' He scowled.

'You'll thank me when the summer comes and you can get into your Superdry trunks that we got for Andy and Mel's barbeque last year.' She kissed his cheek.

'I love you, Rosie, you know that, but the only way to shift weight is to actually do something about it. Reading articles isn't enough.' His tone was soft.

'I know.' She smiled. 'But it's not about how much you love me. It's about how much I love myself and I don't all the time, not looking like this.' She ran the flat of her palm over the roll of stomach that pouched over her jeans. 'I need to lose it for me and for my health.' She felt embarrassed, hated having to discuss the subject, especially as she'd been that way since having the girls and could have lost it ten times over if only she'd stuck to her good intentions.

'Well, I'll support you, of course, but I can't guarantee that I won't stop for a sneaky pasty on the way home.' He laughed.

'Well just don't tell me about it!' She laughed too. 'Where you working today, still up at Mortehoe?'

'Yep.' He nodded. 'You should see it, Rosie. My word, it's something else. The architect is up there every day. Poor bloke's being run ragged. She keeps changing her mind about the colour of the tiles in one of the bathrooms, the way a wall curves by the pool, could he make the laundry room wider, is it too late to have a real fire in the bedroom? She's a right pain in the arse and I swear to God it's like as soon as she's got something she's had to argue and fight for, she doesn't want it any more, has us all running around in circles, just because she's got all the time in the world. I hate to think how much she's spent, must be at least three million all in.'

'God! You are kidding me?' Rosie gasped. 'Three million!'

'Yep, and that's just on the rebuild and refit, mind, not what it cost to buy the land and the house that sat on it.'

'Mind you, prime bit of land, that. Right on the clifftop,' Rosie mused.

'True. And it's not her only home; apparently she's got a place in London and one in Florida. But I bet the others don't have the view she's got up at Mortehoe. It's beautiful.'

'It would have to be for three million quid. Did you say it has a swimming pool?' Rosie tried to picture it.

'It's got two. One outside – an infinity pool that makes it feel like you're swimming off the cliff – and another massive one in the basement, where there's also a gym and a sauna and all sorts of other bells and whistles. It's like a bloody hotel!'

'No hotel we've ever stayed in.' Rosie lifted her shoulders excitedly. 'I'd love to see it.'

'If she's not around, I'll try and get some photos on my phone. I find it quite amazing how one person can have so much, all that space. Mind you, if we weren't constantly shelling out for kids and what not, we might be able to have a swimming pool.'

'Where would you put it, exactly? In the front room? The back garden's just big enough for my washing line!'

'Good point, think we'll leave it. I'd only keep falling in every time I went to reach for the remote control.' He smiled.

'How'd she get so much money?'

'Apparently she and a couple of others started a smallish company that got floated on the stock exchange and she got millions.'

'What's she like?'

Phil exhaled. 'Don't know how to describe her really. I've not spoken to her much. She looks like one of them women who spends a lot of time in the hairdresser's – you know, bouffy hair and nails all painted, and loads of make-up. The kind of woman you could never snog or you'd end up with a mouth covered in lipstick.' He puckered his lips theatrically and leaned in towards her. Rosie backed away, holding up her palms, unwilling to kiss him before she had cleaned her teeth.

'Oi! I should think you wouldn't want to snog anyone!' She laughed.

'I don't want to snog anyone but you, Rosie, you know

that.' He pecked her cheek despite her protestations. 'But I'll say this about her: for all her fake nails and teeth, she gets things done. Got half the contractors in Devon running around like ants at her command, and that takes some doing.' He gave a nod of approval.

'What was her company, then, that she put on the stock exchange?'

Phil shrugged. 'Something to do with computers, I think. I don't know.'

Rosie laughed. 'Well, I know *you* don't know, you can't even work the satnav!'

'I tell you what, love, I'll have it programmed for the Red Barn quicker than you can say sesame and soy dressing if you keep making me eat this.' He waved the lunchbox in her direction before placing it in his tool bag. 'I could murder one of their breakfasts.'

'Can I come to the Red Barn?' Naomi waltzed into the little kitchen, in her uniform and ready for school. Thankfully, her face was glitter-free.

'No. And I'm not really going, I'm only teasing Mummy.' He winked. 'But if I went, I would definitely take you with me. Have a good day, my girlies, and I'll see you all tonight. Hopefully it will be less eventful than last night.'

'Bye, Daddy!' Leona sloped down the stairs.

'Bye, darling. I was just saying, try not to shove anything up your nose today.'

'What about my finger?' She stared at her dad as she held her index finger in the air.

Phil scratched his head. 'Your finger is okay, as long as there's nothing on the end of it.' He kissed her head and shut the front door behind him.

'Daddy was just telling me, he's working on a big house that's got two swimming pools in it! Can you imagine that?'

Naomi considered this as she hopscotched around the kitchen floor. 'What's the point of having two? You can only swim in one at a time.'

'Don't know, Nay, and I don't think it's anything that I am going to have to worry about. Not in this lifetime.'

Two

Rosie had a favourite place to sit. It was a wooden bench on the headland overlooking Combesgate Beach, set back from the cliff edge. If she stretched her neck, she could see from one bay to the next, watch the tide rolling in and spot the weather long before it arrived. She thought of it as her bench. They had history that seat and her, and she had to admit, if ever she arrived to find someone sitting on it, she felt ridiculously aggrieved.

According to her dad, her mum had liked to sit and think on the same bench. Apparently they'd done some of their courting there too, which made it extra special to Rosie. When she was younger, she would sit there and chat to her mum. She would tell her all about her day, if there was anyone she fancied at school, what she wanted for her birthday, that kind of thing. Those were special times for Rosie. The fact that she had never met her mum and had absolutely no idea what she looked like wasn't relevant. The mum she created in her mind, the neat, smiling, attentive listener, was just about as perfect as a mum could be; and she smelt of apples.

At the age of six, sitting in the bathtub in their colourless, austere bathroom, where the tile grouting was grey and the towels were thin and stiff, Rosie had opened a bottle of apple-scented shampoo. Its sweet, synthetic smell was one of the most glorious things she had ever sniffed. Inhaling it until she was utterly intoxicated by the mouth-watering aroma, she decided there and then that this was the way her mum would have smelt. In her mind, anything that smelt of apples could only be good.

All Rosie knew was that her mum had disappeared just a few hours after she was born. There were no photos and sadly, no memories. Ever since she could remember, her dad's stock response had been, 'Something happened, Rosie, and she just couldn't live with me any more,' and that was always the end of the conversation. Rosie spent her childhood trying to imagine what her dad could possibly have done to make her mum run off like that. During her bench chats she often used to apologise on behalf of her dad, for whatever it was that he'd done to scare her mum away.

Sometimes Rosie used to secretly wonder if, actually, she had somehow killed her mum when she was born and her dad was just covering that up, pretending it wasn't her fault, to make her feel better. In her fertile, childish mind she would let her imagination run wild with images of her mum slipping away, deathly pale but still beautiful, hands reaching out, lips trying to tell Rosie something really important, eyes fixed and bright, looking at her and trying to convey what her mouth could not.

As strange as it sounded, it was easier in some ways to imagine her dead. Better that her mum was gone and unable to get in touch than that she was alive somewhere but had chosen to remain hidden, scared off by Rosie's dad.

Or, when she wasn't imagining her dead, she imagined her with a lust for travel, too far away for contact. She pictured her in the jungle, living wild and tanned among beasts, in tropical heat, carving out paths with a rusty machete and sipping water from clear waterfalls, crouched on slippery rocks with one eye on the lookout for snakes. At other times she pictured her wrapped in furs, trekking across ice floes, navigating icy cold plateaus with frozen lashes and teeth that chattered in the cold, her trusty rifle stuck to her palm in case of polar bear attack. Rosie often placed herself in these imaginings, having either built a tree house high in the jungle canopy or a cosy, concealed igloo. In both, she would have the kettle boiling and a red and white tablecloth set for tea and when her mum stumbled, through the door, relieved and grateful, she would hug her tightly and kiss her face. 'How I've missed you! My beloved daughter!'

The reality was, though, that Rosie had no idea what happened. All she knew was that, not long after her mum went, her dad upped sticks and relocated them both to a new house further out of town. To the adult Rosie it seemed as if he was trying to outrun the memories of his wife, escape the guilt. As a child, it had worried her greatly that if her mum had wanted to return home, wanted to come and find her only child, she wouldn't know where they'd gone. Rosie used to imagine hiding a note with their new address on it, and she knew just where she would leave it, behind the wonky brink at the back of the coalhole. She was confident that her mum would know to look there, that she could read Rosie's mind, just as Rosie could read hers. This she still maintained, even now.

Growing up in a house with no mother was confusing. Despite being normal to her, it fascinated her peers. '*Why haven't you got a mum? Who does your hair?*' Although she'd never known any different, she still felt her absence keenly. It was like being cold and never having owned a blanket but knowing you could do with one. It was just how it was. Her mum had gone and this was her lot and she accepted it.

That was until Rosie met Phil and became a mum herself. For her, giving birth threw up more questions than it answered about her mum's disappearance. *Her mum...* She was a real person, with a real name, and that name was Laurel. This made Rosie laugh. She couldn't imagine her dad, Roy, who liked Rich Tea biscuits and watching the darts, being with someone as glamorously named as Laurel. In her mind, they didn't go together at all: Roy and Laurel, Laurel and Roy. She thought her mum should have been with a Damien or at the very least a Brett.

Rosie had hoped that when she herself gave birth, it would provide a moment of clarity, explain her mum's actions in some way, as if looking through the magic portal of parent-hood might reveal secrets. If anything, the opposite was true. Watching her two daughters racing through their childhoods made the breath stutter in her throat. Rosie looked at the lean, rangy limbs that wrapped around her and listened to the steady beat of hearts that were yet to be broken and she knew that nothing, no circumstance on earth would keep her from them. Nothing.

Laurel was obviously cut from different cloth.

She wondered if her mum had gone on to have more chil-dren. Was she replaced? This idea had haunted her dreams on occasion. Was there a girl a couple of years younger than her with the same dark irises and a kink to the near-black hair at the nape of her neck that meant she too could never carry off a slick, neat do? Did she have a key in her purse that gave her entry to their mother's house, a world that she too should inhabit? Did that girl hover in a kitchen in which hands that had briefly swaddled her pulled open drawers and touched shelves in front of which she would never stand, forever unwelcome, a stranger in that kitchen, the heart of the house. And did that girl ever knit her eyebrows in a flash of confusion as her mother accidentally called out 'Rosie!' for her to 'Come eat supper! Get that phone! Bring down the laundry!' And just for a second, as the two syllables danced on her tongue, did Laurel imagine a different life, one in which her firstborn had not been abandoned and there had been no need for the inter-loper who slept in Rosie's bed, fed from her breast and got to share all the things that Rosie could only dream of?

Mostly, though, Rosie was now simply too preoccupied with her own life to spend much time thinking about her mum. She'd given up the obsessive face-scanning and paper-reading of her teens and no longer caught herself staring at women of a certain age on the bus or the television, wondering if they might be Laurel. She'd even begun to forgive her dad, who she could see had tried very hard to make amends for the situation of his own creation.

She could no longer hear the constant hum of abandonment and confusion that used to sit like a background noise to her thoughts. Although, as she had come to realise of late, just because it didn't intrude so much any more, that didn't mean it wasn't still there, like a silent wasp, resting. She still longed for the opportunity to look Laurel in the eyes and say, *'I'm sorry. I'm truly sorry, Mum, for whatever happened and you don't need to feel guilty or worry, because I am married to an amazing, amazing man. I am happy and I am loved.'*

And this was true.

Three

Rosie bustled into the coffee shop and scanned the tables for her best friend.

'Psssst!' A sound came from behind a raised, laminated menu in the booth in the corner.

'What you doing, Mel?' she quizzed. Her friend and work colleague appeared to be trying to hide. 'Are you incognito again?' She laughed. 'Although I have to say, I think you'd be a crap spy – you've still got your name badge on.' She pointed to the little plastic oblong with the holiday-park logo on the top. Then she laid her bag and jacket on the vacant seat and slid into the booth to sit opposite her.

'Maybe I'm a better spy than you think, maybe this isn't my real name!' Mel placed her fingers over her name badge.

'But it is your real name!' Rosie was confused.

'Or is it?' Her friend gave her a sideways look. 'Anyway, I'm not incognito, I just need a bigger menu.' She ducked down. 'I'm hiding!' she whispered.

'Who are you hiding from?'

'All right, you two?' The gloomy voice of Ross's wife floated over Rosie's shoulder, making her question redundant.

'Hey! Hi, Kayleigh, how are you?' she enthused, trying to erase any hint of meanness, as that would be her very worst thing, to be mean.

Mel shot her a look. She had broken the golden rule by asking that one question, knowing it could invite hours of detailed response. She sat back, closed the menu and waited for the depressing download.

Kayleigh was married to Phil's cousin, Ross, who was also a friend of Mel's husband Andy. When jobs allowed, Ross worked with Phil and Phil's dad, labouring on site. In all the years that she and Mel had known Kayleigh, the only time they'd ever seen her light up from within was when she learnt of another person's misfortune. It wasn't a nice quality. She had, as Phil had once described her, been a bit short-changed in the positivity department.

Kayleigh sighed and looked downcast – her default setting. 'I'm not so good. Did Ross not say to Phil?'

Rosie faltered, not wanting to get Ross into trouble for not having shared his wife's latest petty ailment but at the same time hoping to avoid a rerun of the details.

'Erm... he might have, but you know what it's like, we've had so much going on, what with our mad dash to A&E last night.'

'Why were you in A&E?' she asked, with a combination of interest and envy.

'Oh, it was nothing, really.' She regretted mentioning it. 'Leona put some small objects up her nose and we had to get them hoovered out by a professional.' She flapped her hand in the air, as though this were an unimportant, regular occurrence.

Mel screamed her laughter. 'Small objects! I love it! How small are we talking? Like pea-sized or baby antelope?'

'More pea-sized, thankfully, Mel.' She shot her friend a look.

Kayleigh stared at Mel, trying to work out if she was being funny or was just stupid. 'Last time I was at A&E, it wasn't for nothing, it was when I had that suspected tumour.'

'Oh God!'

'That's awful!'

Kayleigh nodded.

'Was it benign?' Mel was suddenly interested.

'No, it was just an infected gnat bite, as it turned out. But I did come over all peculiar. And my foot was itching something terrible. It's still not right.' She sighed again.

Rosie looked again at Mel, imploring her not to make a funny remark, and quickly filled the silent pause. 'In answer to your question, she had a rubber shaped like a little poo with a face on it up one nostril and part of a compass up the other.'

'Terrible, really, wasting the NHS's money like that.' Kayleigh tutted and Rosie swallowed the many retorts that sat on her tongue, the main thrust of all of them being that Kayleigh practically owed rent on the doctor's surgery, she was in there so often.

'S'pose you've heard all about the big place they're working on in Mortehoe?' She pursed her lips and clasped her hands in a sign of disapproval. Ross and Phil were both working with Phil's dad on the rebuilding project. They were all very grateful, knowing this would keep the wolf from the door in the coming months.

'Ooh, what big house?' Mel sat forward, always excited to glean a bit of news.

Kayleigh nodded her head to the left, as if indicating the site with her gesture. 'Apparently some multi-zillionaire has bought an old farm building and a chunk of land, has knocked down the bungalow and is putting up some huge mansion. Ross said it took him all day just to lug the bags of plaster into the kitchen. More money than sense, if you ask me. Who needs all that space and two swimming pools? Bloody ridiculous.'

'Two swimming pools!' Mel was impressed. 'Whose house is it?' Gossip like this was grand entertainment in a small town like Woolacombe. 'Please tell me Daniel Craig has seen sense and not only decided to respond to my emails but also bought us a love nest!'

'Poor Andy!' Rosie felt the need to express her loyalty.

'Poor Andy? He's a massive James Bond fan, I think even he'd understand if I left him for Daniel Craig!' Mel sighed. 'I tell you, that bit in *Casino Royale* where he walks out of the sea... Oh my word! That image has warmed me on many a cold night.'

'It's not Daniel Craig.' Kayleigh shattered her dreams matter-of-factly. 'It's Geraldine Farmer. I've seen her!' Her eyes widened. 'She's got an enormous Range Rover and she was smashing it down the lanes like she owned the place!'

'Well, she does own a great big chunk of it, to be fair.' Rosie thought it prudent to point this out. 'Made her money from something to do with computers.'

'Don't care how she made it, she's only been here five minutes and you can't go racing around like that. Ross said she looks like a footballer's wife – you know, all teeth and tits – and the way she's decorating the place…!' Kayleigh drew breath, as if offended. 'Apparently she's going for silver and white and crushed velvet and glitter. If you can imagine that!'

'Ooh, Naomi would love it!' Rosie pictured her daughter's face the previous day.

'No class, if you ask me,' Kayleigh said, as she grabbed a handful of sugar sachets from the little bowl on the table and stuffed them in her pocket. 'They're useful for when we're camping,' she offered by way of explanation. 'Anyway, best be off. I've got a terrible period, feel drained, wipes me out, it does. I've been to the doctor's, but there's nothing they can do. I think it's just as my mum would say: a woman's lot is to suffer. Oh well.' She sloped off, barely able to lift her feet, her expression morose, her gait lumbering.

'I'm glad she shared that with us. Poor Kayleigh, imagine having a period! It must be terrible.' Mel pulled a face.

'I hope you or I never have to have one. I couldn't cope with being wiped out and drained, and how would you manage, Rosie? Having to clean caravans with an actual period?'

Rosie laughed, felt instantly guilty and checked to see that Kayleigh had indeed left the building.

'I always feel so lifted after bumping into our Kayleigh, she's so full of sparkle!' Mel continued. 'It's like being given an injection of joy!'

'I feel a bit sorry for her really. She's obviously missing something if she feels the need to harp on about her many illnesses all the time.'

'You're right. I think she's missing a marble and quite possible has a screw that needs tightening.' Mel gave her unfavourable assessment. 'Now can we please get the bloody jacket spuds ordered. I'm starving.'

An hour and a half later and now full of coffee, jacket potatoes and up to speed with the latest gossip, the two friends zipped up their jackets and made their way along the shiny pavements, wet with rain, heading towards school. Mel's son Tyler was two years older than Naomi.

'Do you think you'll try again?' Mel asked, thinking about the pregnancy-test result Rosie had shared with her.

Rosie thought about how rarely she and Phil had sex, let alone in an effort to conceive. 'I don't know, really.' She considered how best to continue, conscious as ever that Andy and Phil were good mates and had been since they were teenagers. 'I'd like to, but Phil's not keen. Says we can't afford it and haven't got the space.'

'He's right. You can't and you haven't,' Mel said. 'But since when did that stop people having babies?'

Rosie laughed. 'I don't know, Mel, maybe he's right, maybe I am getting past it.'

'Shut up! Who are you? Kayleigh? Don't give me that rubbish! You are the best mum. Christ, your world revolves around those girls and Phil. He's a lucky man. He should be doing all he can to keep you happy!'

'Not sure he always sees it that way. I wish I could lose a few pounds.' She looked up at her friend through the fine mist of rain. The air was tinged with salt as it blew in from the sea.

'What is wrong with you today? You are beautiful, you've always been beautiful, inside and out. You've got gorgeous curves, and your face, your hair... Blimey, girl, you are sexy!'

Rosie shrugged, embarrassed by the compliment.

'This weather's proper shit!' Mel changed the subject.

'It's February, what do you expect? And anyway, it's a trade-off, isn't it?'

'How do you mean?'

'Well, if the weather's crap, there are no visitors, so we can park and get a seat in the coffee shop, but if the sun's out, the place is busy and we get the sun but no seats or parking spaces.'

Mel stopped in her tracks and stared at her friend from underneath her hood. 'You are a right ball of sunshine today, Rosie May Shitstar!'

They both crumpled into laughter and Rosie wished she hadn't shared Naomi's favourite swear word with her mate, hoping it wasn't a moniker that was going to stick.

*

Rosie placed the mug of tea on the side table by her husband's chair and sat back down on their denim sofa, an impulse-buy from a few years ago. It grew saggier and comfier with each passing year and was now so imperfect, no one cared about the odd splash of coffee or swipe of felt-tipped pen. It was a far cry from how she had guarded it when it was new, whipping off the kids' shoes and banning food and drink from their tiny sitting room. This was far nicer, relaxed.

'I bumped into Kayleigh earlier.' She held her mug with both hands and tucked her feet beneath her legs.

'Oh, sorry to hear that. What ailments is she suffering from today? Should I be dusting off my black tie? Again?'

'Ah, don't be mean, Phil. Mel thinks she's got a screw loose.'

'Bloody hell, and that's coming from her!' He enjoyed ribbing his best friend's wife. 'It's Ross I feel sorry for, having to put up with that! Bloke needs a medal.'

The two watched the adverts on the television, the silence broken by Rosie after some minutes.

'Do you think we should have more sex?' she asked, without taking her eyes off the screen.

'Blimey, Rosie, what, right now?' He laughed. 'Can I finish my cup of tea first?' He raised his mug.

'No, you dafty, not now! I've just been thinking about it and I wondered if you think we have enough sex.' She nibbled the shortbread biscuit she'd taken from the packet and turned to watch Phil do the same to its twin that she'd placed by his mug. The health kick had lasted approximately twelve hours. Neither of them mentioned it. She had, however, noticed that his salad had been returned in the Bob the Builder lunch-box, untouched.

'When you say more sex,' he pondered, sipping his tea, 'do you mean more frequent or longer, or—'

'I don't know!' She felt her cheeks flare. 'As I say, I was just thinking about it today. How many times do you think we have sex a month?'

'I'm not sure. Let me just go up and count the notches on the bedpost.' He chuckled.

'Seriously, Phil, how many times would you say we do it?' She bit into her shortbread.

Phil took a deep breath and looked skywards, as if count-ing. 'I'd say maybe once or twice a month.'

'Yes, that's what I reckon.' She paused. 'Do you think that's normal?'

'God, I don't know! What's normal?'

'I don't know either,' she confessed. There was another period of silence before she continued. 'Do you think we have more or less sex than our friends?'

'Rosie! I don't know! Do you want me to phone Andy and ask him?'

'No.' She giggled. 'I suppose I just want to know that we're having the right amount for you and that you're happy.' She held his gaze, but he didn't say anything. She noticed the slight rise and fall of his Adam's apple and felt a wave of love for her man. The last thing in the world she wanted was for him to feel inadequate. 'I was just thinking that when we first met we had lots of sex, probably every day.'

'Yep, probably.' He nodded at the TV.

'But it's got less and less, hasn't it? And then we had the kids, and now it's just once or twice a month. I worry it's not enough.'

He flashed her a smile.

'I love you, Phil.'

'And I love you too. Mind you, thinking about it, if there's a bit more sex on offer, I'm not going to refuse.' He winked at her.

'Play your cards right, Mr Tipcott, and after *Big Brother*'s finished, I might just make you an offer.' Rosie finished her biscuit and enjoyed the warm glow of love that swirled in her stomach. She was happy. This was all she needed: a squidgy sofa, a cup of tea, a stick of shortbread, crap telly and the promise of an early night with the man she loved. *I'm a lucky woman.*

They heard the creak on the stairs long before Leona popped her mussed head around the sitting-room door. Rubbing her eyes and swallowing her tears, she trotted in wearing her pink Dora the Explorer pyjamas.

'Oh, Leo! What's the matter?' Rosie placed her mug on the floor and held her arms wide open as her little girl took a flying jump and landed next to her on the sofa.

Phil sat forward. 'What's up, my little girlie?'

Leona lifted her head and tried to stem her tears. 'I… I had a bad dream.'

'Oh no! What did you dream about? Ssshhh…' Rosie cooed into her daughter's hair, trying to calm and reassure her.

'I thought that Naomi's poo-face rubber was really big… and… and under my bed and it was trying to get me and shove me up its… its nose!' she managed through her tears.

Phil pulled his head into his shoulders and fought the laughter that wanted to erupt.

Rosie narrowed her eyes at him. 'Don't cry, little Leo. Don't cry, baby. It was just a dream. You are safe and you are here with Mummy and Daddy and no one and nothing can hurt you.' She held Leo tight until her tears slowed and her body relaxed.

'C… c… can I sleep with you, Mummy?'

'Of course you can.' She kissed her child.

Phil sighed and finished his biscuit.

Four

It was March, a whole month later, and the weather had brightened significantly. It was the time of year when Woolacombe began to have a buzz about it. This was especially so at weekends when incomers from Exeter, Bristol and further afield arrived with their cash and in their cars, queuing for the car parks in an orderly fashion before walking their dogs on the beach. Busy cafés churned out platefuls of bacon and eggs to stave off hangovers, and sticks of rock had last year's dust wiped from them and were arranged just so in jaunty coloured buckets on the counter tops of the convenience stores.

The Hunter-wellies-and-waxed-jacket brigade walked arm in arm, whistling for their Labradors to catch up and watching with fascination and envy as the long-haired surfies unloaded their vans, zipped up their wetsuits and waxed their boards. The whole place had the sniff of summer about it. It was the seasonal equivalent of waking on the day of a special event and knowing there was so much to look forward to, an unspoken promise of what would be arriving in just a few short months.

It was early one Saturday and Rosie had just arrived at work. She had tramped up the hill and was a little out of puff. The caravans were, as ever, fully booked. It wasn't the grandest of holiday parks, the facilities were sparse and the trek to the beach a hike, but the caravans were spotless and the view was the best in the area. The sea was flanked by the curve of graduated hills, each peppered with fat sheep boxed in by full and ancient hedgerows. A farmhouse sat in the foreground, its chimney billowing smoke that filled the air with the distinct aroma of a real fire. The whole scene shone against its backdrop of clear, crisp, turquoise sky. Rosie smiled, thinking that if someone wanted to bottle an image of the perfect English countryside and pop it in a snow globe, this would be it.

With her tabard on, her long, thick hair fastened into a messy knot on top of her head and her bucket full of cleaning products in her hand, she walked to caravan 9A as per her worksheet. She knocked, then tried the handle. Receiving no reply, she let herself in and made straight for the kitchen, knowing that she might need to start by giving a grotty grill pan a good soak. She checked the cooker. It was pristine. Clearly the guests in 9A preferred to eat out, which was absolutely fine by her; less to clean. The kitchen areas were her nemesis. She had many horror stories of fat-clogged pans and bean-caked saucepans that could take her an hour to get clean. She ran her sponge under the hot tap and squirted kitchen cleaner on the small areas of work surface and the stainless steel sink drainer.

'Oooow! Good Lord!' a voice yelled from the bathroom at the other end of the caravan.

'Shit!' Rosie switched off the hot tap and gathered up her bucket and other bits and pieces as fast as she could. She had got as far as the hallway when the bathroom door opened and she came face to face with a middle-aged man, who thankfully had had the foresight to wrap himself in a large towel. He was, however, naked from the waist up. She tried not to look at his bare, hairy chest; it was strange and embarrassing to see a man who wasn't her husband in this state.

'Who are you?' he yelled, more in shock than anger. His accent was distinctly American.

'I am so, so sorry!' She spoke with her free hand raised in supplication and the bucket in her other hand. 'I knocked and waited, but there was no answer, so I came in to clean.'

'I was in the shower!'

'Yes, I can see that now.' She cowered.

'The shower ran *really* cold.' He pointed behind him, as though this might be of interest and as though he wasn't standing wearing a towel, chatting to her in a rather confined space.

'That was my fault too. Sorry. I ran the hot tap, to do the surfaces. I am so sorry to have disturbed you. I'll let you get on.' She stepped gingerly along the hallway, towards the front door.

Rosie laughed as she rattled down the wobbly steps, off to tend to 9B, where she would make a much more thorough job of checking whether it was occupied. She hoped she might bump into Mel. Working opposite shifts meant this didn't often happen, but she couldn't wait to tell her, knowing her friend would find it hilarious!

She was all done by midday and after hanging up her overalls and placing her bucket in the cleaning cupboard, she said her goodbyes and started down the hill for home. Her phone rang.

'Daddy is taking us to soft play and so we won't be home!' Naomi shouted, her haste and volume a combination of excitement and lack of telephone skill.

'Oh, right! Put Daddy on, Nay.' Rosie listened to the clunks and rumble as Phil was passed his phone.

'Hey, love.'

'I hear you've been badgered into taking them to Barnstaple.' She laughed.

'I don't mind really.' He sighed. 'I mean, it's not like I was actually looking forward to putting my feet up and watching a bit of sport on the telly.'

'Oh, love, look, hang on five minutes and I'll come home and take them if you want a rest.' She knew he'd had a busy week.

'No, you've just finished work and I am kidding, kind of. It'll be nice to spend time with them and if I'm lucky we'll get to put the One Direction CD on repeat all the way there and all the way back!'

'Well, look, have fun, drive safely and I'll see you when you get home. Love you.'

'And we love you. Say goodbye to Mummy.' Phil held the phone out and it was hard to believe that it was just her two little girls who screamed and shouted words of farewell and not a football team. It made her smile, imagining the girls hounding him into taking them. They would all be exhausted by the evening. Poor Phil. She vowed to cook him a nice supper and spoil him a bit.

The day was too nice to waste and Rosie decided that rather than hide from the sunshine at home, alone, she would walk the long way round and stop for a while on her favourite bench. In fine weather, the view over Combesgate Beach and beyond was especially lovely.

The Esplanade was busy. Converted vans and campers were parked side by side, with wetsuits hanging on airers hooked to windows and the aroma of bacon sizzling in pans mingling with the whiff of gas that crisped it just so. Rosie always thought the vans looked very cosy. She smiled and nodded at the blanket-wrapped adventurers with pruney toes who sat close together, huddled inside with camping mugs full of tea, looking cold and tired, salt water dripping from their hair, but slowly warming as they stared out over the rolling waves they tried to master.

Rosie felt her chest tighten and she huffed and puffed as she picked up the pace. Wishing she was fitter, her thoughts turned to the cheese on toast she would devour as a late lunch when she got home. It seemed that a picture of the grub she loved almost instantly replaced every thought of dieting or healthy living.

With her bench in sight, she pushed on. Reaching it finally, she peeled off her jacket and placed it on her lap, partly to cool herself down and also using it as a cushion to cover her pouchy tum. She closed her eyes briefly and threw her head back, feeling the scorch of early spring sunshine on her cheeks. It was lovely. The sound of circling gulls echoed overhead and the distant giggle of a child rock-pooling below made it perfect. She placed her left hand on the bench and wondered if her mum's fingers had touched the same spot.

And there she was! Laurel, sitting on the bench, smiling, as if to say, *'There you are, Rosie. I've been waiting for you.'*

She imagined her mum's face, lit up with happiness at the sight of her, as the comforting scent of apples filled her nostrils. She pictured Laurel turning in her direction, her expression quizzical, as if enquiring about her day.

Rosie beamed and spoke out loud. 'Funny thing, actually, Mum, earlier I nearly half scalded a man to death and then he ran out in his towel. Didn't know where to look!'

Her mum tipped her head back and smiled.

'I know!' Rosie grinned. 'I'm a little pickle. No wonder my girls are always up to mischief – they take after me, don't they!' She looked at her mother and swallowed. 'Am I your best ever thing, Mum?'

Laurel nodded.

'I knew it!' Rosie smiled, beyond happy. 'I would have

liked you to brush my hair,' she confessed, as her mum leant towards her with her hand reaching out—

There was a jolt and spring to the wood, as someone sat on the other end of the bench. It pulled her from her day-dream. She smiled, opened her eyes and tried to look delighted, swallowing the mild irritation that a stranger was robbing her of her brief time of solace and her precious time with Laurel. That was the trouble with a special place like her bench with the view: it tended to be special to a lot of people.

Rosie glanced to the left. *Oh shit!* It was the American! She turned her head sharply to the right, looking over towards the Watersmeet Hotel, trying to ignore him, wanting to budge up and fill the spare two inches to her right, putting as much distance between them as possible but without him seeing.

'Hello there.' He craned his neck, trying to catch her eye.

'Oh, hello!' She looked over her shoulder, making out she'd only just noticed him.

'Do you mind if I sit here? I know it's a drag sometimes when you think you've got the place to yourself and along comes a random stranger.'

'No, not at all!' *You big fat liar, Rosie.*

'Although we're not complete strangers, are we? I thought it was you – it's the big hair.' He twirled his finger near his own. 'You have lots of it!'

She nodded. Yes she did.

'You gave me quite a start earlier!' He laughed now, seeing the funny side.

'And you me.' She smiled.

'Well, sorry if I alarmed you. Just a few more hours and the place will be free for you to come and go as you please.'

She gave a small nod. 'I left in such a hurry, I didn't get to empty the bins or check you were all right for towels.' She felt the creep of embarrassment, regretting mentioning towels, considering how he had presented himself earlier.

'Don't you worry. I am more than capable of dealing with both. This is a lovely place to come and sit.'

She nodded, glad of the verbal change in direction. The wind kicked up and the sharp breeze grazed her face.

'It's where I come to think.'

'And here's me interrupting you.'

'No, not at all.' This was less of a lie. With the awkwardness now gone, she was happy to chat to the grey-haired man, who actually seemed quite pleasant.

'I love the view from here. I like watching for tankers on the horizon – they fascinate me. When you first see them, you can't tell if they're coming closer to you or moving further away. Isn't that something?'

'Yes it is.' She nodded, having never considered this before.

'Are you local?' he asked, twisting on the bench to see her better.

'Yes, I am. Born and bred, never lived anywhere else.'

'What keeps you here?'

She smiled at him, interested by his assumption that she wasn't anchored to one place, that she could just up sticks and follow the breeze and live anywhere! Even the idea of it made her laugh. 'Love keeps me here.'

'Ah, that magic potion.' He studied her grin.

'Yep. Married for nearly twelve years now, two girls. So, yes, it's love that keeps me here.' She pictured the three people she loved most in the whole wide world and her heart soared. She couldn't wait to see them later.

'So, safe to say you like it here?'

'Is this twenty questions?' She watched his face turn puce. 'Oh! I was only joking.'

'No, you're quite right, I do ask a lot of questions, I know. I'm sorry.' He placed his palms on his thighs.

'I'm only teasing. I do like it here very much.' She shrugged, thinking how best to describe her relationship with Woolacombe. 'It's where the only people I know live. I can't picture being anywhere else. I've been coming to sit on this bench for longer than I can remember and my mum used to do the same. I think that's what first drew me to it.' She smiled. 'I used to bring my girls and their friends up here when they were toddlers. It was like trying to herd cats. They'd dart all over the grass and dip into the picnic bag and one of them would need a wee the moment we arrived, usually Naomi. They'd be dancing and laughing one minute, falling over and crying the next. I loved it, though: the mayhem, the busyness.'

'What a lovely thing.' He gave her a warm, genuine smile.

'I'm lucky,' she acknowledged.

'Yes, you are, for many reasons, not least for having this,

the most perfect spot to come sit. Especially today when we have been given this little gift, a bit of sunny residue, warm crumbs that the weather gods found in their pockets and decided to lob in our direction. Lovely.'

Rosie looked at him. He had the most unusual way of speaking, as if he were reading aloud. 'I shall remember that: "warm crumbs that the weather gods found in their pockets..."'

'This is my first time here but hopefully not the last. I'm quite taken with the cliff walks, the wild sea. It's unexpected. But as I say, I leave later today.'

'Are you going back to America?' she asked, always interested to hear about lives very different from hers.

'Yup, eventually, but I have a few more months of travelling the British Isles first, and then it's back to Portland, Oregon.' He ran his hand over his neat, short hair.

Rosie extended her finger and looked into the distance, as if picturing a map.

'So that's on the opposite side of the country from New York, almost a straight line across, but up a bit, towards Canada, to the south of Seattle.' She drew a right angle in the air, raising an eyebrow at him, pleased to be able to demonstrate the geography that lurked in her brain, only usually useful for pub quizzes and *Pointless*.

'Well, I am impressed, there aren't many people I've met around here who could pinpoint my home city on a map!'

She smiled, chuffed. 'What are you doing here? Are you on holiday?'

'More of a working holiday. I'm a writer.'

'Oh. What do you write?' She had never met a writer before.

'I write for the American market: travel books, guides, walks, cuisine.' He raised his hand and slapped his leg, as if trying to summarise what he did was a tough call.

'And you're writing about here?'

'An article, yes. I must confess to coming up here just before daybreak most mornings. It's the one joy of jetlag – I get to explore while the rest of the country sleeps. Have you ever been up here at dawn?'

'I don't think I have.' She shook her head.

'There's something about it. It's like the planet is sharing a glorious secret with you: the still, the quiet, even the air is different, as if it's yet to be stirred. The slow creep of sunlight into a world of hushed expectation. It's like a blank page and who knows how it's going to be written? I find that very exciting, the most exciting thing. I think if it were my last day on earth, I would be happy to go if I got to see the dawn.'

'You really are a writer, aren't you?'

'Yup, really, really.' He smiled at her; he had neat, even teeth.

'I'm trying to imagine Americans coming all the way over here just to sit on this bench. I guess it's hard to see the draw of a place I know so well when there are so many other places in the world to visit. I mean, I get why people in the UK would come here, it's one of the best places in the country and not too far if you're in the southwest, but to come all the way from America, when you could go anywhere...?'

'Where would you suggest they went instead?'

'Oh, I don't know – the Seychelles, Bali, Norway.'

'Interesting combination. Which do you prefer?'

'Oh, I've never been to any of them. I've never been abroad. But I really want to. They're on my list to visit one day. I've always loved the idea of travelling, looking at maps, planning trips, trekking through jungles or building an igloo. I spent a lot of my childhood imagining just that. It was a dream of mine to open a travel agent's actually...' Rosie shook her head, remembered who she was talking to and straightened. 'Anyway, I better be getting off, and sorry for scalding you earlier.'

'Don't mention it. It's been nice to chat, and skin heals, right?' He laughed.

'Oh, don't! I feel bad enough as it is. I best be going.'

'Sure.' He raised his hand.

She heard the catch of lament in his voice. 'Are you here on your own?' she asked.

'Yes, recently divorced. Well, actually, not that recently. It's been eighteen months and I'm only just coming up for air, learning how to breathe again.' He swallowed, as if this was a rare admission.

Rosie stood up and put her jacket back on. 'I'm sorry to hear that.'

He sighed. 'It's just part of life, I guess, and I'm still set-tling into the new me. It's been scary, exciting, horrible all at the same time, but I'm coming out the other side.'

She shoved her hands in her pockets. 'I really had better

go. Kids and husband have been to soft play and they'll be wanting their tea when they get back. Well, good luck.'

'Thank you. You too.' He smiled.

Rosie took a few steps, skirting the path that headed back along the Esplanade.

'I'm Clark, by the way,' he shouted after her.

'As in Kent?' She smiled, turning her head.

'Yes, but without the superpower or the glasses, worse luck.'

'I'm sure you could get glasses if you really wanted them...'

Clark chuckled. 'And what's your name?'

'I'm Rosie, Rosie Tipcott.'

'Now there's a name.'

She waved. 'Safe travels back to Portland.'

'Eventually.' He reminded her.

'Yes, eventually.' She smiled.

As she made her way back to Arlington Road, Rosie couldn't stop her mind wandering to her childhood bedroom and the vast travel-themed montage that she'd created on its walls. The rest of the house had been non-descript and full of mismatched furniture donated by well-meaning neighbours, but her bedroom was special. She spent hours ripping pictures from magazines and brochures and gluing them to the wall. The images that gripped her were of tropical oceans, deserted beaches, skyscrapers in unfamiliar cities, bowls of street food eaten with chopsticks and of course the planes, trains and ships that carried people back and forth on their adventures. She added to her collage over the years and eventually her dad glossed over it with a light varnish, leaving a wall of travel-related decoupage for her to escape to before she fell asleep at night.

In her dreams, she would walk hand in hand with her mum as they stepped from gangways onto foreign soil. Once ashore, they would eat ice cream and nod at the locals as they strolled and chatted, with all the time in the world...

Rosie had laid the table and was stirring the pot of chilli on the hob as the front door banged open. 'Mummy!' Naomi yelled, then came crashings and bashings in the hallway. Trainers were discarded, coats dumped and a knackered husband threw his car keys on the windowsill.

The girls ran into the kitchen.

'Mummy, I did a massive jump into the ball pit and landed on this boy's head and his dad said to Daddy that I was a maniac and Dad said he should watch his mouth and I watched his mouth but nothing happened, and the boy was sick and we had to get out of the ball pit and the man said it was my fault, but I don't think jumping on someone's head can make them sick, do you?'

'Naomi Jo Tipcott, do you ever take a breath? Goodness me, I'm gasping just listening to you!' Rosie swooped forward and kissed her daughter. 'Go to the loo before tea and wash your hands, there's a good girl.' She tutted and patted her daughter off to the cloakroom.

'Suppose you've heard about our little adventure?' Phil leant against the work surface and folded his arms. 'I tell you what, Rosie, that girl is a human wrecking ball! She creates chaos everywhere she goes. There's me nearly scrapping with a bloke near the ball pit. It was a bloody nightmare – never again! I was half tempted to leave them there and escape to the pub.' He shook his head.

'I know, Phil. I look after them every day.' She walked past and kissed him too. 'And where's my baby?'

'I'm here, Mum!' Leona called from the hallway. 'I'm trying to get my tattoos straight.'

Rosie watched as her daughter peeled the backing plastic from the images and rubbed the transfers of a skull and crossbones and a large cutlass onto her dainty forearm. 'You're still being a pirate, I see?'

'Aye aye, Captain.' Leona winked. Her eye patch was firmly anchored to the centre of her forehead.

'Well, shipmate, when that scoundrel Naomi comes out of the cloakroom, can you please use the loo and wash your hands and then I'll dish up supper.'

'Are we 'avin' grog?'

Rosie looked at her slight, pretty five-year-old as she stood on wobbly legs and grabbed the bannister. 'I reckon you might have already had some!'

There was a rare moment of silence in the Tipcott household as the four tucked into the chilli and rice. 'This is lush,

Rosie. I'm starving.' Phil scooped a large forkful towards his mouth.

'I met an interesting man today. A writer,' she began.

'What do you mean, a writer?' Naomi asked.

'Don't talk with your mouth full.' Rosie used her fork as a pointer. 'He writes things – books, and articles for the newspapers, stuff like that.'

'But that's just a stupid thing to say.' Naomi looked at her mum.

'Why is it?' Phil snapped.

'Because everybody writes things. I write my news, Mummy writes lists. I don't say, "I'm a writer". I talk as well, we all talk, am I a talker too? And I walk, am I a walker and I wee, am I a wee-er? And I poo, so am I a—' These last two she added for Leona's benefit and it did the trick, as her little sister dissolved into fits of giggles.

'We get the message, thank you, Naomi!' Rosie interrupted, fearful of where her daughter's train of thought might take her.

Phil put the fork down and placed the back of his hand against his mouth, trying to swallow his supper while he talked. 'I reckon you are a talker, Nay, you never shut up.'

Rosie smiled; trying to reassure her daughter. 'It's a bit different, love, it means he writes things for his job.'

'For his *job*?' she yelled. 'Writing stuff isn't a proper job!'

'For the love of God, Naomi, stop shouting and just eat your chilli.' Phil pointed towards her bowl, his jaw tense.

'Anyway...' Rosie shifted on her seat, trying to regain the floor. 'He was from America, on the West Coast.'

'Was it Washington?' Naomi shouted.

'No, it wasn't Washington,' Rosie answered.

'Was it Florida?' Leona asked. 'That's in America.'

'Yes, it is in America, clever girl, but no, it wasn't Florida.'

'Does he know Buzz Lightyear?' Leona asked, wide eyed.

'I didn't ask him.'

'Was it Disneyland?' Naomi was warming up.

'No more guesses!' Rosie held her hands up. 'He was from a place called Portland in Oregon, which is on the opposite side of the country to New York and up a bit, as if you were heading towards Canada. And as I was saying, he said something quite amazing.' She paused until she had their full attention. 'He said that the weather gods had found some warm crumbs in their pockets and that's why we got that little sprinkling of sunshine on a cold March day. Isn't that lovely?'

'Have *you* been on the grog, Rosie?' Phil snorted and tucked into the remainder of his rice.

'Daddy was on the phone to Gerald the farmer, who doesn't have pigs or a horse or a farmer's wife,' Naomi said.

'What's she on about?' Rosie smiled at her husband.

'Geraldine Farmer, who's got the big place in Mortehoe, she phoned about a new polished concrete floor she wants putting in the basement.' Phil concentrated on his supper, chasing the grains with his fork.

'That's a bit of a liberty, phoning you on a Saturday. I mean, you'd think it could wait until Monday. What a cheek.'

'She's the boss.' He pushed the chair back from the table.

'Not at the weekend, she isn't.' Rosie tutted.

'That's the thing, when you've got as much money as she has normal routines don't count. Her life isn't divided up into a treadmill of nine to five with the weekends off for good behaviour.' He looked up at the ceiling. 'She just breezes through, doing what she wants when she wants. Wouldn't that be nice, no slaving away, someone to babysit the kids on a Saturday afternoon… Money like that gives you choices.'

'I'm sure it does. I did offer to come and take the kids off your hands.' Again she smiled at her girls, wary they were being discussed like a commodity to be traded. 'But I stand by my view, if she thinks she can choose to eat up your family time on weekends, she's mistaken. I don't care how much money she's got.' She paused. 'I reckon we should get you a nice cold can of cider and watch some telly, how does that sound?' She smiled at the man she loved.

He smiled back, but behind the smile he looked distracted and tired.

Five

May had arrived with promise: trees were heavy with blossom and the mornings were lighter earlier. But one week in, this changed; the signs of summer were snatched away and the rain-lashed beaches were far from appealing. The early-blooming petals were no match for the relentless raindrops and they lay in clusters on the kerb, a fragrant pink cushion waiting to be washed into the drains.

Rosie had made the packed lunches and walked the girls to school, pulling her hood up over her hair as she tried and failed to keep Naomi from puddle-jumping and showering her sister in muddy droplets in the process.

She popped into the coffee shop on her way home and as her wet coat steamed in the warmth of the place, she scanned the tables to see if Mel was around. It had been over a week since she'd seen her friend and she missed her. She fired off a quick text. *Oi! Coffee mate! Missing your gossip, no fun eating a jacket spud alone! Love, your friend, Rosie Shitstar X* She looked forward to her friend's response and the chance to arrange a get-together.

The response came almost immediately. *Ha! Hello Rosie Shitstar! Up to my eyes, see you soooooon. X*

It was rather more noncommittal than she had hoped for, but she understood. Family life could sometimes swallow you up.

Back home and having dried off as best she could, Rosie filled the kettle. She spied Phil's Bob the Builder lunchbox on the work surface.

'Bum.' She didn't like the idea of him going without his packed lunch, especially on a cold, rainy day like this, knowing how much he preferred a sandwich and a bit of cake to just about anything else. Acting on impulse, she grabbed the lunchbox and the car keys and set off to her in-laws' house.

Mo and Keith lived on a smallholding on the way out of town, heading towards Braunton. Their spacious 1950s house, Highthorne, was quite ugly; the beauty of the place was in the 2.4 acres that surrounded it. It had a grey pebble-dashed exterior and four evenly spaced, shallow bay windows with pale green window frames. The front door was recessed inside a wide, space-grabbing porch lined with the original and now rather dulled red tiles. This was usually cluttered with shoes, boots, newspapers and the odd recycling trug waiting to be sorted, along with peelings for the compost, which Keith used to fertilise his locally famous courgettes and marrows.

To the right of the house sat a large metal-framed structure commonly known as 'the yard'. It was from here that the Tipcott men ran their building business, and when work was scarce it was where they gathered to play pool and drink tea, ferried in and out of the house on a laminated bamboo tray, while they waited for the phone to ring. Which it always did, eventually.

The inside of their home was packed with family memorabilia. The walls were crammed with photographs of the two boys growing up, some featuring embarrassing haircuts that were a rich source of ridicule. These were encircled by wedding pictures of Rosie and Phil and images of Keith and Mo's two adored grandchildren, who in their baby stages looked remarkably similar. Anything that arrived from the wandering Kev – a postcard or memento from his travels, usually a picture of him bare chested on sand, holding an aquatic specimen – was set in pride of place on the mantelpiece, giving the bulky, brown-glazed fireplace an almost altar-like status. Rosie loved getting updates about the places he saw and the people he met. She always pored over the latest shots, taking in the sun-bleached, shoulder-length hair and weathered face; the laughing eyes of her school friend staring right at her.

The windowsills and shelves were crowded with ornaments, the chairs and sofa in the sitting room were piled with hand-embroidered cushions, and nick-knacks crowded the top of the television, each holding a special memory of someone dear to them. It was a busy house, full of love, and Rosie was, as ever, grateful and happy to be a part of it.

The house had been her haven throughout her teens, a source of the warmth and cosiness that wasn't apparent in her own home. Her dad was not the demonstrative type. He was never mean or unkind, but it was as if he parented with a sense of embarrassment, going through the motions, like he had read a book on how to be a dad but lacked the softer skills, the spontaneity. She figured that was because he carried the guilt of whatever it was he had done to drive her mum away. This and the fact that he was a Roy and not a Damien or a Brett.

He now lived on the outskirts of Exeter with his partner, Shona, who was a little odd, like him, but in a different way. They were big into ballroom dancing. Shona dragged him around the country with her feather and net creations nestling in the boot. Rosie smiled to think of him in sequins and shiny, shiny shoes.

'*We need to start afresh...*' She was eighteen, just, when he had said that and he left, making it obvious that it wasn't 'we' that needed to start afresh but him. Rosie wasn't quite ready to be abandoned, even though she said she was. She lied to make it easier for him, knowing it was going to be harder for her, but she also knew that sometimes that was what you had to do. In her experience, everyone left her eventually.

Her dad used to mention Laurel's departure as if it was incidental, as if this might lessen the blow. Something of interest, certainly, but not the life-changing event that it was. He simply lumped it together with other days that stood out in his memory. Maybe that made it bearable for him, but for her it was almost comical. *'Do you remember that Pete Sampras win in straight sets? 6-4, 6-2, 6-4 – a bloody walkover, fantastic! And what about the day your mum did a runner after having you? Just picked up her coat and off she trotted. Who wants a cup of tea?'*

'Yeah, sure,' is what she wanted to say. *'What did you say to her, Dad? What did you do?'* But she never found the confidence.

Life at Highthorne was very different. It was safe, predictable and warm.

She smiled at the sight of the two large white vans parked on the driveway, feeling a flicker of pride at the Tipcott name emblazoned on the sides. She may have been a Tipcott for only twelve years, but this was her family, her daughters' heritage, and it thrilled her.

She pushed on the side door of the yard.

'Only me!' she called out as she walked into the large office space that backed onto the storeroom, where the walls beneath the corrugated roof were lined with racking and shelves. It was an Aladdin's cave, holding all manner of tools, paint, plasterboard and odds and ends that her father-in-law was confident they would need one day. He was a stickler for organisation. Salvaged doors leant against the wall, three deep and in height order. Boxes of various sizes and old ice-cream containers were adorned with sticky labels giving the measurements and inventories of what lay within. Plastic drawers sat in portable frames, stacked all the way up to the ceiling and carefully labelled with descriptions like *Butterfly Rawl*. She was sure the contents were a lot less pretty than they sounded. A fine layer of sawdust covered the floor and the whole place smelt of chemicals and wood and reminded her of her childhood, bringing to mind the many projects her dad used to start in the kitchen and then abandon weeks later.

'Is that you, Rosie?' her father-in-law called from the back. 'I thought I heard the car.'

She ducked her head and spied him in his overalls, at the top of a ladder against the back wall. 'Yep, only me, Keith. Don't let me disturb you. Phil forgot his lunch!' She held the box over her head and wiggled it.

'Oh, you're a good girl. Pop it on the desk and I'll make sure he gets it.' He waved from his perch.

'Everything all right with you?' she called.

'Yes, thanks, love. Glad to get that bloody job in Mortehoe out the way.'

'I heard she was a bit of a nightmare!' Rosie laughed.

'A bit? She was a right fussy madam. I had a full head of hair when we started the job.'

They both laughed at his favourite joke as Keith ran his hand over his bald head.

'Phil's just finishing off up there, then we go to the new flats on the front. Should be a breeze by comparison.'

'Oh lovely, I'll walk that way home from school with the girls and then you can see them.' She smiled at the idea.

'I'll hold you to that. Kettle's on in the house, if you fancy a cup of tea? Mo's in, I think.'

'I just might.'

As she walked around the front of the building to the main entrance, Rosie smiled in anticipation of seeing her mother-in-law. She rang the bell, then instantly regretted doing so as Kayleigh sauntered down the hall and let her in. It seemed that when Ross was up working for his uncle, she saw the need to accompany him, loitering at Highthorne, as if it was a day out. 'Shit,' she muttered under her breath.

'All right, Rosie? How *are* you?' Kayleigh smiled, her bright demeanour and upbeat mood as surprising as it was unnerving. 'Everything all right with you, then?'

'Yes. Good, thanks. How are you?'

'Great!' came the unexpected response.

Rosie wished Mel were there to share this; the only possible explanation was that Kayleigh had been abducted by aliens and this imposter hadn't been outed yet. This was, to her mind, far more likely than the fact that Kayleigh was simply happy.

'Mo's nipped out. Gone to get a few bits up at the farm shop,' Kayleigh chirped.

'Oh right, well don't worry about putting the kettle on, Kayleigh. I wasn't staying, just popped in to say hi.'

She glanced around the spacious kitchen with its lidded china hens, raffia coasters, cluttered pinboard and trusty Kenwood Chef. It had been state of the art in the late nineties: blonde-wood cupboard doors with wrought-iron handles, a clunking great waste-disposal system and a heavy square wooden rack that hung on chains from the ceiling, dripping with copper pans that were only for show, and the whole contraption topped with fake plastic ivy. Mo and Keith didn't seem to notice the wear and tear, or if they did, they simply didn't care. And anyway, nearly all available wall space, cupboards included, was covered in their grand-daughters' artwork, along with a tea towel that bore the words: *Only the best mums in the world get promoted to Grandma!* This Mo had pinned to a wall, in pride of place. Rosie smiled to see the ever-growing collection.

'Are you sure? I'm having one!' Kayleigh grabbed a mug from the wooden mug tree by the kettle.

'No, I can't. I was only dropping off Phil's lunch and I thought I might catch him.'

'He's up at Mortehoe,' Kayleigh offered, unblinking.

'Yeah, Keith said. Well, no matter, he'll get it up to him. Right, Kayleigh, give Mo my love and I'll see you later.'

Rosie jumped into her old banger and laughed. She couldn't wait to share this with Mel.

Weaving her way along the country lane wet with residual rain, she smiled to see Mo, her diminutive mother-in-law, tootling towards home, her eye line only just above the steer-ing wheel of her Renault. Both women slowed their cars, lowered their windows and beamed, happy to see each other. Rosie reached out through the window and took Mo's prof-fered hand.

'Rosie! Have I just missed you?' Mo asked regretfully.

'Yes, sorry, Mo, I just dropped Phil's lunch off and I was going to have a cup of tea, but—'

'But you didn't want to hang around. I get it, lovely.'

She pulled a face, indicating that she wasn't looking forward to being trapped in the kitchen with a certain someone either.

'She's in a suspiciously good mood!' Rosie picked up the thread.

'Yes, she is. It's quite unnerved Keith, I can tell you. He's hiding in the storeroom!' Mo clamped her top teeth over her bottom lip, as if to stop her speaking. It wasn't her style to gossip in this way, but she and Rosie shared a special friendship.

'So I saw. He was saying they're moving to the flats on the front next. I told him I'll bring the girls by every day to say hello.'

'Oh, he'll love that! I can write them little notes for him to pass on, and send sweeties and things.'

'You spoil them, Mo!'

'Can't help it. I love them so much.' She raised her shoulders as if mentally hugging them.

Rosie smiled. 'I know you do. Lucky girls.' A car approached and beeped, slowing as it came up behind her. The driver was clearly unhappy at the hold-up in the middle of the lane, raising his arms as if something catastrophic had occurred. 'Ooh, better get going.' She let go of her mother-in-law's hand and waved her apology in the rearview mirror, then made her way back to town.

Rosie wandered round the local shop with the basket on her arm. She had popped two tins of baked beans in it and a bottle of sugar-free squash when her eye was drawn to the papers and magazines, sitting on the bottom shelf next to the drinks fridge.

There, on the front page of *The Times*, was a thumb-sized photograph of Clark, the American! Rifling through the unwieldy pages, filling the aisle with her outstretched arms, she turned to the right section, held the paper close to her face and read the first paragraph.

North Devon may not be the obvious choice when it comes to worldwide holiday destinations. But here's why I think Woolacombe and the surrounding area has as much to offer as the Seychelles, Bali or even Norway...

'Anything interesting?' The woman's voice caught her off guard.

Rosie lowered the paper and came face to face with Geraldine Farmer. It had to be her: she looked shiny, immaculate and out of place in the local shop. She was a diminutive woman, a vision in skinny black jeans, loose black V-neck sweater that slipped off her tanned shoulder, and high-heeled boots. Her arms and neck rattled with sparkly silver jewellery.

'Oh, not really! A friend of mine wrote this article – well, not a friend exactly...' She blushed. 'Someone I met on a bench... well, actually, I met him before that... in a caravan.' Her blush intensified. She felt instantly inadequate in the presence of this petite, gleaming, shiny-haired millionaire.

'How funny.' The woman beamed, showing her perfect teeth. 'I'm Geraldine by the way.'

'Yes.' Rosie nodded. 'I guessed as much. I'm Phil's wife. Phil Tipcott? He's working up at your place?'

'Phil! Yes, of course! Oh God, you must hate me, keeping him and the whole crew working till all hours. I'm sure my name is mud.' She gave a loud laugh and let her eyes roam over Rosie's stretch denim M&S jeans.

'Not at all. I think they've quite enjoyed the project,' Rosie lied.

'It's so nice to meet you in person at last. I've heard a lot about you from Phil and you're exactly as I imagined.'

Rosie felt a warm glow at the thought of Phil telling this sophisticated woman all about his family. 'Do you know, it's nice to chat to someone. I only get to speak to grubby workmen, don't know a soul.'

Rosie nodded. Geraldine grabbed her arm. 'Oh God! Not that Phil is grubby! I'm just putting my foot in it today.' She laughed again, loudly.

Rosie laughed too. 'No, you were right the first time – he can get quite grubby.'

'I should let you go.' Geraldine smiled. 'Really, really lovely to meet you. Give my best to Phil, won't you?'

'I will.' Rosie smiled and waved as Geraldine left. 'Ha! Well I never,' she muttered, then felt the bloom of self-consciousness at having laughed out loud in the local shop.

'You okay there, Mrs Tipcott?' Mrs Blackmore's busty granddaughter asked from behind the till.

'Yes thanks, love.' She folded the newspaper and laid it on top of her shopping. 'I'm fine.' She couldn't wait to show Phil.

Rosie fed the girls and ran the bath so they could both have a quick soak before bed. As they splashed in the bubbles, she sat on the loo and read Clark's article. Naomi filled her cheeks with water and spat it at Leona, who wailed loudly.

'Please, girls! Can't I just have five minutes' peace to read this? Naomi, please stop gobbing water at your sister. It's not nice.'

'I didn't!' She held her hands up with an expression so virtuous it was as if butter wouldn't melt.

'What do you mean? I saw you do it!' Rosie glared at her.

'I always get the blame!' Naomi's protest increased in both vigour and volume.

'Because it's always you!' Rosie replied.

'It's not fair!' Naomi slapped her palms down on the surface of the water and, to everyone's surprise, bubbles leapt from the bath and began raining down on them.

'For goodness' sake!' Rosie shook the droplets from the paper and folded it quickly to avoid another soaking.

Leona pointed at her mum and laughed so hard, she couldn't catch her breath. Naomi followed suit until they were giggling and smiling, back to being the best of friends.

'What are you two laughing at?' Rosie couldn't help but smile; their happiness was irresistibly infectious. It was only when she stood up and looked in the mirror that she saw the large crest of fluffy white bubbles that had landed on the top of her head, making her look part punk, part ice-cream cone.

'Oh my goodness!' She laughed, relishing the joy that often came from the smallest of things.

'Well, I'm glad someone's had a good day.' Phil's voice came from the landing.

'Mummy's got bird poo on her head!' Naomi shouted.

Phil pushed on the door and shook his head at the sight of his wife. 'Hey, guys. I'll be downstairs,' he added, sounding far more downbeat than the situation warranted.

Rosie put the girls into their pyjamas, turned back their duvets and clicked on the nightlights in their bedroom.

'Right, you can have five minutes chatting to your dad and then it's bed.'

The two little girls hotfooted it downstairs, wanting to make the most of those five minutes, which, if they were canny, they knew they could stretch to ten.

They actually managed fifteen. As Rosie wished them goodnight and closed their bedroom door, a welcome blanket of hush descended on the house, smothering the flames of chaos that had crackled brightly only minutes earlier. She closed her eyes briefly, feeling the day's tiredness wash over her. Retrieving the newspaper from the bed, she crept downstairs and into the lounge.

'You'll never guess, Phil... Two things. Firstly, I met that Geraldine Farmer and she said to give you her best. She's lovely! I think she was glad to have someone to chat to.'

He stared at her.

'And secondly, that man I spoke to, the one who was staying in the caravans, I saw his article today, the one he was writing.' She held up the paper.

'What is it I have to *guess*, exactly?' He looked up at her, his expression weary.

'What?' She was a little confused.

'You said I'd never guess?' he shot back irritably.

'Well, nothing. I'm just saying, it was really strange, he said he was writing an article and then there it was in the paper!'

'So, let me get this straight, you meet a man who says he's writing an article, he writes the article he told you he was writing and then you see it in the paper. I don't see what's strange about it.'

Rosie placed the paper on the sofa. 'What's the matter with you?'

Phil pinched the bridge of his nose and sat back in the chair. 'Nothing. I'm just tired.'

'I brought your lunch up today, dropped it with your dad, and not a word of thanks.'

'I never asked you to!' he snapped.

Rosie stared at him. 'No, you're right, and more fool me for worrying that you might not get your lunch. Lesson learnt, Phil. Next time you forget your lunch or need something running up to your mum's, which I do all the time, you can bloody whistle!'

She left him alone to stew and went to wash up the tea

things and stack the dishwasher. She worked quickly, agitated by his mood and his remarks.

It was ten minutes later that he trod the cold kitchen floor and came up behind her.

'Sorry, Rosie.'

She shrugged and carried on sorting the cutlery into the allocated pots in the dishwasher. 'Doesn't matter, it was only a stupid article, I just felt involved in some way, because I met the man who wrote it. Stupid, really.' She was embarrassed.

'It's not stupid. It's quite exciting. And I shouldn't have taken it out on you. I'm sorry.'

'Taken what out on me?'

'Everything – you know. I had a bad day, but it doesn't give me the right to come back here and be grumpy.' He ran his hand up her arm. 'Forgiven?'

'Course you're forgiven. Everyone's allowed to have a grump in a while, but let me help you. Talk to me. What's up?' She closed the dishwasher and faced him, tying her thick hair into a loose knot at the nape of her neck and giving him her full attention.

'Nothing really, just… everything.'

'Is it having to go up to Mortehoe?'

'What?' He creased his forehead.

'Your dad said you were up there on your own, finishing off, and he also mentioned that you found Geraldine a bit of a handful. Is it that? Because if it is, you need to tell Keith that it's not fair on you. Tell him to send Ross or, better still, if she's going to be demanding, go up as a pair, support each other, would that help? I can't bear the idea of her giving you the runaround – you're worth more than that. Although I have to say, Phil, that she was so nice to me today, I reckon if you took the time to get to know her, she'd be lovely.'

Phil looked at the floor and ran his sock over the tiled surface. 'I love you, Rosie.'

'And I love you, you dafty! Go sit in your chair and I'll bring you a hot drink, how about that?' She smiled, her voice soft, motherly.

Phil nodded and sloped back to the comfy chair in the sitting room.

Six

It was the first week of July. All the windows of their little house on Arlington Road were open, making the whole place feel different. With the back door permanently ajar, the garden and house became one and their usable space doubled. She loved this time of year. The girls had just ten days left at school before they broke up for the summer holidays and they were already giddy with thoughts of what the summer might hold. Rosie, like most locals, had practically abandoned her car. To try and travel by road was a challenge too far. The town centre was gridlocked, not only with holiday traffic but also with idling pedestrians who had all the time in the world. They ambled across the roads, distracted by ice creams, chocolate-covered waffles and shared bags of fudge, their arms wide and draped with all manner of beach paraphernalia. They were too focused on getting to that wide stretch of golden sand to notice that cars, buses and tractors also needed to go about their business. The taxi drivers smiled for the first time in the year, but after a week or so of pulling fourteen-hour shifts, they were soon moaning about the lack of rest, unlike the other forty-odd weeks of the year, when they moaned about the lack of business.

Mel was in situ and filling out her timesheet when Rosie slid into the booth.

'I've already done mine.' She nodded at the sheet of paper on the table.

'Someone get this woman a cloth to shine her halo! She's already done her timesheet!' Mel shouted into the busy café.

Rosie laughed and hid her eyes, employing Leona's strategy. 'I was only saying!'

'I always, always forget and then it's this mad rush to get it in on time. I have to make half of it up.'

'You can't do that,' Rosie tutted.

'You are such a rule follower.'

'I am,' she acknowledged. 'If I thought I'd put the wrong hours in, I wouldn't be able to sleep. I need to have everything organised, planned. Talking of which, what weekend is the big barbecue this year? Mid August as normal? I've got to ask Mo if she and Keith will do the usual and come and collect the kids after they've eaten. Then we can boogie the night away. They'll take Tyler too, I'm sure, give you the night off. Plus I want to get my outfit planned.'

'Oh God! I've just remembered the Baileys cocktails that

Phil made last year. I was wrecked.' Mel stuck out her tongue and winced. 'They tasted like milkshakes, but, my God, I had the worst hangover I think I've ever had.'

'I think one or two would have been fine, but it was the eighth or ninth that did it. Or it could have been that we'd had the bottle under the sink since Christmas.'

'Please don't remind me.' Mel closed her eyes, as if even the memory was enough to make her queasy.

'What can I do to help? Coleslaw and salads as usual? I was thinking of doing a fancy one I saw in my magazine, with couscous, lemon and mint.'

'Ooh, couscous – get you, Miss Fancy Pants! Yes, please, that or coleslaw would be lovely. I'll let you know the date when we've fixed it. Andy's been dithering about the details, shock horror.'

'Well, can you remind him that I need to put it in my social calendar. In fact...' She considered this. 'It is the *only* thing in my social calendar. How sad am I?'

'Not sad, just too busy to fit everything in.' Mel waved at the waitress. 'Coffee and a jacket, Miss Shitstar?'

'Of course.' Rosie smiled at her friend.

'So, is Kayleigh still sprinkling glitter with every smile?' Mel asked as they waited to order.

'Seems to be. I've only seen her in passing a couple of times, but, honestly, it was weird. Even spooked Mo and Keith, and you know it takes a lot to get them flustered.'

'Unless we're talking about a visit from the prodigal Kevin – they always go into a big flap over that.'

'True. I suppose it's a bit unfair, really. I mean, I'm fond of Kev, you know, and he is the baby and all that, but when I think how hard Phil works... And then when Kev turns up, it's as if Phil's invisible, and he's a good son to them, as well as a good husband and dad. We're lucky really.'

Mel waved again at the waitress and changed the subject. 'I'm bloody starving,' she said.

It was late afternoon and the girls skipped ahead. 'Don't cross any roads!' Rosie shouted the usual warning as they made their way along Bay View Road. They started jumping up and down with excitement when they spotted their grandad's van parked at the bottom of a driveway. Rosie texted him to make sure it was safe and within a minute Keith was strolling down the drive in his overalls.

'Hello, girls! What a lovely surprise.'

They both ran forward and nearly sent his crouching form toppling as they flung their arms around his neck.

'We break up in nine days,' Naomi held up all her fingers and shouted, even though she was only inches from his face.

'Not that we're counting.' Rosie smiled.

'I know! Then what will you do for six whole weeks?' He beamed.

'I'm going to learn to skip and Mummy is getting us a new paddling pool because we stuck a fork in our old one.'

'Don't ask.' Rosie closed her eyes briefly, pre-empting his questions.

'And we are going to the beach and we are going to get a pony,' Naomi finished.

'We are not going to get a pony.' Rosie corrected her daughter.

'You said we could get a pet!' Leona reminded her.

'Yes, a pet! Not a pony! I was thinking a hamster, but preferably a fish.' She rolled her eyes at her father-in-law.

'Oh, come on, Rosie, don't be mean, I think a pony is a great idea.' He winked.

'Well, Grandad, there's only one person with enough land for a pony and that's you.' She threw it back at him as the girls shouted, 'Yes! Yes! Yes!' and ran around him, as though it was a done deal.

He chuckled. 'Actually, do you know what, on second thoughts, I think a hamster or a fish sounds like a great idea.'

'Phil not here?' Rosie looked up at the three-storey building they were converting into six apartments.

'No, love, he left early. Is he not home?'

'I must have just missed him. I went for a coffee and a late lunch with Mel, then straight on to fetch the kids. What a shame – he could have come with me. Never mind, I expect he's glad of the peace and quiet.' She laughed as Naomi and Leona raced around the driveway.

The street in which the Tipcotts lived was like many within walking distance of the town centre, with six out of its fourteen houses owned by out-of-towners and used as second homes. Many of these families were city dwellers who visited on the odd weekend, at New Year and for most of the summer. Rosie, unlike those who were quick to bemoan the rising price of property and the lack of community spirit, rather liked it. Her street was quiet in the non-occupied months and if her house was going up in value because Woolacombe was getting more fashionable, well, so much the better. It made her laugh, though, to see how the houses had been altered. Originally identical to hers, they now boasted glass-roofed extensions out the back that ate up the gardens, loft conversions to provide master suites, and Juliet balconies to make the most of the glimpse of sea from the upstairs windows. That was if you stood on a bucket and craned your neck. Tipcott and Sons had themselves worked on a couple of the houses, adding a few quid onto the price of the job – 'the townie tax' they called it.

As the three rounded the corner, nearly home, their occasional neighbour was unloading her Mercedes estate. Children of various ages, all wearing blue-and-white-striped items from the Joules catalogue, were ferrying bundled duvets and boxes of food across the pavement. They reminded Rosie of modern-day von Trapps.

'Hi, Rosie!' Mummy von Trapp shouted as she unfurled her skinny limbs from under the tailgate. 'How *are* you?'

'Good, thanks. Is it that time of year already?'

'Yes, thank goodness. Just *had* to get out of town.' The woman swiped her brow as if her life was spent down a mine and not sprinting up and down Chiswick High Road in search of organic quinoa. 'It's nice to see you.'

'And you.' Rosie nodded, noting that she looked

decidedly younger than she had the previous year and was now suspiciously wrinkle-free.

'We should get the kids together for a play date!' Mummy von Trapp smiled at Naomi.

'Oh, they'd love that – wouldn't you?' She directed her question at the girls.

'I wouldn't, no,' Naomi said bluntly.

Rosie felt her cheeks flame. 'Don't be daft, Nay, of course you would. She's kidding!' She addressed the last bit to the rather taken aback Mummy von Trapp.

'I'm not, Mum. I don't want to play with them. The last time I went there, she gave us rice cakes and told us they were biscuits, but they weren't, they were rice cakes and I hate rice cakes.'

'I only give them organic, sugar-free,' Mummy von Trapp whispered, almost apologetically.

Rosie couldn't get into the house fast enough. Phil was in the kitchen.

'Oh my God, Phil, I have just nearly died. You won't believe what Naomi said to the woman two doors down.' She looked up for the first time. 'Oh, you've had a haircut!' She deposited bags, summer cardigans and lunchboxes in the usual fashion.

'Yep, went this afternoon. I needed it.' He ran his hand over his newly shorn locks.

'Very swanky. Different. Looks nice.' She smiled. 'Your dad said you'd left early.' She opened the freezer to grab the oven chips.

'What, you checking up on me now?' he said.

'Course not! I just took the girls to the site to say hello and you weren't there. No big deal.' She put the corner of the plastic bag in her mouth and ripped it open with her teeth, before shaking out the entire contents onto an oven tray.

'Well, it shouldn't be a big deal, but apparently it is, if you need to go and ask my dad where I am! What do I need, a note?' He raised his voice.

'Are you and Daddy having a row?' Leona called from the sitting room.

'I think Daddy might be, but I'm not,' Rosie called in response.

'Very funny.' Phil grabbed his car keys and swept out of the kitchen.

She heard the front door close behind him. 'What on earth...?' she whispered as she shoved the chips in the oven and tried to think of something to serve with them.

He was gone for three hours. Rosie put the girls to bed and tried to keep the mood light, hiding the rising tide of angst that threatened to engulf her. She found herself continually glancing at the clock on her phone and she sent him three messages, asking simply, *WHERE ARE YOU?* To which he declined to reply. The lack of response sent her anxiety rate even higher.

It was just after nine o'clock when she heard his key in the door.

He crept into the sitting room and flopped down on the other end of the sofa, holding his hand over his eyes.

'I'm sorry.'

Rosie twisted her body and tucked her legs beneath her, so she faced her husband. 'What's going on with you, Phil? I'm worried about you.'

'Don't be.' He reached out and took her hand, laying it on his thigh; he ran his fingers over hers.

'But I am and saying "don't be" won't stop that. You need to talk to me, Phil, tell me what's up. You're not yourself.'

He opened his mouth as if to speak but closed it again. She continued to prompt.

'Is it because of the baby thing? Because I understand that it's a pressure you don't need and I purposely haven't mentioned it, not since that day. I can see that the timing's not right and you know what? I've got more than I ever imagined I would have with my little family in our lovely house and if the thought of having another child is making you feel—'

'It's not the baby thing.'

'Oh. Is it work?'

'Why does it have to be something, Rosie? Why do I have to have one reason for feeling a bit out of sorts?' He let go of her hand.

'Because I've known you since I was a teenager and we've been married for nearly twelve years and I've never seen you like this – stroppy, snappy. It's just not like you.'

'I think I'll go up.' He smiled briefly and stood up, making it clear the conversation was over, or so she thought.

'It's not even ten o'clock.' She pointed to the window, trying to emphasise the summer evening light and the relatively early hour.

As if she hadn't spoken, he walked slowly to the door and with his hand resting on the frame he turned to her. 'Don't you ever want a life that's more than cleaning caravans?'

'I do have a life that's more than cleaning caravans. That's just one tiny part of my life.' She sat up straight, her face tilted to one side, as if in question.

'You know what I mean.' He placed his hands on his hips. 'More than eking out a living in the summer, with me working on houses I could never afford for people rich enough to know they should get the hell out of here in the winter. We haven't even got a proper supermarket!'

'You want us to move near a supermarket?' Rosie stared at him; she was trying to follow his thread.

'No! Jesus Christ, Rosie!' He twisted his jaw and shook his head, as though she was stupid, and she thought she might indeed be stupid, because despite him talking, using words she understood, she was no closer to understanding what was going on.

She studied her husband. He turned his body to the left and right, almost pacing on the spot, highly agitated, as if warming up for a run. His eyes darted to the clock and the window, as if he had a place to be. Rosie would have found it hard to describe how he looked to anyone that didn't know him as she did. But it was as if he was already a stranger. She felt no more able to touch him, hold him, kiss him than any man on the street, and at that realisation, she felt the beginnings of fear.

'I want more. I just want more for us both.' He turned his head in her direction, but she noticed that he looked to the left of her, avoiding her face. 'Don't you ever just want to jump in a car and...' His mouth flapped as he searched for the words. 'Go to London!' He raised his palms.

'London?' She let out a little laugh. 'We're not the sort of people who go to London! Not on a whim. I mean, that takes big planning and you know we'd rather be here, at home, away from the hustle and bustle.'

His expression told her this was not the response he wanted. Her mind rushed into solution mode. She loved him, and he was probably tired, what could be done? She thought about a particular weekend a couple of years earlier, when Naomi had asked her what it was like to be on holiday in their town and not live there, and why so many people came there in the summer. After a quick word with Doug up on the site, the grand plan had been launched and she had surprised her husband and two kids with a weekend break in a silver-category six-berth caravan with the best view. It had been cosy in a way the house wasn't. The gas fire had pumped out heat and they had played cards and eaten chips as their laughter steamed up the windows.

'Do you want me to have a word with Doug, see if we can get a caravan again? The kids loved that night and it might be a fun thing to do?'

He gave a slow blink and for a second she thought he might be about to cry. He composed himself and shook his head, tapping his wedding ring against the wood, whispering his response before he left the room and trod the stairs to bed.

'No, Rosie, I don't want to do that.'

Seven

As Rosie threw her bag in the car ready for her annual daytrip to see her dad, she became aware of the racket the girls were making. She pictured the stripy von Trapps having their peace shattered and she cringed, convinced they'd be sitting tutting beneath the wisteria that clambered over their aged oak arbour.

The girls were running in and out of the back garden, jumping into their paddling pool, screaming, splashing around until they were sodden and then darting through the kitchen and diving onto the sofa to huddle under a fleecy blanket for warmth.

'Girls! You are literally soaking the whole house!' she yelled from the kitchen. 'Can't we keep the water outside? Just dry yourselves off with your beach towels before you come inside, please!'

'You sure you don't want the girls to come with you?'

Phil asked as he made the sandwiches for lunch. 'It might be nice for them to spend a bit of time with your dad and Shona and it's company for you in the car.'

'That's lovely of you to think of me, but I'd rather they didn't. It's going to be a pig of a drive, in a hot, stuffy car and it's not exactly fun when we do arrive. The girls are more than happy here and I'll worry less knowing it's only me that's having a rubbish day. God, I feel awful saying that.' She wrinkled her nose. 'Besides, Dad and Shona are off to one of their dancing competitions this afternoon, so it will literally be a quick cup of tea, show my face, have a bit of cake and back in time for supper.'

'Well if you're sure.'

'I am.' She nodded. After the unnerving events of the previous month, things still hadn't returned to normal, but what with the summer holidays and everything, there just hadn't been the time to get to the bottom of it. She hoped that having the day with the girls might cheer him up a bit. Quite probably he was a little jealous of her being able to spend time with the kids while he was busy up at Mortehoe or wherever, this she understood. Mel had quite rightly pointed out that men were allowed a funny five minutes too, and that Andy had had similar wobbles in the past. Rosie took comfort from her words.

'Right, girls, I'm off. See you later and please be good for Daddy.'

'We will.' Naomi tutted, as if offended by the very suggestion. 'Have you said goodbye to Moby and Jonathan?'

Rosie smiled. She might have guessed that allowing the girls to name their own goldfish would produce hilarious results. Moby she understood, but Jonathan? According to Naomi, he was a boy in the year above her at school who looked a bit like a fish.

'Yes, I did. I said goodbye earlier.' She had to admit that the two little fishes were a lot less bother than a pony.

As she sat at the Mullacott roundabout waiting to pull out, a large shiny black Range Rover swept past. The registration was GF38. Geraldine Farmer. Even in the few seconds Rosie had to take in the car and its driver, she could see that both looked very impressive. She raised her hand to give a little wave, a hello to the friend she had made in the Spar, but Geraldine didn't look in her direction. The car simply zoomed past. It was the kind of vehicle that would always look brand new and stand out in the car park. And the woman with the red lipstick and big black-framed sunglasses, well, she would stand out anywhere. She had the upright posture and particular flick of the head of someone who was confident in this knowledge.

The drive to Exeter took just over two stifling hours, far longer than usual because of the holiday season. At one point her car was chugging up a hill behind a caravan, a bus and a tractor. She had laughed loudly, wondering if a couple of cyclists were going to appear, just to give her a full house.

She texted Phil to say she'd arrived, then took a deep

breath before abandoning the car on her dad's precariously sloping driveway.

'Hello there, Rosie.' Shona opened the frosted-glass front door to their flat-fronted nineteen seventies home and ushered her in. A burgundy-and-gold-patterned runner sat in a narrow strip in the middle of the hall floor and the white walls were devoid of pictures, making the place feel cold despite the sunshine.

The house Rosie had grown up in had been similarly soulless, but in a different way. Her dad had had little clue about making the environment cosy, and items were functional rather than pretty. Kindly neighbours donated their unwanted furniture to the poor motherless home, which meant that nothing matched and everything echoed with a history that wasn't theirs. When Rosie had set up her own house-hold with Phil, she had worked hard to make sure Arlington Road was as welcoming and personal as possible.

The house Roy shared with Shona was not so much odd and mismatched as too clean, and chilly, like a sparsely fur-nished holiday home, as if they too were only passing through. There was a similar lack of warmth in the way Shona behaved towards Rosie. She was always polite and attentive, but even though she'd been her dad's partner for some eighteen years, Rosie still found it hard to relate to her. She always felt like a visitor rather than a daughter returning to see her dad.

She followed Shona down the hall, slowing her pace accordingly. Shona always moved as if she was about to take her place on the ballroom floor, keeping her legs stiff and giving a little kick at the ankle after every step. She took her hobby very seriously and was always well turned out, never without her spray-on perma-tan, which kept her skin a nice shade of mahogany. Rosie was thankful she'd not encouraged her dad to follow suit.

The house was silent. It was so different from the warm hug and raucous welcome that awaited her at Mo and Keith's or indeed the chaos she had left behind at home. The vertical blinds of the rectangular lounge were drawn, leaving the room in shadow. As Rosie entered, her dad placed the remote control symmetrically on the arm of his chair and got up. She noticed his burgundy velvet house slippers and wondered if they had been deliberately chosen to match the rug in the hallway.

'Hello, love, how are you?' Roy smiled and hesitated before giving her an awkward hug.

'Please, sit down.' He gestured to the sofa with the floral arm caps and sat back down in his chair.

'Cup of tea, Rosie?' Shona offered from the doorway.

'Lovely, thank you.' She smiled.

'How are Naomi and Leona?' The way her dad spoke his granddaughters' names was oddly formal – he only really knew them from photos.

'Oh, you know, creating mayhem! But happy. They're on their summer holidays, so they're permanently excited. They've got the paddling pool out, so it's hard to stop them tracking mud and grass cuttings into the house. Place is a mess.' She bit her lip, embarrassed at her confession in light of her surroundings.

'Ah, smashing. It's nice they're having fun. How was the A377? Busy, I expect?'

'Yes, slow in places, took me an extra forty minutes, but could have been worse.' She gave a nervous laugh.

'Yes, not too bad at all, really. Longest it's ever taken me was three and a half hours – that was a slog. They're starting work on Crediton High Street, that's going to slow things down, but needs must, it's sewer renovation.'

'Ah, right.' Rosie looked at her lap. They were silent for several beats.

'And how's Phil?' her dad asked eventually.

'Yes, he's good. Bit stressed at the moment, but I'm sure that'll pass when work eases off a bit and I think he misses having time with the girls but, you know... good.' She smiled again. 'You said on the phone that you and Shona are off dancing later? Where's that?'

'Oh, we have a regional heat in Torquay. Should do quite well. Mind you, we've been putting in the hours. Word on the street is our rumba is the one to beat this year.' He winked. 'We're a proper Fred and Ginger.'

Rosie tried to picture her dad dancing and couldn't. 'It must keep you fit.' She was aware of the banality of her response.

'It does, and look at those beauties.' He turned and pointed proudly to a lone pine shelf screwed into the wall. At least six trophies in various shades sat on faux-marble plinths; they were topped with gold couples mid dance, skirts billowing and heads angled just so.

'They're lovely.' She nodded.

Her dad sat up straight, acknowledging that yes, they were lovely. 'We've got more upstairs, in the spare room. I keep saying we're going to need a trophy cabinet at this rate.'

'Kettle's on.' Shona popped her head in and out again, like a cuckoo in a clock that gave a tea-making update instead of the time.

'Funny thing, Rosie – well, actually, not funny at all, but that's the expression, isn't it? I got a letter from Laurel's brother.'

'From…?' She had heard him perfectly, but she felt as if the blood had rushed from her head, leaving her a little woozy and needing him to repeat what she thought he'd said. He hadn't mentioned her mother for a number of years. To hear her name pass his lips so casually was disconcerting, plus there was a new snippet of information: her mum had a brother, which meant Rosie had an uncle! And maybe cousins! It made her feel uncomfortable and excited all at the same time.

'From Laurel's brother. You know… your mum.' He nodded.

She held her breath. As if she needed reminding, as if she could for one second not know who he was talking about!

'Anyway, sad news really.' He paused, looked at her and then at his hands, as if lack of eye contact might make it easier to say.

'She died.' He paused again. 'Nearly eight months ago

now. Cancer. He was going through her things and thought he should maybe let us know.'

He tutted and shook his head slightly. Rosie wasn't sure if this was in response to the news of her death, the time it had taken to alert them, or the fact that Laurel's brother had contacted them at all.

He looked up. 'It's sad, I know, but there we are. Are you okay, Rosie?'

She stared at him, trying to fathom how this news, this vital piece of information could be just casually dropped into the conversation after an update on the impending sewer works in Crediton, while they waited on a cup of tea.

'I...' She swallowed. 'I wanted to see her.'

'You wanted to see her when, love?' He sat forward and lowered his voice, either out of respect for Laurel's demise or simply to keep their words from Shona's keen ears.

Rosie shook her head. The enormity of the realisation that she would now never get to see her mum started to sink in. 'I don't know when exactly, but I just wanted to see her. Just once.' *And I wanted to talk to her.* She stared at her dad. The lump in her throat was making speaking difficult.

'Oh, Rosie, love, I'm sorry.' He glanced over at her, hesitated, then added, 'But she made no effort to see you, did she, in all those years. Made no contact at all. Even so, I'm sure she wouldn't want you to feel sad. She'd want you to soldier on, trust me.'

His words made her skin shiver and her limbs twitch. He'd never been so blunt about the lack of contact before.

A storm of feelings tumbled inside her and she suddenly felt very lonely and very angry.

'Well, I'll never know what she would or wouldn't want, will I? Because for some reason she left before I got the chance to know her. Trust you? I've never had any choice but to trust you, Dad. You were all I had, remember? That was why I went through school learning about periods from my mates and having to rely on friends' mums to tell me about stuff! I just *had* to soldier on then and trust that it was all for the best.'

Shona had walked in with the tray.

'Oh dear, I don't know if that kind of talk is really necessary when your dad's only trying to do the right thing.'

Rosie scowled at her dad's partner in her nylon ski pants and tight-fitting shirt. 'This is between me and Dad, Shona.'

She knew it was mean, but she didn't care. She had lost her mum and the last thing she needed was a reprimand for using the word 'period' from Mrs Strictly.

'Shona's only trying to help,' her dad said meekly.

He crinkled his eyes in a smile at his partner. Shona dropped her chin to her chest and took a seat on the sofa.

'Is she? I tell you what, Dad, if I had something of importance to tell my girls, I would explain beforehand, prepare them, set the scene, and if they were adults like me, I'd suggest they bring someone with them, to support them and take care of them on the way home. This is absolutely typical – you were always so blasé about Mum going, and now you're being blasé about her death and yes, she left me, left us and only *you* know why, but she was still my mum.' Her tears began to fall. 'She was still my mum and I would have liked the chance to meet her, just once.'

She gulped back her sobs and stood up.

As she made her way towards the door, her dad began fumbling in the drawer of the unit to his right. 'I *did* think about it, Rosie. I thought about it a lot, day and night, and I didn't really know what to say to you, or how, but I found this and…' He held out an envelope, which she took from him. 'It's a letter from Laurel. To me. I thought you should probably have it.'

Rosie stared at the yellowing envelope in her hand. 'When… when did you get this?'

Her dad looked skywards, as if trying to remember. 'About four or five months after she left.'

'And you waited till now to tell me about it?'

'I wanted to protect you. I've always wanted to protect you.' He smiled, briefly and affectionately, the glint of tears in his eyes. 'And you always seemed so fine about things, happy, that I thought dragging this up would only spoil that.'

Rosie clenched her jaw, wondering just how blind her dad would have to have been to get it so wrong. Had he really not seen how much she yearned for her mum, what lay behind all her walks to the bench, her apple-scented daydreams, her reliance on Kev and the rest of the Tipcott family?

She just about managed to mutter her goodbyes before practically running out of the front door. With the engine running, she carefully placed the envelope in her handbag. She pictured herself on the sofa at home, with Phil's arms around her. That would be the time and place to find out what her mother had had to say.

The drive home was slow and that suited her fine; she needed the time to reflect. Rosie hated to admit that Shona was right in a way – you didn't miss what you'd never had – but now they could never put things right. She had spent so many years daydreaming about meeting her mum that she'd thought it might actually happen, and she knew exactly how it would go. Her mum would be contrite but resolute, her reasons for leaving powerful and convincing. Rosie would finally learn how her dad had messed up and her mum would confide details about her pregnancy and Rosie's birth, things that only Laurel would know. They would find out that they had so much in common. But now this would never happen and that felt like a huge loss.

As she joined the steady stream of traffic making its way into Woolacombe, the sun began to dip below the horizon. The vivid red sunset sent a spike of joy through her: she was nearly home.

The first thing she heard, before her key was even in the lock, was Naomi's wailing.

'What's going on here?' she called out as she walked into the hallway, having hoped that just for once she might be greeted by an atmosphere of tranquillity.

'Mu-um!' Leona ran from the kitchen and threw herself against the solidity of her mum's legs.

Phil appeared at the kitchen door. 'We've had a bit of a disaster.' He grimaced.

'What on earth has happened?' Rosie bent down and lifted her youngest daughter until she rested on her hip, then kissed her face repeatedly, as if she could erase her sadness with her lips. She walked into the sitting room and sat on the end of the sofa, on which Naomi was curled.

'Moby and Jonathan are dead!' Naomi yelled before placing her head back on the cushion.

'Oh no! That's terrible.' She sought out Phil's face, hoping he might be able to deliver the details in code.

'We... we took them out of their bowl and put them in our paddling pool.' Leona hiccupped. 'Nay said they'd like it because it was a big lot of water, they might think it was the ocean.'

'Right.' Rosie nodded her understanding.

'Then we took them out of the paddling pool and put them in a mug, to take them upstairs.' She sniffed.

'Why were you taking them upstairs?'

'To put them in the bath!' Naomi again lifted her head to explain.

'But we put the mug on the bedroom floor and I didn't know it had been kicked over and we went to the bathroom to run the taps and put the bubbles in and when we came back they were on the carpet and they weren't breathing or talking!' Leona sobbed again.

Phil rolled his eyes. Rosie decided there was no value in explaining to them at that point how the fish should not have been removed from their bowl in the first place. She figured it was best to let them calm down and to give them that salutary lesson when they were better equipped to receive it.

'We want to bury them, Mummy.' Naomi sat up, her eyes red and swollen with crying.

'Yes, of course.' She looked at Phil. He surprised her by not showing the slightest hint that he found the idea of a fish funeral amusing.

'We are going to do it tomorrow,' Leona explained.

'Would you like to see them?' Naomi seemed to brighten a little at the prospect.

'Okay.'

Naomi jumped up and came back into the sitting room with the little square shoebox in which Leona's summer sandals had arrived. She carefully laid it on the floor and removed the cardboard lid to reveal folds of green tissue, in the middle of which sat two little goldfish that looked more grey than gold; death had inevitably dulled their iridescent sheen.

'Ah, that is sad, poor little fellas. But we'll give them a nice send-off tomorrow and we'll think about all the reasons that we're glad we had them – how pretty they were to watch and how happy it made you to know you had pets. In the week and a half that we had them.' She caught Phil's eye and gave a small smile.

Naomi replaced the lid and put the box back in the garden, where it would await burial.

With the girls finally in bed, tears dried, hugs issued and promises of pet replacements wrung out of her, Rosie flopped down on the sofa and tied her thick hair into a knot.

'What a bloody day.' She sighed. 'I can't believe they

killed Moby and Jonathan! They didn't last long. Just glad we didn't go for a pony. I hate to think of those little fish suffering. I blame myself, I should have explained better about fish care. I'll turn it into a lesson when things are a bit calmer, even if it is a bit late for that. It's the worst possible end to a really crappy day.'

'You got off lightly – they wanted me to give them the kiss of life.' Phil came through and sat in his chair.

She laughed. 'I know it's not funny, but I'm picturing you administering CPR to those iddy-biddy things!' She replicated their size with her thumb and forefinger.

His aftershave was strong and danced up her nose. 'You smell nice.' She smiled at her man. Then she remembered the letter in her bag and thought about her mum. The fallout from the great fish massacre had robbed her of the moment until now.

'I've got something to tell you,' she began.

'Me too.' He looked at her.

'Oh, you go first, love.' She yawned and rubbed her eyes with the back of her hand. The long drive and the day's events were taking their toll. She pictured a bath full of bubbles and couldn't wait to climb in.

'No, you go first.' He looked at the carpet, his hands resting on his thighs. He seemed tense.

'No, go on, Phil, mine's a bit of a weird one and I need to prepare, so you first.' She smiled.

Rosie had been wrong. The passing of the goldfish was not the worst possible end to a really crappy day.

Eight

Jamie Oliver burbled away in the background. He was wearing a brown checked shirt and his hands were waving about as he sprinkled something from a great height. He was cooking outside; she caught the green of a garden in her peripheral vision. Naomi and Leona's brightly coloured floral beach towels were strewn about the floor and the Lego table was on its side, the tiny bricks littering pretty much the whole carpet. A blonde-haired boy, possibly one of the von Trapps, whizzed by on the pavement outside. She heard the rhythmic bump of his skateboard over the paving stones and noted the way he seemed to bob up and down under their window like a well-spoken jack-in-the-box.

Phil's scent was woody, unfamiliar and quite overpowering; not as pleasant as she'd first thought. A torn corner of green tissue paper sat on the arm of the sofa. She picked it up and rolled it between the thumb and forefinger of her right hand. Her toes, splashed with remnants of bright pink nail polish, poked like fat, pale sausages from under her tucked legs and she noticed that her heels were a little grubby around the areas where the skin was cracked. She unwittingly stored away the smallest of details, as if she knew they would become important. It would in the future help her to replay this scene, this moment, replicating it perfectly until the day she died.

Rosie thought she had to worry about the impending burial of her kids' dead goldfish, she thought she was nervous about reading a letter from the mum she had never known. But she had much, much more to worry about than this; she just didn't know it yet.

Call it sixth sense, call it intuition, but as Phil sat up straight, rubbed his palms on the thighs of his new jeans, looked at her and opened his mouth to speak, Rosie raised her left hand and splayed it. As if this little shield could prevent the devastation that was about to come at her, could ward off the tsunami of hurt that was on its way, already set on its unalterable course.

There was, however, nothing she could do.

It was coming at her faster than she could run, quicker than she could think and this realisation was enough to paralyse her. Her breath quickened as he began.

'Rosie.' He swallowed.

No! No! No! No! No! No! The word screamed inside her head. She stared at him, noticing that he looked a little different: new haircut, new clothes, new scent.

Oh God! Oh my God! Please! No, no! Please, no! Don't say it! Don't!

'Rosie,' he repeated.

I can change! I can change! I can! I'll be better, I will. Please, please! Stop it! Stop talking!

'I've met someone.'

His words were clearly delivered, calmly rehearsed. She heard them, but it was as if he was speaking another language. She stared at him and a smile formed on her face. It was a strange feeling, as the last thing she wanted to do was smile. It was as if someone had pulled the rip cord without warning, only to find there was no parachute, as if she was in freefall, not knowing if the ground was an inch or a mile away. Her body felt heavy, as if it was made of rock and might plummet through the sofa, the floor and the foundations, all the way down into the middle of the earth. And strangely, this thought, as she tried to make sense of his words, was quite comforting. *Let me disappear...* Her head, however, was light, floating above them, looking down on proceedings. This feeling of disembodiment was to last for quite some time.

She stared at him, unable to speak or move. The atmosphere was eerily calm, with none of the hysterics she might have imagined. The exchange that followed was delivered slowly, punctuated by uncomfortable pauses and punches of pure shock. It was as if someone had pressed the button on the remote and slowed everything down.

'It's been going on for a while.' He filled the silence with words of self-incrimination and then he coughed, quite unnecessarily. A nervous cough and she was happy that he was nervous. A sound like a high-pitched note rang out in her head, clouding her thoughts.

'But... but... I'm your wife. And I love you.' She whispered the words, as though this cure-all that she'd been uttering in apology, lust, celebration and greeting since she was a teenager might make a difference. 'We... we can get over this. We'll work it out. Work harder. Things haven't been easy, I know, but we can move on, Phil, we can go on holiday, maybe? I'll get your mum to have the girls and—'

'No, Rosie. I'm leaving you.'

And that was when the fear bit.

Rosie opened her mouth to speak, but no words came. She fought the instinct to throw herself on him, pin him down and keep him anchored to the place where he belonged, the house where he lived with his family. Instead, she pointed to the ceiling, eventually finding the words that her mind rummaged for among the jumble of confusion. 'The... the girls...' she managed, as if the two little children upstairs might be the glue that could make him stay. *If not for me, for them, please!*

His tears came then, as he nodded. 'I know, but I'm not going far, I'll still see them.' He wiped his eyes and took a deep breath, as though the tears justified the words, proof of his own hurt. 'It's not unusual nowadays. They have friends in similar situations.'

His almost flippant justification floored her. 'I...'

She tried but failed to speak. *Please don't do this! Please, please, Phil...*

'I'm going in the morning. I've already packed.' He nodded towards the hallway, where his bags were waiting. She hadn't noticed them, too preoccupied, as ever, with life, the kids and the next mini-crisis that needed attending to. *I'm sorry, I'm sorry for not listening more...*

'It's the woman in Mortehoe, with the two pools, isn't it?' She stared at him. 'The one who was nice to me in the Spar. Geraldine.'

'Yes,' he confirmed, his eyes downcast.

'But... but you said she was a pain in the arse, you said you could never kiss a mouth covered in lipstick—'

'Please don't do this.' He shook his head, too embarrassed to have that conversation. Now he held up his palm, also in self-defence.

'I saw her today. She looks...' The words failed her. They were silent for a second or two.

'I'm sorry,' he whispered.

'I don't know what to do now. I don't know what I'm supposed to do.' She spoke aloud.

'I am sorry, Rosie.' He sounded cool, calm.

She wished he would stop saying that. Sorry was what you said when you were prepared to act to put things right; sorry was the first step towards making amends. But that wasn't what Phil meant; he was just trying to make himself feel better, although it gave her a glimmer of hope that all might not be lost.

'If you're sorry, then don't do it. We can… we can figure it out. We are married and we have two lovely girls and we can work it out, Phil, we always do. You're my husband! You're my family. I haven't got anything else. I love you. I love you. And I forgive you, I do, but please don't go.' She slithered forward until she was on the rug. 'I am begging you. I'm on the floor and I am begging you, Phil, not to destroy our little family. Please, please don't do this to my girls, to me, please…' Her tears came in a steady trickle.

'Get up, Rosie. You need to understand, as harsh as it sounds, that those words don't mean anything when there's been a change of heart.'

And there it was, the silver bullet: he had had a change of heart.

He stood up, unable to meet her eye as she grovelled and begged, lying on the Lego bricks that were strewn all around. With her hand touching his ankle, she looked up at him. From where she lay on the floor he appeared very tall and powerful. He stared out of the window, seeming uncomfortable and… something else, an expression she recognised. It was irritation; he was irritated at having to have this exchange, offended by her collapse. And this made her feel ashamed. Once again, she wished that she could just disappear. She pictured Laurel smiling and yearned more than ever to fall into her arms.

Rosie stared at his distracted face, could see that he was already miles away – less than two miles, to be exact. A change of heart indeed. She realised then that it was too late;

his love for her had drained away and been replaced by a new, all-consuming love, making theirs appear tarnished, unfit for purpose. When he pictured love, sex and a future, it was not her face he saw, but the Mortehoe woman's, whose name had gone clean out of her head.

'Are... are you going to come to bed with me?' *For the last time, Phil, for the last time!*

He coughed. 'I was going to sleep on the sofa.'

'I need you to hold me,' she managed, her voice faint, desperate and ashamed of her need.

Rosie clambered up, holding the side of the sofa for support. She swiped at the two Lego bricks that had stuck to her palms and trod the creaky stairs. She didn't clean her teeth, wash her face or close the bedroom curtains. It was as if all her normal rituals had to be ignored in recognition of the fact that there was nothing normal about this night.

Still in her clothes, she crept into her side of the bed and laid her head on the pillow. Her thoughts were so numerous and noisy, it was hard to focus. There was a pain behind her eyeballs and no matter how hard she tried, she couldn't get rid of it; the more she tried, the more it hurt. Her muscles were tensed and a ball of nausea sat in her gut. Staring at her husband's pillow, she let hot tears run over her nose, along her temple and into the pale blue pillowcase. A strange mixture of numbness and panic rendered her silent, but she was screaming on the inside, her fear balled in fury, trying to escape.

Time was skewed. It might have been an hour, might have been three, but eventually she heard the familiar sound of his footfall on the stair treads as he made his way upstairs, granting her her last wish. He hesitated, first poking his head around the door, already a stranger in the room he had entered thousands of times. He had changed the rules and this was no longer his home. She blinked, taking in his form. The light from the streetlamp along the road sent his shadow leaping up the wall. She stared at the dark, smudged shape of him, knowing that after tonight, that would be all that remained.

She heard his loud swallow as he eased off his suede slip-on deck shoes and, still fully clothed, pulled back the duvet. The weight of him next to her, which had reassured her since the very first time, made her tears flow faster. She cried, missing him before he had gone.

'Please don't cry, Rosie,' he whispered into the darkness.

'I like you being my husband,' she sobbed. 'I never thought, Phil... I never, ever thought in a million years... Not us. I can't believe it. I can't believe it.'

She felt his hand snake along the mattress until it found hers and he gripped her fingers under the duvet, knitting them together, secretly, as if hers was no longer a hand he could hold. And that was how they stayed. She was sickened by how grateful she was for the contact, unable to process that this might be the last time.

She lay there trying to control her wild, disordered thoughts. In the background was a flickering movie playing on a loop. She saw the day that he came home on leave, remembered the way she had looked up from the table in his parents' kitchen where she and Kevin were playing Uno and eating toast, recalled the way he had looked and then looked again, his double-take sending a frisson of joy right through her.

Her friend Kevin had dimmed, becoming as misty in her thoughts as the faded chintz curtains at the window. The only thing that was bright and distinct was the dark-haired soldier. He filled her completely and it was still that way. She recalled his face, wet with tears, as he held his tiny, damp babies for the first time; recalled the way he had looked at her, as though she was something special, something so special that no one would ever want to leave her, not her mum and not him.

His face, scent, smile, voice were never far from her thoughts; every task she undertook, every decision she made had him at the heart of it and try as she might, she couldn't conceive of a life where this would not be the case.

They spent the night side by side, hand in hand. She continued to cry silent tears, thinking of all the nights she had lain next to him, taking him for granted, all the early mornings she'd woken next to him, knowing he was there to nudge if she heard a noise or had a bad dream. It felt like her heart had been ripped from her body. Her sadness was all-consuming and she didn't know how she was going to rise from the bed and face the day that was creeping far too quickly over the horizon.

Like a condemned woman, she lay listening to the sounds of the night. The drunken bleats of late-night revellers gave way to the chug of diesel engines in the early hours as the fishermen made their way to the harbour, where their boats bobbed in wait. The clink of the milkman's deliveries and the shrill gulls who greeted the day with their tuneless cry – she wanted to rage at them all.

She took a deep breath, trying to accept what awaited her. Phil turned onto his side, mirroring her posture and they stared at each other, inches apart, both with their faces resting on hands in prayer position.

'I don't know what to do,' she repeated, hoping that if she said it enough times, the answer might come to her.

'You'll be okay.'

'I don't want to be okay. I want you.' She sniffed up her tears that spilled. 'Please, Phil, I am begging you. Please don't do this.' She felt her face crumple again.

'It's already done. It was done a while ago.' He blinked.

This was the piece of information that told her there was no point in begging any more. It was like running to catch a train that she'd only just been told had actually left the station ages ago; all she could do was stand on the platform, stare at the space where it had been and listen to the rattle down the line, hinting at its presence, now long gone.

'What did you want to tell me?' Phil asked. 'You said last night that you wanted to say something.'

'My mum died.'

He opened his mouth as if to speak, just as the bedroom door opened. For the first time in her life, Rosie felt intense irritation at the presence of her daughters. *Please no, just five more minutes...*

'It's funeral day,' Naomi announced with a mixture of sadness and excitement.

'Can I wear my party dress?' Leona asked.

Phil let his eyes rove over his wife's face, as if taking her in for the last time, then he leapt from the bed. 'Of course you can!'

She hated his joviality, the eagerness to get things rolling.

'Why have you got your clothes on in bed, Daddy?' Naomi pointed at his shirt. 'And you, Mum!' She giggled at the sight of Rosie's jeans, visible where Phil had flung the duvet back.

'We were too sleepy to get our pyjamas on,' he answered.

That's your first lie to them today. How easily it slips from your lips. How many more to follow? How long have you been lying to me?

'Mummy, your face is all balloony. Have you been crying?' Naomi stared at her mum, her little fingers twisting the edge of her pyjama top, her mum's tears the cause of her agitation.

'Yes.' Rosie coughed to try and clear some of the croak. 'Yes, I have.'

'It's okay, Mum, I cried too. But we can bury them now and we won't let it spoil our day.'

Rosie's heart went out to her girls and their sweet natures as they ran down the stairs to go find their dead pets. She closed her eyes briefly, still feeling quite disembodied, and wished that their day wasn't going to be spoilt; wished that their dad wasn't going to leave. But she knew wishes didn't come true, otherwise her mum would have collected her from school every afternoon and cooked her tea, they'd have had enough money to take the girls to Disneyland and Phil would not be casting her aside in favour of another. Geraldine Farmer. The name was now back in her mind, never to be forgotten again.

As she glimpsed her blotchy face in the mirror, she remembered the day he had taken the girls to soft play in Barnstaple. *'That's a bit of a liberty, phoning you on a Saturday. I mean, you'd think it could wait until Monday. What a cheek.'* She recalled the indignation she had felt on his behalf. *You bloody idiot, Rosie.*

Half an hour later, the family made their way out into the back garden and chose the perfect spot under the Japanese maple that thrived in the corner of their narrow plot. Phil dug down into the rich soil and placed the shoebox securely in its final resting place.

'Goodbye, Moby.'

'Goodbye, Jonathan.'

The girls cried, each clinging to one of her legs, as their dad loaded up the spade and patted the dirt back into place, cushioning Moby and Jonathan for their final sleep. Rosie stared, dry eyed, unable to think straight or get upset, unable to feel much. She did, however, cradle her girls to her, holding their heads in her hands and whispering 'Ssshhh...' into the air, as if that might somehow dampen their distress.

What followed next was quite unceremonious. There was no fanfare, no drama or swell of emotion. Naomi and Leona were entirely unaware that this was anything other than a regular day. Fully expecting to see their daddy sitting across from them at the tea table later, they waved him off, distracted by what was on the telly and the crumpets that their mum had toasted. Phil simply loaded his bags into the van, came back, kissed the girls one last time and almost ignored her, as if that might make things easier for all of them; it certainly spared him any embarrassment. He then stepped over the threshold and closed the front door behind him, walking out on twelve years of marriage.

And just like that, he was gone.

Rosie stared at the door long after he had shut it. It felt so much like any other day; it was hard to feel the full force of the situation.

With the girls settled in the sitting room, fed and watered and with the television for company, she trod the stairs. Carefully and quietly she locked the bathroom door behind her and climbed into the bath. Without the water to separate her body from the cold plastic, it wasn't entirely comfortable, but Rosie didn't care. She rolled a towel and placed it under her head and there she stayed for an hour, maybe more, fighting the urge to vomit and shivering despite the warmth of the sunny summer's day.

Nine

Rosie had been glad to see an end to the longest day and yet despite her exhaustion had only managed to sleep fitfully. The day had seemed to go on for ever. Zapped of all energy, she found it hard to look after the girls and resorted to sticking them in front of a DVD with the promise of pizza, giving her a few precious minutes to sit in the kitchen and cry. Her thoughts were jumbled. Her grief sat like heaped spaghetti in her brain, strangling all rational, coherent thought.

Then, as night arrived, she'd found herself swamped by fear, a new emotion to sit on top of the sadness. They had lived in the house for years, she was familiar with every square inch of it and knew practically every permanent resident in the town – heck, she could stand on the doorstep and holler, knowing that people would come running – but on her first night without him, she checked and double-checked the windows, secured the locks and drew all the curtains.

She then lay in bed with a mist of worry around her. What if someone got into the house? What if they were burgled? How would she keep the girls safe? She missed the presence of her husband in a million different ways.

Closing her eyes, desperately hoping for sleep, she couldn't stop images of Phil and Geraldine Farmer from floating into her mind. She pictured him and the super-rich woman who had sped by in her flash car, saw him unloading his bags from the van, for which *she* was insured and had travelled in countless times, saw him dump them in a grand hallway that looked like something out of *Downton Abbey* before celebrating his new-found freedom by sipping champagne in one of her two swimming pools. She knew they would, of course, in the first throes of romance, have sex that night, knew that he would whisper to her the sweet words of courtship that had been rehearsed in her ear over a decade ago. These imaginings caused her physical pain. Her gut twisted with jealousy and longing. It was torture, but she couldn't help it.

And now, after her first night alone, she lay awake in their bed, the imprint of him still in the mattress, his presence lingering on the sheets. Still in the jeans and T-shirt she had been wearing for forty-eight hours straight, she ran her hand over her pouchy stomach, feeling ashamed and disgusted that she had expected him to sleep with her when he had a well-kempt WAG-lookalike to rush off to. *Did they laugh at me? Talk about me?* This thought brought on another bout of sobbing.

Rosie pulled his pillow into her chest and that was how she stayed, clinging to the scent of him, an aftershave bought for the benefit of another woman. She felt desolate and desperate and if she looked towards the future she could see nothing but a big black hole of despair and loneliness. She didn't want to see anyone, didn't want to tell anyone. She simply wanted to disappear. And with this idea in her head, she thought for the first time about her mum, her dead mum, who had done just that.

With a start, she sat up in the bed and pictured Kayleigh's face, remembered her smile, her recent cheeriness, and slowly realisation dawned: it was because she had known. *'All right, Rosie? How are you? Everything all right with you then?'* Kayleigh had a secret and she liked it. *Who else knows? Who else is laughing at me?* She rubbed her forehead, hoping this might alleviate the thumping headache that she had nursed throughout the night.

Rosie reached out her shaking hand for the glass of water resting on the windowsill. Her brain jumped when she felt a flash of worry as to whether Phil had enough clean underwear with him and then quickly realised it was no longer her concern. She knew what he had worn and eaten every day for the last twelve years, but now it was nothing to do with her, some other woman would be choosing his supper and eating it with him, and even that small detail was like a knife to her heart.

She trod the landing, hoping for a bit of time alone downstairs, wanting the silence of the morning to ease her into the day ahead. But no sooner had she filled the kettle than she heard the clatter of little feet on the stairs. It was hard to find a smile.

'Mum?' Naomi began, the moment she was in sight. 'I had a very funny dream that you got me two puppies because my fish died and we called them Moby and Jonathan just like the fish and they were so cute and we took them for a run on the beach and they loved it. Can I get two dogs?' She did this, launched the day as she meant to go on; she never had the need for a period of easing in.

'I don't think so.' Rosie was aware of her cracked voice, her lowered tone.

'Well, I will let you think about it and when you've made up your mind, we can go to the big pet store near B&Q and see if they have books on how to look after your new puppies, so that I don't do anything wrong with them like I did with Moby and Jonathan when I put them in the mug.' She smiled.

Rosie opened her mouth to speak but literally didn't know where to start. Trying to find the right words through the fog of confusion and sadness was too hard.

'Where's Daddy?' Naomi asked as she picked up a little rubber ball and bounced it on the hard, tiled floor, catching and dropping it repeatedly.

'Mum, where's Daddy?' she repeated, in case she hadn't heard her over the noise of the kettle.

Leona sloped into the kitchen. 'He's not in the loo, I just looked.' She rubbed the sleep from her eyes.

'He's at work,' Rosie managed.

'I've told her we want two baby dogs.' Naomi updated her sister on events, this seemingly more pressing to her than the fact that Phil wasn't around.

Rosie was glad of the change of topic, a hiatus before having to disclose the truth.

'I do want two baby dogs, but I want breakfast as well!' Leona looked a little distressed, as if it was an either/or choice.

While the girls ate their toast on the sofa, Rosie sat in the kitchen and sipped at her cup of tea. Her mobile rang. It was Mel. She took a deep breath and answered the call.

'Are you okay?' her friend asked urgently.

'I guess you've heard.' She closed her eyes; it was somehow easier to have this conversation without looking at the world around her.

'Andy spoke to him. Oh God, Rosie, I honestly don't know what to say.'

She had never heard her friend at a loss for words before. 'Me either.'

'I'm coming over.' There was no time for a response: the phone went dead.

Fastening her hair in a knot, she opened the front door to her best friend. Mel rushed forwards and put her arms around her and there they stood, locked together while she cried.

'It's okay.' Mel spoke into Rosie's thick hair.

The two made their way into the kitchen. As soon as the girls got wind of their visitor, they rushed in, hopping on the spot at this much excitement this early in the morning. Rosie once again filled the kettle as if on autopilot.

'Well, if it isn't my two favourite girls!' Mel beamed.

'Mel,' Naomi began, 'we are going to get two dogs called Moby and Jonathan because we accidentally killed our fish and you and Tyler can help us take them for a walk if you want to?'

'Oh, we'd love that!' Mel looked at Rosie, who shook her head.

'We're thinking about replacement pets, but it won't be dogs.'

'But you said!' Naomi stamped her bare foot on the floor.

'Please, Naomi.' Rosie closed her eyes and leant over the sink.

'But you did-da!' she whined.

'You did, Mum,' Leona added.

Rosie slunk down until her head rested on her arms. Mel and the girls stood staring as her shoulders shook.

'I... I'm sorry, Mummy!' Naomi started crying.

Mel bent down and spoke face to face with the girls. 'I think Mum's a bit tired, why don't you go and sit on the sofa and I'll make her a cup of tea, okay?' She hugged them both and wiped Naomi's tears, then the two girls trudged towards the sitting room.

Mel guided her friend to a chair at the table. Rosie placed her head on her forearms and continued to sob. It was some minutes before she found the energy to talk.

'I can't believe it, Mel. I just can't take it in.' She sat up and shook her head, 'I don't know what I'm supposed to do.'

'Well, what you can't do is fall apart. You've got two little girls who need their mum right now.' Mel pointed towards the sitting room.

'They don't know what's going on.' She wiped her face with a tea towel.

'They don't need to know the details to know that something's up. You can feel it in the air, Rosie, and you look terrible.'

'I can't cope with you being mean to me right now.' She felt her bottom lip tremble.

Mel got up and held her again. 'Oh! I'm not being mean to you. You're my best friend! But I am trying to help you and you need to be tough now. I know it's not easy, but you really do.'

Rosie ran her hands over her jeans, realising that not only had she not changed her clothes, she hadn't showered either. She smelt, she knew she did, and her hair hung in greasy coils either side of her swollen, tear-stained face.

'Have you eaten anything?'

She shook her head and grimaced. Even the thought of food made her feel sick.

'Can you just have a piece of toast, just for me? You need to keep healthy, honey,' Mel said, as if Rosie was six. She rummaged in the bread bin, pulled out two slices of white and shoved them in the toaster. Clearly she wasn't going to take no for an answer.

'I can't believe it,' Rosie repeated.

'It feels terrible right now because it *is* terrible, but these things happen and you will move on.'

'I don't want to move on!' Her tone was sharper than she intended, but her friend, no matter how well intentioned, clearly had no idea of the extent to which her life had been destroyed.

'You have no choice.' Mel's tone was softer now. She sat at the table and placed her hand on her friend's arm. 'I know you loved him—'

'I love him. Not loved. I love him!' Rosie corrected, picturing his face again and crying afresh. 'I saw her again, you know, as I was driving out of town. She looked very fancy, the kind of woman that would make me feel crap about myself even if she wasn't sleeping with my husband. And all I can think of, having seen her looking so glam, is that I can't imagine her being with someone like my Phil.'

The two women sat in silence for a second or two, both considering how to proceed.

Rosie scooped her hair to one side and sat up straight. 'Did you know, Mel?'

Mel cast her eyes downwards and looked at her fingers on the tabletop. 'I knew bits. He told Andy a few weeks ago apparently and Andy stewed over telling me and then he told me at the beginning of the week that Phil had been playing away.' She looked up, regretting her casual choice of phrase. 'I was so torn. I didn't want to say anything in case it blew over – least said, soonest mended and all that. I thought saying something might cause more trouble.' She shook her head. 'I've hated knowing that much about it without you being aware of it. It felt disloyal, horrible.'

'Because it was, that's why. You should have told me!' she snapped.

'Oh my God, Rosie! How could I? I didn't know if it was going to blow over, I had no idea of the details and how on earth was I going to sit you down and break that? You have always thought the sun shone out of his arse, I wasn't going to be the one to shatter that for you. I love you too much for that. It didn't feel like my business.'

'So how did you know he'd gone?' She stared, her tone gentler, her mouth fixed in a pre-crying twist.

'He called Andy and said he was going to tell you and that he was moving in with that tart!'

The toast pinged and shot upwards in the toaster. Neither made any attempt to fetch it.

'I don't know if it's just a phase. As you said, it might all just blow over.' Rosie's tears came again. 'I just want him back! I want him to come home!'

'You can't think like that. You need to get on with your life and what will be will be. You are so much more than that little band of gold on your finger. You are more than your husband's wife, you are Rosie and you are fabulous. Your marriage doesn't define you, it's not all you are!'

Mel spoke with strength and conviction, but frankly it was more than Rosie could cope with. She closed her eyes as if unable to hear any more. 'That's all well and good, but the… the trouble is…' Her voice was small. 'It was all I ever wanted to be. Just that. Phil's wife and the girls' mother. It is enough for me and it's all I want.'

'But...' Mel tried and failed to find the right response.

'But what, Mel?'

'Mummy?' Naomi called from the sitting room. 'Leona's cut her foot on the fireplace and there's blood on the carpet, the curtains and on my pyjamas and on her forehead!'

'How the hell does she get blood from her foot to her forehead?' Mel asked, and they both laughed briefly, then raced into the lounge to deal with the latest crisis.

Later that afternoon, with Leona sporting a large bandage on her cut foot, Rosie decided to take them for a quick stroll along the beach. She tried not to look at the families sitting bunched together on towels and blankets or hovering in the entrances of ridiculously extravagant beach tents, tried not to eavesdrop on the parents and kids and couples who tossed Frisbees, batted balls or read out snippets from the newspaper. And she tried not to think of the countless trips she had made down there with Phil since her teens.

She wanted to scream at the top of her lungs, *'Enjoy it! Enjoy it all, because it can all be gone in minutes. The person you love and trust can have a change of heart and just like that you're discarded!'* Instead, she plonked herself on the shoreline while the girls chased the waves in and out, squealing with joy when they mistimed their retreat and their feet and ankles got wet.

Leona sat on the wet sand, peeled the crepe bandage from her foot and ran back to her mum, flinging it at her before trotting back to the water. Rosie gathered it and rolled it carefully before popping it in her pocket. She realised she hadn't told Phil about Leo's little accident and reached for her phone, before remembering that he wasn't really at work but had left. He'd gone. She slid the phone back into her pocket, unsure of the rules and trying to comprehend that, after speaking to him day and night since she was a teenager, this too had now stopped, she was not allowed. This thought caused her tears to pool. She pulled her sunglasses down from her head and pushed them up on the bridge of her nose, thankful for the privacy they offered.

Naomi picked up a length of seaweed and proceeded to chase her sister with it. Leona screamed so loudly that the lifeguard stopped and turned his head.

Rosie was preparing supper for the girls when her phone buzzed. It was the call she had been waiting for.

'Hello, Mo.'

'Oh... oh...' Her mother-in-law tried to speak through her tears.

'Don't cry.' Rosie smiled weakly to herself; this advice was far easier to give than act upon. The truth was she had barely stopped crying all day. The girls had made her a card with a sad face on the front and big fat blue tears running down the orange cheeks. An arrow pointed to the face with the word *Yoo* written next to it in green felt tip. She got the message. Now she glanced again at their work of art, which was propped against the window behind the sink.

'Oh, Rosie!' Mo's sobbing made it hard to converse and this in turn set Rosie off again.

She tried to fill the pauses as best she could. 'I can't... can't imagine you not being...'

'I will always be there for you, Rosie. I have been there since you were a young girl and that won't change,' Mo managed.

Rosie gripped the phone with both hands, beyond grateful to hear that the woman she loved was not going to cut her off from the only proper family she had ever really known. 'I can't believe it, Mo. I can't.'

'I know. Us too. I don't know what to say.'

Rosie heard the sharp intake of breath and was quietly pleased at her mother-in-law's displeasure, happy that she would be putting pressure on Phil to end this nonsense and come home. Just thinking of him being elsewhere was torture.

'Why don't we come and get the girls tomorrow and bring them back here, give you a chance to get your head straight and they can have a run around?'

'Thank you. They'd love that.' She nodded, thinking ahead to a day alone and the peace it would offer.

Rosie found it hard to see her father-in-law the next morning. There was a new awkward tilt to his movements and a faster blink rate that made them both uncomfortable. She knew that this was just the beginning. As he shepherded his beloved granddaughters into his van, she caught a glimpse of the future, saw herself handing over the girls to a family that might be embarrassed, torn by her presence. Despite Mo's kind words of comfort, and her obvious distress, she knew that Phil leaving had removed the cornerstones from the walls that kept her safe. She felt vulnerable and afraid of the isolation that loomed. Naomi and Leona waved goodbye furiously as Keith pulled out of the road with a friendly beep of reassurance that did little to reassure.

With the house to herself, Rosie sat on the sofa and stared at the detritus that littered the floor, a mat of toys, clothes and the odd wrapper and toast crust. Stooping low, she gathered a stray sock and sat back on the sofa; even this small task took more energy than she had to spare. Her pale leather handbag was on the floor and from the top poked a little white triangle. *Of course!* Until that point she had all but forgotten about her mum's letter.

Lying flat on her stomach and with her arm outstretched, she reached across the floor, hooked the bag by its handle and dragged it back towards her. This required far more effort than simply standing and picking it up, but there was nothing logical about her actions or the situation in which she found herself.

Pulling the envelope out of the bag, she laid it flat on her palm and ran her fingers over the loose, gummed strip, thinking that her mum must have held it in her hands, licked the edge. It was overwhelming to be in contact with something that had felt her mum's touch. Their old address was written on the paper, which had yellowed around the seams. The neat blue biro script had also faded. On the reverse there was a round stain from the bottom of a carelessly placed damp mug. She found it irritating that someone had considered this precious thing a suitable coaster. *Typical.* Angrily, she pictured her dad.

It was one single A4 sheet that had been folded and folded again, not the beautiful cream vellum or watermarked Basildon Bond that she had pictured. The paper choice itself made her feel sad. She tried to imagine writing a letter of such importance and simply grabbing the nearest pad and tearing a sheet from it. Especially if that letter concerned her five-month-old daughter. She pictured Naomi and little Leona, at that exact age. The idea of not seeing them made her shudder. She tried to picture herself on the day the letter arrived: tiny, vulnerable, sleeping, trying to smile, looking at her environment, keen for input. She would have lay, unaware, as the postman, hardly a figure of interest, slotted through the letterbox this letter now in her hands.

Unfolding it, she was instantly disappointed by its length. One measly paragraph. Rosie turned it over, but the reverse was blank. She held the sheet up to her face and read the lines that had been hidden from her for over three decades.

Roy,
It's been five months now and I wanted to say, don't hate me. I didn't want any of it, not marriage, not kids, not the routine of laundry and housework, not the small seaside life, none of it. I wanted more than to be known as my husband's wife. I wanted a life for me. I wanted to be me. I know you thought that a baby might make everything okay, you said as much, but it didn't. Not even a bit. I knew if I came home with you both, I'd be trapped, possibly forever. It's best for you both that I went when

I did, a chance for everyone to have the life that was meant for them. You included. This is kindest. I don't love you, Roy. I know this will be hard for you to read now, but eventually it will help bring clarity. A caged animal will eventually fight for freedom and I would never want to fight like that with you.

L

Rosie read and reread the words. Her mum hadn't even mentioned her by name – there was not a single enquiry as to her welfare, nor any words of love or regret. Not only that, but it was obvious that Rosie had misunderstood the situation all these years. It wasn't her dad who had been at fault after all, it wasn't something he'd done or said that had forced Laurel to run off; quite the opposite, in fact. Laurel simply hadn't loved him, hadn't wanted him and so had packed her bags and gone. Her dad, hurt and abandoned, had been the one that stayed. And he'd decided to take the blame, presumably to make life easier for her.

In her present state of mind it was almost too much to process.

Replacing the sheet inside the envelope, she thought how much she would have liked to share the letter with Phil. But then she was struck with a cold spike of dread as she realised that the sentiments it contained might be ones with which he wholeheartedly agreed.

*

It was late afternoon when the telephone woke her. She lumbered from the sofa and was delighted to hear Naomi's breathless gabbling.

'Nanny said we can have a sleepover and go and get eggs from the chickens in the morning for our breakfast. Can we, Mum? Can we?'

'Let me think about it a second.'

She rubbed her face, trying to wake up, trying to think if there was anywhere they had to be or anything they had to do that might interfere with the grand plan. She opened her mouth to speak, but Naomi halted her flow with her words. 'And Daddy said he will come and read to us before we go to sleep because he isn't living with us any more and he can see us at Nanny's, so can we, Mum? Pleeeease?'

It was as if she had been punched in the stomach. She leant against the wall. It was the first time since Phil had gone that she felt pure fury. Over the last couple of days she'd spent hours trying to figure out how much to tell the kids and when to do so, and yet he'd seen fit to tackle the topic while they were away from her and without her knowledge. She felt sick.

'I guess so, Nay. And you know, there's nothing to worry about. Everything will be fine.' Her reassurance was met with silence. 'I'll pick you up in the morning. I love you.'

'Love you, Mum!' And she was gone.

Rosie wasted no time. With anger as her fuel, she slid the screen with her shaking finger. As she waited for him to answer, she tried to steady her pulse. He didn't pick up. Immediately she pictured him in the Downton Abbey-style home of his lover, sipping champagne as they swam and laughed together, ignoring the phone that went straight to answerphone.

Rosie considered the prospect of being all alone until the morning; it filled her with a quiet dread. She made her way once again to the sofa, lay back down and closed her eyes. Half an hour later she came to, alerted by the sound of a key in the front door.

And just like that, he was back in their house.

She propped herself up, wishing she'd cleaned her teeth and that the house was tidier. Feeling awkward in front of him, the man who'd held her hand through their wedding, childbirth, minor surgery and loss, was a new sensation.

'I knocked but...' He gestured towards the hallway.

'I must have dozed off.' She shuffled around into a sitting position, wishing she had opened a window, freshened the place up a bit.

It had been less than seventy-two hours since they had seen each other, but it felt like a lifetime. He was changed. They were changed. The tiny fissures had already cleaved into chasms too great to be crossed and the frightening thing for Rosie was how quickly this had happened. Her tears came unbidden and she was angry at the display.

Phil sat down on the sofa. 'Don't cry,' he said.

'Don't cry? Why does everyone say that to me, as if I have any choice? You think I want to cry? I don't. But then there are lots of things I don't want.' She glared at him through her sobs. 'I've done nothing but cry. You have no idea what you've done, do you? And how... how can you tell the girls that you don't live here any more without talking to me first, without agreeing a plan? I can't believe you did that! Is this what it's going to be like?' She sniffed.

He looked at the floor, taking in the mess, which seemed to offend him. 'I didn't mean to. They asked me some questions and I didn't want to lie to them.'

'Of course we don't lie to them! But they are little girls and we do what we have always done: wrap things up to protect them, soften things. And I'm interested to know how you work out what it's okay to lie about and what's not?'

His eye roll that followed, as if what she'd said was illogical or unreasonable, made her shout.

'I am their mum and I say how this is handled. Me! Do you understand?' Her voice was shrill.

'And I'm their dad.'

'That's right. You are. But you chose to abandon us. You've left – remember? Gone to live God knows where without the slightest clue about how you have smashed up our lives!' She was shouting now, resisting the urge to throw herself at him and beg him once more to stay. 'You make me sick.'

Phil stood up and in that second she realised that this would always be his default setting, to get up and go, because he could.

'You can't just walk in and out of here as you please; you lost that privilege when you packed your bags. Give me your key!' she demanded with her palm outstretched. Her fingers flexed impatiently.

He reluctantly pulled the key from the key-ring and placed it in her hand. 'I don't want to fight with you, Rosie.'

'Well you should have thought about that before you left us.'

'I didn't leave them, I left you – there's a difference!' He raised his voice.

She was silent for a second as she stared at him and the words sunk in. Her sadness boiled over into anger.

'Is that what you think? That you can pick and choose like that? Because you can't! We are one family, one little unit and you chose to leave it! You are not welcome here and the girls will know it's you that messed up, they won't need me to tell them that, they're not stupid and it doesn't matter how much you try to get in there first with your skewed story. You have made this happen!'

Phil ran his palm over his face and took a deep breath. She noticed for the first time that he was wearing clothes that she had never seen before: jeans and a new pale blue T-shirt. Gifts, no doubt.

'I know you don't meant that,' he whispered, 'and I hate how upset you are. And if it's any consolation, I'm upset too.'

She couldn't help the involuntary giggle that left her mouth. 'Is that right?' She looked up at him from the sofa, again picturing him in that bloody swimming pool.

'I didn't plan this.' He bit his bottom lip.

'You didn't plan it? That's amazing! So how did it happen? Just a random series of events over which you had no control? You just found yourself packing your bags and buggering off? Someone planned it, Phil, and it sure as hell wasn't me.'

He sighed. 'I just meant to say that I haven't been happy for a while, but I thought it was just how things were. I didn't question it, until...'

'Until you met her.'

He nodded.

'Do you love her?' She held his gaze, twisting her lower jaw to try and stem the next wave of tears. It was a difficult question for her to ask, but she had to know.

'I... It's early days, so...' He raised his hands and let them fall to his sides.

She knew then that he did love the woman to whom he had run because no was the easiest answer to give.

'I'm in shock, Phil. I'm gobsmacked. I trusted you and I believed in us. I never thought in a million years that we would be just like those couples we've talked about, the ones who stray, throw in the towel. You used to say it was cowardly, easy, and that the hard bit was staying. Well, I think you're right, you are a coward.'

'There is nothing I can say that you will want to hear, so I think it's best if I don't say anything.' He sighed.

'How convenient.' She snorted. 'I'd hate to make you feel uncomfortable in any way.'

'All right, Rosie, you win.' He changed his stance so that he now stood side on, with one foot twisted towards her and his open palm gesturing in her direction. 'I haven't been happy for the last couple of years and the fact that you haven't noticed says it all, really.'

'Well, I'm sorry for being so busy working my arse off for this family that I didn't stop to double-check everything was okay with you. And talk about mixed signals – we were trying for a baby!'

'No. No, we weren't. You were trying for a baby. Jesus Christ, I kept saying we didn't have the space or the money, but you were hell bent on driving ahead with that because it was what you wanted!'

'So it's my fault?' she squeaked, hurt to know that the child she had longed for might have been unwanted by the man she loved and, worse still, the catalyst for him leaving.

'No, I'm not saying that. I'm trying to tell you that I've felt so hemmed in.' He pulled his fingers together at the tips to form a collar around an imaginary neck, as if a visual aid was needed. 'I just want more.'

'Well, it seems like you've got more. Two swimming pools and what was it…?' She tapped her mouth with her finger. 'Oh yes, a gym, a sauna, a laundry room, like a bloody hotel! Sounds like you've got a whole lot more.'

There was a pause while Rosie swiped at her tears and her runny nose and he looked around the room.

'Like I said, I don't want to fight with you,' he whispered. 'I think anything we say right now is going to hurt.'

She hated his calm, rational tone. 'You shouldn't have told the girls! It's you that's left, not me, and you don't get to control what happens next.' She sniffed.

Phil raised his palms. 'Okay. Look, I can't talk to you

when you're upset like this, so I'm going to go. We just wanted to make it as easy as possible on everyone.'

He had used the word 'we' and the pain in her chest was so acute, it left her breathless. She struggled to get the words out. 'Don't you dare let her meet my kids! You can't do that, Phil! Promise me! Not yet. No. Please don't do that. It will confuse them and I need to explain and they're not ready, they're not...' She sobbed.

She knew that it was her that wasn't ready and she doubted she ever would be.

'Okay.' It was an agreement of sorts. He trod the Lego-strewn floor and closed the front door behind him.

Rosie replayed his visit over and over, thinking of all the things she wished she'd said. *I am stronger than you think, Phil!* That would have made her feel better now. And there were more questions too: *'Why didn't you tell me you were so unhappy and at least give me the chance to put it right?'* She held his front-door key tightly in her scrunched-up palm, silently cursing herself for having asked him for it. Because if she had his key, that meant he wouldn't be able to come home when he wanted to, wouldn't be able to let himself in if he changed his mind. She wanted to leave him a note telling him that he would always be welcome. She pictured hiding it behind the wobbly brick at the back of the coal hole, as if he too would know it was there, as if he too could read her thoughts.

A picture of her dad loomed large in her mind; did he have similar questions for Laurel when she went? Laurel, who like

Phil, kicked at the door of domesticity until it gave way, Laurel who felt similarly trapped and overwhelmed at the prospect of settling down to a predictable, family life? The letter had certainly stripped her mother of some of the saintly veneer with which she had painted all fantasies of her, yet still she yearned to be close to her, occasionally lighting an apple-scented candle to inhale the scent of her, giving her comfort in this small way.

It was quite a shock to drive to her in-laws' house the following morning and feel none of the joy that she had always associated with the place. The happy bubble of anticipation was replaced by a nervous dread of what might await her. It wasn't that she expected hostility or rejection, not from Mo or Keith; it was more the prospect of their pitying expressions, sensing their awkwardness, and the thought of having to face Kayleigh.

Pulling into the driveway of Highthorne, she was relieved to note that neither Phil nor Ross's vans were there, nor the flashy Range Rover. She knocked on the door and listened to the thunder of feet as the girls ran the length of the hallway.

'Mummy!' Naomi answered the door and flung her arms around her mum's waist. It was just what she needed.

'I missed you,' Rosie said.

'It's only been one sleep,' Naomi replied.

'I know.' *But it feels like a lot longer.*

Mo called from the kitchen. 'In here!'

Rosie took a deep breath and took a seat at the table, just like she always did.

'Kettle's on.' Mo smiled brightly. 'We've had great fun. They were up till goodness knows when, giggling and laughing.'

'Daddy came and read us a story!' Leona said.

'Ooh, smashing! What story did you have?' Rosie painted her smile wide.

'We had two chapters of *Awful Auntie* and Daddy did her voice.' She giggled.

Rosie caught Mo's eye and the two women pursed their lips to suppress the words that threatened. Both were thinking of Kayleigh.

'And Daddy said we can go and have tea with him next week and that if you don't want us to go to his place then he'll take us for egg and chips at The Beachcomber, but I'd rather go to Daddy's house, Mum, so I can see where he sleeps.' Naomi spoke quite matter-of-factly, without any of the upset or concern that Rosie had envisaged.

'Goodness me, so much for your mum to process, little Miss Noisy! Why don't you two go and watch a bit of telly, while Mummy and I have our drink.'

The girls ran out of the room and Mo made the coffee and took a seat opposite her daughter-in-law.

'I'm very proud of you, Rosie.'

'What for?' she croaked. Her mask of jolliness had slipped now that the girls were out of the room.

'For making this the best it can be for my grand-daughters.'

Rosie kept her eyes on the bone-china floral mug with the fine gold edging. 'I can't fully explain how I feel. It's like my mind and my body aren't joined together, like I'm floating.'

'You're in shock, love.'

She nodded. 'Yes, probably. I thought maybe it was just a momentary blip, that he'd come back quickly, embarrassed and we'd have a row and then make up and figure out how we move forward, but it's not, is it?' She looked up at Mo and held her gaze, waiting for a rebuttal, but it didn't come.

Mo's tone was anguished. 'Keith and I feel so helpless.'

'Did you know?' Rosie readied herself for the answer.

'It's been terrible. Keith found out a couple of weeks ago and just went silent on me. I didn't know what on earth was up – I was worried it was his prostate again and he just wasn't telling me. So we were both awake all hours but for very different reasons.' She tapped the tabletop. 'And then he told me the day before Phil told you. It's awful, Rosie. We don't know what to say for the best. I can't say I agree with what he's putting you through, but he's also my son and I have to be there for him.'

'I understand that.'

'I don't think you do, love. I feel like I'm grieving. I just want my family to be happy and safe and you are part of that family. And aside from what this is doing to you and the girls, I'm so sad for me and Keith, and I know that sounds selfish, but the older you get, the more important it is to picture all those you love in the future. You just want to know that when it's your time, you've left everything neat.'

'You don't have to think like that, Mo.' Rosie thought of her own mum, who had never given the neatness of her life any consideration.

'I can't help it. I think about the upset, the upheaval and I feel like I can't face it, so goodness only knows how you feel, Rosie.' She paused. 'All I can say is that you are young, and I know this feels like the end of the world...'

'It does.' Rosie started crying again, the feel of tears on her cheeks now so familiar.

Mo reached across the table and took her hand. 'But it's not. It's not, love, I promise you. You will forge a different life.'

'I don't want a different life.'

'I know, love.' Mo patted her hand. 'I know.'

'And how can I let the girls go and have tea with the two of them next week? How can I do that so soon?'

'You don't have to do anything you don't want to, of course, but I suppose it's new to you and to us but not to Phil. He's probably been biding his time and we are just playing catch-up, aren't we? He wants to show the girls where he's staying, and that will probably help them settle, if they can picture him in his new surroundings.'

Rosie withdrew her hand and nodded. Mo's words reinforced the fact that she would always be treading a fine line between peacekeeper, confidante and Nana, but at the end of the day, first and foremost, she was Phil's mum.

Ten

Three miserable weeks passed and Rosie returned to work. While Mel watched the girls, she scoured three caravans from top to bottom, ready for their new occupants, finishing each one with a spritz of room spray that smelt like fresh laundry. The hard physical toil was just what she needed. She took out her frustration on the limescale in the shower, scrubbing until her fingers ached, and she was happy to reshape the bench cushions by thumping them mercilessly. While her muscles ached and her hands were busy, there was less time for her to think. She tried to picture Naomi and Leona going to the house that their dad shared with a new woman. It was the hardest thing.

She walked up the steep hill to the clubhouse with her bucket in her hand, noticing that her jeans had slipped down onto her hips. She hoicked them up and reminded herself to find a belt. Tightening the thick knot of hair that sat messily on top of her head and tucking the stray tendrils behind her ears, she knocked on the office door. Her stomach sank when she saw that Doug was alone. She'd been hoping that Susan, his assistant, might be there too.

Doug Hanlon was a lush; he also happened to be her boss. He was unpredictable, often too sloshed to keep order, and Rosie had seen him snake many a tenner from the bar into his grimy trouser pocket instead of the till. Every night, he greeted the regulars as if they were old friends that had popped by specially to see him.

There were some caravan parks in the locality with kids' clubs, sporting facilities and family entertainment, but this was not one of them. It would have been too costly to lay anything on for the twelve caravans and the smattering of campers who drifted in. The best a family could hope for was a quick spin on the laminate-floored dance area beside the sticky-topped bar, where a few twinkly lights hung in front of a black cloth. Parents could wait for their dancing divas on a sunken sofa behind some iron railings that had been left over from the patio extension. Middle-aged women sat quite contentedly, swaying to 'Careless Whisper' and lamenting the days when they would have been the ones dancing. Rosie had seen them close their eyes in dreamy recollection as they sipped large glasses of wine that came in a box, while their men downed pints and scoffed curry and chips as if their lives depended on it.

'Ah, Mrs Tipcott, what can I do you for?' Doug had always said this and it had never been funny. Rosie did, however, like the sound of her name. It made her feel safe being referred to as a Mrs, as if people knew she had back-up if it were needed. Now, though, she wasn't so sure; that back-up had made other arrangements and she felt adrift. Her maiden name was Watson; she'd forgotten what it felt like to be Rosie Watson.

'Can I have a word, Doug?'

'You can have several!' He smiled, his humour as unamusing as it was predictable.

'I was wondering if you had any more hours? I don't mind if it's not cleaning. I can do the bar, or litter patrol, anything...' She felt her cheeks flame, aware how desperate she sounded.

'How many more hours are you thinking?' He leant back in his chair. His polo shirt rode up to reveal a cushion of hairy white stomach that sat over the top of his waistband.

She looked away, directing her gaze over his shoulder and praying that Susan would come back soon. 'I don't really know. I just need to earn more.'

'Well, yes, I must admit I'd been half expecting you to come by.'

'Oh?'

'This is a small town, Rosie, and people talk.'

People like you... She swallowed the sentence.

'I haven't said anything to the staff, because it's your business. All I can say is, the bloke must want his bumps feeling. I mean, he's got the lot, hasn't he? You and them two little 'uns.' He shook his head and she realised that what Doug probably wanted more than most was just that. 'I shall do my best to shuffle things around and see what I can come up with. I take it you want school hours?'

'After the holidays, yes.' She nodded.

'Well, as you know, that's when we get quieter, but some of the casuals are off then, so it might be possible. Leave it with me. I'll see what I can do.'

Doug stood up and for a horrible moment she thought he was going to try and hug her. She shrank back against the wall. He arched backwards and gurned as he reached into the tight front pocket of his jeans.

'Here you go. I want you to take this and treat the kids to some chips or whatever.' He waved a twenty-pound note in front of her.

'Oh, Doug, no! That is so kind of you, but...'

'No buts.' He walked forwards and placed the money in her palm. 'We're a little family up here on this site and this is what we do, we look after our own. Now go on, Rosie, get out before I get all semi-mental on you.' He winked.

'Thank you, Doug.' She smiled at the man who had shamed her with his beautiful act of kindness.

Back at Arlington Road, Rosie let herself in and tried to ignore the toys, clothes and rubbish that littered the floor. Her grand tidy-up hadn't lasted long. 'Helloooo?' she called.

'In here!' Mel shouted. She and the girls were watching CBBC. Mel's eyes were rimmed with a large stroke of green eye shadow and bright red lipstick sat in a garish circle on and around her lips. 'We've been playing makeovers.' She nodded at her friend.

'So I see. I'm sorry I missed that.'

'We can still do you, Mum!' Leona piped up from where she lay on her front, kicking her legs up behind her.

'Lovely. Maybe after tea.'

'Is Dad coming home for tea?' Naomi asked without prising her eyes from the screen.

'No, darling.' She looked at Mel. 'Not tonight.'

'Is he coming tomorrow night?' She turned to her mum, revealing her own makeover of glitter-covered cheeks and a butterfly sticker on her forehead.

'I don't know.' Rosie cursed the familiar prick of tears that stung the back of her eyes.

'Can I phone him?' Naomi sat up, looking a little overwhelmed.

'Of course you can.' She smiled.

'Can I phone him now?' She sat up straight. Talking to her dad was becoming urgent.

'Yep. I'll grab my phone.' She took her phone from her bag, pressed his number and handed it straight to Naomi. 'There you go, love, it's ringing.'

Naomi stood up and held the phone with two hands under her chin. 'Hello, Dad? Daddy?'

The answerphone message was loud in the room. '... after the tone, please leave your message.'

Naomi swallowed. 'Hi, Dad, erm, we've been doing

makeovers and I want you to come home for tea and I don't know when you're coming home and...' Her tears spilled, her expression of utter distress was torturous to see. 'I've made you a card and it's under my mattress and I'll give it to you when you come home. Bye.'

She handed her mum the phone. As she made to walk out of the room, Rosie tried to catch her.

'Can I have a hug?' she asked, but her little girl slipped her arm from her grip and made her way up the stairs.

'She probably needs five minutes,' Mel offered sagely. 'How was work?'

'Same old. But Doug was really kind to me, said he'd heard.'

'Oh God, he wasn't offering to warm you up on those cold winter nights, was he?' Mel shivered.

'No, actually he was trying to be nice. He's going to see if he can get me some more hours after the holidays when some of the casuals have left.'

'That's good.'

'Yeah. I can't even think about money and things, I can only just about think about tonight.' She sighed. 'I was wondering about the car earlier. I mean, it's our car, our house, how is it all going to work?' She closed her eyes at the enormity of the thought.

'I guess when things are a bit more settled, you guys will sit down and figure it all out. I s'pose that's the one thing about where he's gone, it's not as if they're strapped for cash,' Mel said casually.

'Well, good for them.' Rosie gave a false grin.

'That sounded crap, but you know what I mean.' Mel tried to smooth the awkwardness. 'Anyway, on a brighter note, our barbecue is next Saturday!'

Rosie shook her head. 'Oh God, Mel, do you mind if I give it a miss?'

'Yes, I do. You're my best friend and it won't be half as good for me without you there, plus it'll be a laugh and it'd do you good to get out and see everyone.'

'I really don't want to go out and I definitely don't want to see everyone. I couldn't cope with everyone asking me questions or making out everything was fine and carrying on as normal. I'll skip it this year, Mel. Don't be mad.' She smiled.

'I won't be mad if you're sure that's what you want, and we'll all miss your coleslaw!'

'I can still make the salads if you like?'

'No! I'm only kidding. It's all taken care of. I will miss you being there, though. Who's going to listen to Kayleigh with me?'

Rosie rolled her eyes. 'We can have a coffee after and you can fill me in.' She looked up towards the ceiling. 'Think I'll go check on Nay.'

'I've got to be off anyway. Andy's going out for a pint and will want feeding before he goes and I don't want him dragging Tyler up the pub again – he's the only nine-year-old in the country with his own bar stool!'

The two women looked at each other. Rosie could guess

from Mel's slightly hesitant tone that Andy was meeting Phil. She had so many questions. It was an unfamiliar awkwardness from them both.

Mel grabbed her car keys and phone that sat in a pile on the arm of the chair.

'Thanks for watching them today.' Rosie spoke over her shoulder as she made her way upstairs.

'No worries. That's what friends are for.'

Naomi was lying on her bed, facing the wall.

'Knock knock,' Rosie said as she entered.

'I'm okay,' the little girl managed through her tears.

'Oh, darling, you don't sound okay.' Rosie lay on the bed and spooned the shaking form of her daughter, pulling her towards her and kissing her hair. 'Please don't cry, Nay.'

'I'm crying because I'm sad.'

'I know, darling.'

'I want my dad to come home! I want him to have his tea here with us and not at the new house. I don't like it, Mum.'

'I don't like it either, but you know, don't you, that no matter where your dad is, he loves you very, very much. You and Leo are his best things, his best things ever! And that doesn't change, no matter where he is, and it never will. Whether you are eight or fifty-eight, you will always be his best things.' She saw Mo's smiling face, and heard her words. *'I'm very proud of you Rosie, for making this the best it can be for my granddaughters.'*

Naomi wormed round until she was facing her mum. 'But I miss him.'

Rosie nodded. 'I miss him too.'

'Then why don't you tell him? Tell him that you miss him and he can come home now.' She spoke earnestly.

'I wish it was that simple, honey, but it isn't. I promise you though, Nay, that we will both always love you to the moon and back, and you will always be safe and happy, we will make sure of it, because no matter what happens between Daddy and me, you and Leo will always come first. You don't have to worry.' She tried out a smile of reassurance. 'I promise.'

'Do you want to see the card I made him?' Naomi brightened.

'I'd love to!'

Wriggling off the bed, she knelt on the floor and placed her hand under the mattress, pulling out a piece of folded card with an elaborate picture on the front. She had drawn a line down the middle of the card and on one side was a crudely drawn swimming pool with two stick figures in it and on the other side was a table of odd perspective, flat with four legs splayed at the corners and four stick figures floating around it. The swimming pool had a big red cross drawn through it.

'I've drawn that new house and put this mark through it so Daddy knows that's not where I want him to be, and this is us, having our tea around the table because that was when I used to make him laugh and I think if he sees this he will know that he wants to come and sit around the table with me.'

Rosie turned her face into her little girl's pillow and tried to hide her distress.

Naomi patted her mum's shoulder. 'Please don't cry, Mum.'

She was finishing her rounds of checking the windows, blowing out the candles, and looking in on the girls when her phone buzzed. It was Phil and her heart leapt.

'It's eleven o'clock,' was how she answered the call.

'I just got Nay's message.'

She could tell he'd had a drink; the slight slur to his words was a giveaway. 'Oh, I'll go and wake her up, shall I?' She instantly regretted her sarcasm; thankfully he didn't seem to notice.

'No! No, don't do that. I'll call her tomorrow. I would like them to come to tea. I promised, but I don't want to fight with you. It's hard.'

She snorted. Again, it was as if he wanted sympathy, as if he was in some way suffering. It sent a ripple of anger through her. 'This time last month, my life was perfect.' She spoke her thoughts aloud.

'But mine wasn't.' His response was instant.

'I guess not.' She paused. 'Goodnight, Phil.' It was late and she was in no mood for this discussion.

'Goodnight, love you.'

There was a deafening silence while both reflected on his sign-off. It was he that broached it.

'God, Rosie, I always said that and it just—'

'Go to hell.' She ended the call.

*

It was the weekend before the girls were due to go back to school. Their precious Saturday had been spent traipsing around Barnstaple looking for school shoes, new polo shirts and a pencil case each. Rosie quickly tired of having to explain over and over why glittery silver stilettos were not suitable school attire even if they did come in a whole four sizes smaller, which thankfully they didn't. She glimpsed the joy of their teenage years ahead and it made her smile, despite her exasperation.

'Everyone in my school has got a pair of Ugg boots apart from me!' Naomi said.

'I haven't got a pair.' Leona raised her hand as if answering a question.

'Shut up, Leo!'

'Don't talk to her like that!' Rosie barked.

'But it's true, Mum. I am the only one in my class who hasn't got some Uggs and I'd like some pink ones.'

Rosie knew the price of the boots in question – about a week's wages. 'Do you know what, Nay? I'd like a pair too, but until that lottery win comes in, we will both have to wait.'

The girls had continued to be crotchety until the promise of a Happy Meal, a rare treat, lifted their spirits.

It was now early evening and they were tucked up asleep. A light knock on the door drew Rosie from the comfort of the sofa.

'Mo! What are you doing out at this time of night?'

Her mother-in-law tutted. 'It's only half seven!'

'Oh, I suppose it is. We've had a long day and it feels like midnight. I'm just not used to seeing you out and about so late.'

'Well, talking of out and about,' Mo said, coming in and shrugging off her cardigan, 'I thought I'd come and sit with the girls while you went to Mel and Andy's do.'

'That is so sweet of you, but I've told Mel I'll give it a rest this year. I don't feel up to going out. I don't really want to see anyone.'

'And that's precisely why you should go. You can't hide away here forever, love.'

She smiled at the concern in Mo's tone. 'It won't be forever, just until I'm feeling a bit stronger.'

'You are only going to feel stronger by getting out and doing stuff, no matter how hard it is at first. It's true, so go!' Mo flapped her hand as though her gesture could shush Rosie out of the door – it worked with the cat.

Rosie sighed. 'But I look awful.' She scooped her hair up and let it fall. 'I haven't got anything to wear and I usually make the coleslaw.'

'You look lovely, honestly. You've lost weight, you know.'

'It's not a diet I'd recommend.' She had to admit, though, that she was pleased to have shed some of her excess pounds.

'I'm sure, my lovely, but the fact is, you have and you really do look wonderful. Sad, but still beautiful. And you have lots of nice tops. Besides, it's only a barbeque, you don't need a ball gown. Just go shove a top on and I can whip up a bowl of coleslaw in a couple of minutes!'

'But...'

'But what, Rosie? You are running out of excuses and I want you to go and have a glass of wine and a giggle. It will do you the world of good.'

'I don't want to see Phil.' And there it was, the real reason.

'You won't. He's gone to London.' Mo folded her cardigan and placed it on the bannister, avoiding further questions about why and with whom.

'To London?' Rosie felt her stomach crumple at this. Another reason to feel bereft, lost, left behind. London! She tried to picture him in the big city with his rich girlfriend on his arm and she knew that he had left her far, far behind. She took a deep breath. It might not be London, but this was where her life lay. She decided there and then to go to the barbeque, plus it wasn't as if Mo was going to take no for an answer.

'All right then. You make the coleslaw and I'll go and clean my teeth and try and find a clean top.'

'That's my girl!' Mo clapped.

Rosie smiled at her, the closest thing to a mum that she could ever wish for.

Half an hour later, she trod the stairs, trying not to wake the girls and still getting used to the wedged espadrilles that she hadn't worn for years. She had found a white muslin shirt with a tie fastening and flared sleeves. Very boho. Mo was right, she had lost weight; the top used to be snug on her arms and across her shoulders but now skimmed her shape nicely. With a white vest underneath and two strings of multi-coloured glass beads that she had picked up in Primark, she knew she would pass muster.

'Well, look at you!' Mo beamed. 'You look lovely.'

'I don't feel it, not really.' She felt sick at the prospect of going to a social event without Phil. It wasn't that they stuck together, joined at the hip, but she always took great comfort from knowing he was close by, just in case.

'You're going to be fine. The first time for anything is always the worst. Just take a deep breath.'

Rosie did just that and Mo disappeared into the kitchen and emerged with her mixing bowl full of coleslaw. It looked and smelt wonderful, just the right amount of mayonnaise and a pinch of cayenne pepper on the top to give it a kick.

'Oh, this looks lovely. Thanks, Mo. I will of course be claiming it as my own.' She smiled and took the large bowl into her hands.

'I shan't tell a soul, now off you go! Have a lovely evening and don't worry about the time. If I get sleepy, I'll just nod off on the sofa and if you're really late, I'll stay there till the morning.'

'Mo, it's Mel's barbeque not a nightclub! I'll have a glass of plonk, a raw chicken leg and I'll be home in a bit.' She turned, swivelled the bowl and reached for the front door. Then she hesitated and turned back. 'Do you really think this is a good idea?' Her nerves were making her feel sick.

'Go!' Mo shushed with her hand, and this time it worked.

She decided to walk the ten minutes across town rather than lose her parking space outside her house and then battle to find one in Mel's street. Groups of teens out for the night and surfies with lithe lovelies in tow nodded at her large bowl of coleslaw, which she held protectively in front of her. She had to admit it was an unusual accessory.

Her heart raced as she drew nearer, her nerves palpable. *You can do this!* she whispered to herself, trying to feel strong, courageous. Rounding the corner, she saw the wisps of grey smoke floating up from behind their house, could smell the woody, aromatic scent of food on the barbeque and hear the dull thud of music from the outside speaker. There was the faint tinkle of laughter and the odd shout, evidence of a party in full swing.

She had walked up this driveway and into the house thousands of times, but tonight it took all her nerve to put one foot in front of the other. She stood by the gate, in front of the block-paved space that used to be a front garden, and took a deep breath, pulling the back of her blouse down with her free hand to make sure her bum was covered, then adjusting her glass beads to make sure they sat just so. *You can do this. You can.* She considered phoning Mel and asking her to meet her on the driveway but knew that would sound ridiculous. Swallowing her fear, she turned to her right and there, parked behind Andy's pick-up truck, sat a large shiny black Range Rover. She stared at the number plate. GF38.

She took a step towards it on wobbly legs, thinking that at any moment she might actually be sick. The paintwork was pristine, so glossy she could see her reflection in it, and the seats inside were cream leather and looked comfier than any seat in her house. She was both fascinated and distressed by the car and its presence. They were here, Phil and his girl-friend; they were in her best friend's house. She suddenly felt very alone.

Rosie closed her eyes and longed to disappear, bitterly regretting having left the house and wishing she didn't know that they were just the other side of the garden fence, laugh-ing with the group of people that used to be her friends. It was as if Phil had got himself a newer, blonder, richer upgrade and Mel had gone along with it. She felt the stab of disloyalty and rejection and it was unpleasant.

Suddenly, the front door opened and she was gripped by panic that she would be seen. Ducking, she slid down the side of the fancy car and as she did so she tipped the bowl of coleslaw into her lap. She ran her fingers through the mayonnaise-drenched mess that sat in a pile all over her jeans and shirt, with flecks of red cayenne spreading into a stain on the white cotton. Her head dipped and her hair caught in her eyelashes. She pulled the strands free with coleslaw-slippery fingers, smearing gunk on her cheek in the process. It was everywhere. She closed her eyes, prayed that whoever had come outside would go back in just as quickly and hoped that she was adequately hidden from anyone who was leaving.

She heard the teeter-totter of heels on concrete, the sound made by the kind of shoes she had spent the day arguing with

Naomi about. And then the sound stopped and a clear-cut voice said, 'Are you okay down there? What are you doing?' It was the same singsong tone she had used in the Spar, only now it sounded superior and condescending.

Rosie blinked, the blobs of mayonnaise on her eyelashes making this harder than it should have been. She stared at the peep-toed white stiletto sandals and worked her way up the tight designer jeans, oversized tan leather belt and long-sleeved, baby-pink cotton jersey sitting snuggly over pert, high boobs that had never been grappled and deflated by a feeding baby until she was, for the second time in her life, staring into the face of Geraldine Farmer.

'Have you been sick?'

Rosie was floored by this new question when she was still trying to work out how to answer the first. She shook her head and tried to wipe the piles of mayo-covered carrot and cabbage onto the driveway.

'No, it's... it's coleslaw. I dropped it.'

For weeks now, Rosie had lain awake at night imagining an encounter with this woman, thinking of all the things she wanted to say and what would have the biggest impact. In her fantasies, she was witty, cutting, classy and in control, and above all, she looked amazing. This was nothing at all like that.

'Do you need a hand getting up?' Geraldine's tone was pleasant and this confused and upset Rosie. If this woman was nice, then people would like her and if they liked her, where did that leave Rosie? It was far easier to cope with her nemesis when she pictured her as wicked and vile, because *that* character was one that her friends and family could unite against.

'No, I'm fine.' She kept her tone neutral, hoping that Geraldine would go back inside and leave her on the ground. That, however, was clearly not her intention.

'Shall I take the bowl? Would that make it easier?'

Rosie exhaled. *Please just go away! Go away and leave me alone!* With the bowl in her hand, she awkwardly clawed her way to standing, placing a mayonnaise-covered hand on the dazzling paintwork. When she was finally upright, she was a head and shoulders taller than the neat, pocket-sized Geraldine, especially in her heeled espadrilles. She decided to simply walk away, holding her head as high as possible. She had no desire to spend more time in Geraldine's company than was absolutely necessary, didn't want the woman to see how she had turned her life upside down or realise that her face dominated Rosie's nightmares.

Placing the bowl under her arm, she took a step forwards, just as Phil came out onto the driveway.

'Rosie?' He looked at her through narrowed eyes, taking in her appearance. 'What *are* you doing?'

'Why does everyone keep asking me what I'm doing?' She flicked her hair over her shoulder, oblivious of the two pieces of grated carrot that clung to her fringe. 'It's not complicated. I was coming to visit my best friend.' She paused. 'But instead, I decided to take a coleslaw bath up the side of your girlfriend's car.'

'Awkward.' Geraldine looked at her beau and made a wide mouth.

'Yes, awkward.' Rosie trotted back down the driveway, facing forwards. She carried on walking, looking straight ahead so no one would see her tears.

She made her way through town, ignoring the families and holidaymakers eating chips and laughing, pretending not to notice how they had to step into the road to make way for the lady who was crying, covered in salad and dressing, and carrying a large plastic mixing bowl. She made her way up along the Esplanade until she rounded the headland. With her bench in sight, she headed straight for it and there she sat, crying silently into the encroaching night. *I wish you were here, Mum. I wish I could talk to you.*

She sensed Mel's presence before she saw her: the familiar snort of outward breath as she trod the grass, her familiar outline in Rosie's peripheral vision.

'Rosie!' she called as she came close. 'I knew you'd be here.'

Rosie stared ahead, trying to think of what to say first. Anger and rejection swirled through her and it hurt.

'You said you weren't going to come! I'd have called you otherwise.' Mel was breathless.

'Oh, well, I'm sorry,' Rosie spat.

'That's not what I meant! It's just that Andy asked if you were coming and when I said no, he invited Phil. And then Phil said he couldn't make it, but he had a change of plan last minute. Oh God, I feel like I'm in the middle. I never for a minute thought he'd bring Gerri.'

Rosie jerked sideways. 'Gerri? Well, isn't that nice, you've got a little nickname for your new friend. I can't believe you chose *her*!'

'She's not my new friend! Don't be daft. That's just how she introduced herself.'

'I don't care how she introduced herself!' Rosie shouted, caring enormously and aware of how juvenile she sounded.

Mel looked shocked, trying and failing to recall another time her friend had shouted at her like that.

'You don't know what it's like, Mel, you really don't. I am so lost. I have been Phil's wife for so long, it's all I know. And I know how terrible this sounds, but if he had died, if I'd lost him that way, everyone would be buying me flowers and sending me cards; they'd be on my side. Instead, they're avoiding me, but the end result is the same: he's gone and I have to start over. If he had died, at least everyone would know that he hadn't *wanted* to leave me. This is the most humiliating thing you can imagine. I've been traded in, swapped and I haven't done anything wrong!'

'That's not what people think, not at all.' Mel shook her head.

'Well that's what it feels like.'

The two sat in silence for some minutes, staring out to sea. Then Rosie spoke.

'Someone once pointed out to me that when you see a huge tanker on the horizon, you can't tell if it's coming closer to you or moving further away, and that was like my marriage. Every time I looked up, I thought we were steady.

I thought he was moving closer to me all the time because we shared kids and history. But he wasn't, he was moving further away and by the time I realised, he was too far out of reach. It's not her fault, deep down I know that – if it wasn't her, it would have been another. I want to hate her, but I can't. I don't know her and she wasn't married to me, he was, it was him who broke his vows. But that doesn't mean I want to be in her company or for my best friend to be her mate.' She wiped her nose and a sliver of cabbage fell from her sleeve.

'Why are you covered in vegetables?' Mel asked, as if this were the most natural question in the world, given what her friend had just revealed.

'Coleslaw. I dropped it.'

Mel snickered and shook her head. 'And you wonder where your girls get it from – they're as mad as you.'

Rosie gave a small laugh and rubbed her eyes. 'Oh God, Mel, I'm exhausted with feeling this low.'

'It will pass, Rosie. It will.'

'I hope so. I hate being like this; this bitter. I keep returning to the fact that I thought he was working hard for us, working to give us a better life, putting the hours in, missing dinner, you know, and all the time he was working on getting away from us. I find it hard to accept. How could I have been so clueless, so bloody stupid? I mean, it's so clichéd! If this was someone else's marriage, I'd think the woman must be stupid. All the signs were there, but I guess you only see what you want to see and I didn't want to see it. I was in the dark.'

'And that's why you have to stop beating yourself up

about it and look forwards. And for the record, I choose you. I always choose you.' She reached out and took her friend's hand in the dark. 'Urgh!' she shrieked. 'I don't want to ruin a moment, but what the bloody hell is that all over your hand?'

'Mayonnaise.'

The two curled their legs up on the bench and giggled at the absurdity of the situation, just as they always had.

'Oh God, Mel, I feel like I'm losing the plot.' She let herself fall across her friend, who wrapped her in her arms. 'I've got you. I've got you, Rosie Shitstar.'

Rosie closed her eyes and inhaled the intoxicating scent of apples that seemed to hang in the air.

Eleven

The girls had been leaping around, full of laughter and beans since she had collected them from school. Not only did they have the weekend to look forward to, but tonight they were off to have tea at their dad's. Rosie went through the motions on autopilot, part of her wanting to shake them and say, *'Do you know what he has done to us? To me?'* while her rational self kept on smiling and trying to make it as pleasant as it could be for everyone. And now it was nearly time and the kids' laughter had twice turned to tears as they became a little overwhelmed with excitement.

'Are you going to be okay, Mummy?' Naomi twisted her skirt in her hands.

'Course I am. I've got you.' Rosie kissed her nose.

'I just meant while we're out, are you going to miss us?'

Rosie felt a wave of guilt that her little one was feeling torn, sad that she was experiencing these feelings at such a tender age.

'Miss you? No way! I've got lots to do. You just make sure you have a nice time and tell me all about it.' She even hummed, to show that all was well.

'If we had two baby dogs, they could keep you company while we were gone.'

'We are not getting two baby dogs, or even one baby dog.'

Naomi took a deep breath. 'But—'

'No buts, Naomi Jo. We can't have dogs. Apart from the fact that they're expensive, who'd look after them while I'm at work?' She was grateful for the extra hours she'd been given, which now saw her issuing keys and booking families in and out at reception. Financially, it was a lifesaver.

'We could leave dog programmes on the telly for them so they don't get scared and they would have each other to talk to and we could leave their dinner in a big bowl.'

'That's not going to happen, it wouldn't be fair on them. And when you have a dog, you have to think about what's best for them, not just what's best for you. Who would take them for walks and take them out to go to the loo?' She shook her head, weary of the topic.

'We could teach them to use the toilet!' Naomi clapped, as though this was obvious.

'Right, that's it. I don't want to hear the word "dog" again – you are banned from using it!'

'For how long?' Naomi stood with her mouth turned down.

'Three weeks.'

'Three weeks?' she yelled indignantly.

'Yep, and stop shouting or it will be four.' Rosie smiled, half teasing her little girl. It was actually good to have the distraction of banter while they waited for Phil to knock on the door like the big bad wolf.

The girls had packed their school reading books and swimming costumes as per their dad's texted instructions. Rosie was still plagued by the image of Phil and the petite, pert-breasted Gerri swimming the day away and sipping champagne morning, noon and night, only now she pictured her children swimming alongside them and laughing with the lady with the red polka-dot bikini, flat tummy and no stretch marks.

It was five o'clock on the dot that the knock on the door pulled her from her daydream.

'Daddy, let us out!'

'Daddy! We're here, but we can't get out!'

The girls shouted in unison as they ran to the front door, banging at it in their haste to get to him and sounding very much as if they were being held prisoner. Rosie hoped that Mummy von Trapp hadn't nipped back from London for the weekend and wasn't overhearing all this.

'Mind out the way, please, girls, so I can open the door!' She pulled them backwards and reached over their excited, bopping heads to get to the latch.

Phil took one step forwards and the girls charged at him, throwing their arms around his midriff and holding him tight. She silently berated the punch of jealousy that hit her in the stomach. *Don't be ridiculous, Rosie, he's their dad!*

She couldn't, however, help the feelings of envious curiosity, wondering what it would be like to be the one that had left and was missed so much. It had only been ten days since they'd last seen him, but for them it felt like an age.

Phil looked up and away and then immediately returned his gaze to his wife. 'Hi.'

She held up her palm in greeting.

'Just wanted to say, about the whole barbeque thing the other week… Andy had told me you couldn't make it and we were only there for an hour or so. I wouldn't have gone if I'd thought…' He paused. 'Mel's your mate.'

'Don't worry about it.' She gave a brief smile.

'I'll bring them back by nine, is that okay?' he asked and she was surprised by both his question and his civility.

'That's fine, if Leo lasts that long, otherwise earlier. Whichever. I'm not going anywhere.'

He nodded. 'Thanks for this.'

She ignored him, not wanting to indulge in pleasantries. Civil was one thing, but friendly, which would intimate forgiveness? That was quite another.

'Be good, girls, and see you soon!' She blew kisses and watched as her daughters ran to the side of the vast Range Rover and patted the pristine paintwork with their hands.

'Is this a van, Dad?' Leo asked as she climbed up into the vehicle.

'No, it's just a car.' He smiled.

'This is like a throne! It's so high up I can see everything!' Naomi called from the back.

He shut the door and jumped into the driver's seat, as if he had been doing so his whole life.

Rosie stood on the doorstep with a grin plastered to her face, waving at her kids, who waved back excitedly. This was already quite the adventure and they hadn't left the street yet. She could see their mouths opening and closing as they rambled on to their dad, catching him up with their lives over the past days. As they rounded the bend and disappeared, she quietly walked back inside.

A second later, she took a deep breath, howled loudly and slid down the inside of the front door. Landing in a heap on the welcome mat, she lay there crumpled and sobbing, feeling like her heart might twist out of shape.

'I miss you so much!' she yelled hoarsely. 'I want you back! I want you home! I want it to go back to how it was! Please, Phil, please...' She shouted into the ether, hoping that her words might reach him and make him think.

An hour later she had calmed down. She lay on the sofa with a cup of coffee and her phone for company. She lit her apple candle, inhaling the sweet, calming scent and fired off texts to Mel and her dad, trying to think of anything other than her children and her husband and his girlfriend, all playing happy families in the Downton-style mansion up the coast. *I hope they hate it there, hope it's cold and uncomfortable and they never want to go again.* She shook her head to get rid of the nasty thoughts that leapt unbidden into her mind.

It was a curious emotional state to be in when all she ever wanted was for her children to be happy.

'Don't be like that, Rosie. Don't let them make you like that,' she said out loud.

Her phone rang. It was her dad.

'Thanks for your text,' he said. 'Thought it might be easier to call – I haven't quite got the hang of texts; they always fly off half finished before I'm ready to send them. I think it's my ancient phone. Or my ancient fingers.' He tutted.

She'd spoken to him once since Phil had left, to briefly let him know what had happened, but it hadn't been much of a chat.

'How are you?' His voice was level and sincere.

'Ah, you know, Dad, getting on with it. But I'm sad, very sad. When I'm busy, I might forget about it for a bit, but then I see him, or the kids ask something quite harmless, like "Where is he?" and I'm back to howling.' This sort of confidence sharing was rare between them, but she needed someone to talk to.

'It will get easier, Rosie. Might not be for a while, but it will.'

He was a man who spoke from experience. She thought of Laurel's letter, the rather cool explanation of a woman who had plans and wasn't about to let marriage and motherhood get in the way. *I didn't want any of it, not marriage, not kids, not the routine of laundry and housework, not the small seaside life, none of it. I wanted more than to be known as my husband's wife...*

'Did you feel this bad when Mum left?' She kept her tone neutral. This was new territory for them both, but it was somehow easier to discuss it over the phone with a stretch of the A377 between them.

Her dad gave a small cough. His words, when they came, were barely more than a whisper.

'I did, yes. It was a difficult time. I was taken aback, shocked. She rejected everything I had to offer, and there was no Plan B, no alternative life that I could tempt her with. She just disappeared, and I wanted to run away too, if I'm being honest, but I had this little baby girl to care for and I didn't know how. I really didn't.'

He chuckled with relief, as if he'd survived a near miss. 'Looking back, I think I blamed you at first, in some way. I thought that if you hadn't come along, she might have stayed. But I know that's not true; you were just a little baby, you were an angel, too, placid and quiet, almost as if you knew you couldn't be too much trouble, because I couldn't have coped. And I figured out after a while that she was always going to go, it was just a question of when. I was never enough for her. And so I did what I had to do, battened down the hatches, tried not to think too much and soldiered on. I had no choice, did I?'

Rosie swallowed, taking in her Dad's words of revelation and seeing him in a new light. She thought about the silent serving of her bland food at tea times, remembered his distant stare while she tried to chat and saw his fleeting, disingenuous smile, offered as a weak consolation on her birthdays.

She realised for the first time that he hadn't been cold or uncaring; he'd simply been trying to survive and had done so by putting a lid on the feelings that threatened to bubble to the surface. In fact he put a lid on all his feelings. And all the while she'd blamed him for her mum's departure, assumed she'd upped and left because of something terrible *he*'d done.

'Well, I think you did a good job, Dad. We muddled through, didn't we?'

'We did – just.' She heard the crack of emotion in his voice. 'And Naomi and Leona will be just fine too. You know that, don't you?'

'I guess.' Again she pictured them at that moment.

'I've seen the way you and Phil are with them: they are lucky kids and you'll all come out the other side, all of you.'

'Doesn't feel like that right now,' she whispered.

'I know. But I do think you end up with who you're meant to, Rosie. Look at Shona and me. We are happy. She looks after me, the first person ever to have done that. Your mum said something in her letter, she said that her leaving was to give everyone a chance to have the life that was meant for them, and I can see that now, not that I thanked her at the time.'

Rosie smiled, happy that her dad knew the words by heart. She visualised the coffee ring disappearing from the back of the envelope.

Her situation was, however, quite unlike his. The life she was meant to have was with Phil, there was no better life out there for her, of this she was sure. That life was the one she had always wanted; gorgeous kids, a lovely house and her man by her side. She swallowed the tears that threatened.

Her dad had more to say. 'And she was right, you know. Hard as it was to see and to come to terms with, she was right. If she'd reluctantly stuck around, I would have had a very different life and so would you.'

'It didn't feel like that when I was growing up. I... I missed her.'

'I know. But what you did was imagine a perfect mum.'

She thought about her apple-scented, smiling mummy who used to sit by her side in the darkness.

'And you have become that mum for your girls and that's the absolute best thing you could have done. It's made you who you are.'

Rosie nodded. She had never thought about it in this way, but her dad was right. She had always been determined to give Naomi and Leona the love and care she felt she'd missed out on. So what if they were a bit rowdy and a bit less well behaved than the von Trapps; so long as they knew she would always be there for them, for the little things as well as the big things – ready to fix their hair for parties, to talk about periods and other stuff – that was all that really mattered.

'I don't say it often enough, Dad, but I appreciate what you did, what you went through, and I do love you.'

'I know. And I love you too.'

After she put the phone down, Rosie felt her mood shift a little; she wasn't happy, but she was less fearful. Her dad's words had made an impact, made her feel as if she wasn't alone and that was all she had ever really wanted.

Her phone rang again and she checked the screen. Mo. She must have known that the kids were out and was checking in. Rosie smiled and answered the call. 'Hello, Mrs.'

'Look, I know my hair's a bit long and I have been known to wander round in a sarong, which is technically a skirt, and I do wear a bracelet, but—'

'Kev! Oh my God! You're home!'

'No, I'm still away, but I got Mum to send her phone to Borneo so I could prank-call you.'

'Very funny.' She'd missed his teasing sarcasm.

'So, Rosie Watson, what the hell's been going on? I turn my back for *five* minutes...'

'Oh, Kev.'

'Wait! Don't say a word. Bench time?'

'Yes!' She laughed. 'Bench time would be good.'

Rosie arrived first. It was a little chilly in the evening breeze and she'd thrown on her thick wool poncho for warmth. She lifted her head and smiled in anticipation at every dog walker who passed by, waiting for her old, old friend. Her dad's words were still fresh in her mind as she pictured her teenage self sitting at this very spot chatting to her mum in her mind and meeting Kev for 'bench-time' catch-ups whenever they were needed.

'Get orf my bench!' he shouted as he strode across the grass.

Rosie jumped up and greeted her brother-in-law with a long, firm hug. 'It's so good to see you,' she whispered into his shoulder-length, sun-bleached hair. 'You smell of bonfires.'

'Thank you,' he replied and they laughed.

She resumed her place at the end of the bench, taking in his tanned skin, white teeth and permanent smile. 'You look really well.' She grinned at him. He was ageing, of course, but thankfully had retained his sparkle. And if anything, the faint crinkles now fanning out from the sides of his eyes only made him look kinder.

'And you. Last time I saw you, you were kind of saggy and mumsy.' He waved his arms.

'Flippin' 'eck, Kev! Say what you mean, why don't you!' She shoved her arms inside her woolly cover-up.

'But you did! And now you look really good. Heartache suits you.' He nudged her with his elbow.

'I don't know about that.' She shook her head, unable to joke when everything was still so raw. 'How long are you staying?'

'Give me a chance – I've only just arrived. You trying to get rid of me already?'

'No. I like you being home.'

'I don't know, actually. A couple of weeks, not sure. But I thought it would be nice to be here for Dad's birthday. The weird thing is that it feels less like home the longer I'm away from it. Don't tell Mum that.'

He sounded like the schoolboy of many years ago and it

made her smile. 'Birthdays and Christmas, your usual visiting times.' She nudged him.

'Oh don't, you know I hate Christmas. I find it depressing, always have, all that false jollity and over indulgence. Give me a quiet beach and a good book any day.'

'Don't you miss turkey?' she asked.

'Not even a little bit.' He smiled at her.

'Where are you going next?'

Kev straightened out his long legs and crossed them at the ankles; his desert boots were dull and dusty. 'The British Virgin Islands, or BVI to those in the know. It's got crystal-clear waters, glorious sunshine, incredible fish. It's a tough gig, but someone's got to do it.'

'What are you doing there?'

'I'm gathering and comparing algae samples, which is a lot more involved than it sounds.'

'I'll have to take your word for it.'

'I'm going to be living on a boat, mainly, a beautiful wooden boat that you can moor within sight of any number of isolated beaches. It's paradise.'

'You said that about Borneo!'

'Because it was! I love the travel, I always think the next place I go will be better than the last and it usually is. It's all about keeping this open.' He tapped his temple.

'Don't you ever get fed up of drifting from place to place? I mean, it must be lovely to always have a tan and sit on the sand, but don't you ever think you might want to come home to bricks and mortar?'

'And rain and traffic and television and crowds!' He raised his voice. 'No thanks.'

'But you must want to set up your train set, get all your vinyl out, put pictures on the walls – that stuff was always really important to you.' Memories flooded into her head, of a teenaged Kevin desperate to play her a particular track or show off the latest framed gig ticket hanging above his bed.

He smiled. 'Yes, it was and I will, one day. Anyway, I'm not drifting. I'm anchored to the whole planet and not just one square inch of it. Do you know how big the earth is? How much there is to see?'

Rosie looked up at the darkening horizon. 'No, I don't. It feels very small to me. Especially at the moment. My mum died.' She let the news blurt from her, obviously keener to share it than she'd realised.

'Oh God! Rosie, no! I had no idea! Did you see her? How do you know?' He twisted his body to face her, his questioning urgent.

She was glad of his interest, which was greater than his preoccupied brother had shown. She shook her head. 'I never got to meet her, no.'

She placed her head in her hands and slumped forward as she cried. 'I can't stop crying. I don't even want to cry any more, but I can't stop it. I can't believe he left us.'

Kev placed his hand on her back and palmed warm circles against her skin. 'It's okay, Rosie. Blimey, this reminds me of when we were third years and you sat here crying because Take That were splitting up.'

She lifted her head, crying and sniffing up her tears. 'This feels a bit different.'

Kev removed his hand from her back. 'Oh my God, I'd forgotten that you're such an ugly crier! You look like an angry man when you cry.'

And just like that, her tears turned to laughter. 'An angry man? What are you talking about?'

'No, really, it's bad. I remember it now, jheesh.' He nodded sagely. 'You are never, ever going to get a boyfriend looking like that.'

'I don't want a boyfriend!' The thought was enough to set her crying again.

He carried on, as if she wasn't sobbing her heart out. 'I had a girlfriend, Chrissie, a Kiwi girl, and if I think about her, I picture her in tears. When she cried, her eyes glazed over and her cheeks glowed and she looked serene, beautiful. Of course I never wanted her to cry, but when she did, it was captivating.'

'Did you tell her that?' Rosie wiped her nose on the bottom of her poncho.

'No. How can you say that to someone without it sounding weird?' He pulled a menacing face. 'I like to watch you when you cry! There's no good way of breaking that to your girl-friend. Not that you have to worry about that, Rosie. No one is ever going to say that to you, because as I might have already mentioned, when you cry you look like an ugly, angry man.'

She thumped him on the arm. 'Why did you and Chrissie break up? She sounds lovely.'

'She shagged my mate.'

'And that's not the thing you think about when you remember her?'

'Well, yeah. I mean, it's no biggie.' He pulled a Rizla from the top pocket of his pale blue shirt and rolled a cigarette. 'You see, I believe that everyone has someone they are meant to be with. The one.'

'You so do not believe that!' She waited for the punchline.

'No, I do!' He placed his right palm over his heart, as if this gave his statement solemnity. 'I really do. So when Chrissie goes off and shags my mate, or Raquel leaves the island I'm on, or my best friend, who I've singled out as my life partner, marries my brother...'

'Shut up!' She punched him on the arm again.

He smiled. 'When those things happen, it's fate's way of telling me that they are not the one, because if they were, they wouldn't do those things and would still be with me. So it's no biggie, it just speeds up the process, takes me closer to finding her!'

Rosie stared at him. 'What if you find your one, but you aren't theirs?' Her tears started again.

'Ah, that's the thing, Rosie. It doesn't work like that. It's not possible. It has to be the perfect fit, mutual and for always, or you are not their one and they are not yours. Even if you think they are for a while.'

He pulled her towards him and placed his arm around her shoulders. 'You're going to be all right, you know. Time will help put this into perspective, I promise.'

She laid her head against him. It felt nice to be held. 'People keep telling me that, but it doesn't feel like it.'

'How does it feel?' he whispered.

And she was glad he was there, her friend. She sat up straight, staring out to sea, as Kev lit his cigarette.

'I feel like I'm sitting in a dark place and I have this big hollow space in the middle of my gut that used to be filled by him. I'm self-conscious in a way that I never was before, because he took what little confidence I had and pulled it out of me, as easy as pulling a weed. And I still don't know where my place is in the world because everything I thought I knew and could rely on has gone. And I'm scared. I'm really scared.'

'What are you scared of?' he asked softly.

She coughed to clear her throat, which was clogged with tears. 'I'm scared that I'll never leave this dark place, that I'll be in here forever.'

Kev shook his head. 'Trust me, I have never lied to you and I am telling you now, it will get better. It will.'

'Thank you, Kev.' She meant it.

'But you do need to find a way to sort that ugly crying thing out. It's ba-ad!' He giggled and she laughed too. The sweet sound of temporary happiness echoed around the rocks below and was carried out to sea.

Kev walked her home and punched her lightly on the arm before leaving, like he always used to.

'You know where I am, right, if you need anything?'

She had nodded and smiled. He'd been the best medicine. She'd forgotten how he had the ability to make her laugh, help her escape. The subject of Phil sat between them like the boulder it had always been. It was something they were both keen to avoid.

It was a little after nine o'clock when the headlights swept the room and the roar of a powerful engine heralded the girls' return home. Rosie sat up straight and waited for the knock on the door.

Phil was carrying Leona, who was slumped over his left shoulder, her arms and little legs dangling freely; she appeared to have lost a sock. Naomi held his right hand and was leaning against his hip with her eyes closed and her long hair falling over her face. The sight of the silent trio gladdened Rosie's heart.

'Very tired,' Phil mouthed as he made his way inside, just as he had done a thousand times before.

Rosie bent down, scooped Naomi into her arms and followed her husband up the stairs. She placed her eldest girl in her bed, cradling her head as she laid her against the pillow, pulling off her shoes and socks, then folding the duvet up over her shoulders. Naomi was already asleep.

She turned and watched as Phil brushed the long, shiny hair from Leona's forehead and bent down to gently kiss her cheek. He then blew a kiss to Naomi.

'It's a bit chilly,' he whispered and, without hesitation, he went to the cupboard on the landing and removed the two spare blankets that lived there. They had been a wedding present from Phil's Auntie Sue. Rosie pictured the two of them unwrapping the gift as they sat in the middle of the sitting-room floor, tearing off strips of silver paper and flinging it high in the room like confetti, stopping only to kiss each other. They'd laughed at the blankets, which they'd christened granny blankets, but they were the one gift that they still regularly used. Phil tucked the soft pink wool around the angelic forms of their sleeping daughters; their hair, fanned out on the pillows, looked like strands of spun gold.

Turning off the light and leaving the door ajar, Rosie and Phil made their way out onto the landing. The familiarity with which Phil moved around the house, the comforting presence of him and the way he treated his children made her doubt Kev's words. She was certain that she had found her one, which made his betrayal even harder.

'They've had a great time.' He smiled, like the proud dad he was.

She felt her jaw tighten. 'So, Kev's home.'

'Yeah, haven't seen him yet.'

'He's on good form.' She leant against the wall with her arms folded against her chest.

'When isn't he?' He smirked.

'Does your...' She didn't know what to call her and felt uncomfortable using her name. 'Does your...' She tried again. 'Does she have any children?'

'No.' He shook his head. 'I think it was all a bit of a shock to her – you know what those two are like, tag-team tornado.' And he laughed, as if he'd forgotten who he was talking to, as if he was sharing an amusing snippet with a mate. Glancing at her expression, he straightened, adopted a more sober stance and lowered his voice.

'I know that none of this is easy. But it was the right time for them to meet Gerri. I didn't make a big deal out of it, she was just there but not forceful in any way. I think we handled it well.'

She stared at him, astounded by how completely unaware he was that his every word, his every reference to Gerri and the life he lived with her was like a knife to her flesh.

'I hate having to leave them. It's hard for me – and before you say it, I know it's me that's made this choice and I know you're hurt, but not seeing my kids...' He closed his eyes briefly.

'Everything has a cost, Phil, and that's the price you have to pay. And as you said, it's your choice.'

'But I don't choose that. I want to be happy, but I want my kids!'

'Well, you know where they are and you are welcome to see them any time, for as long as you want, just like you used to every day when this was where you lived!' Her eyes blazed.

Phil exhaled. 'You can't keep punishing me.'

She snorted her derision, as if whatever he might be experiencing could only be a fraction of the pain she was in.

'I said they can stay next Saturday night if it's okay with you.' He pulled the car key out of his pocket. It sat on a silver ring along with a cluster of other keys, little slivers of metal she had never seen before, giving access to rooms and doors that were alien to her, proof of his new life, right there in his palm.

She walked past him and opened the front door.

'As I have mentioned before, I'd appreciate it if you didn't make any arrangements or suggestions with them directly, no matter how casual, because if I don't think it's right or if it's not possible for whatever reason, they will be disappointed and I will be cast as the baddie, and I'm not having that.'

'So are you saying they *can't* come and stay?'

'I'm saying I'll think about it.' She kept her eyes downcast as he swept past her.

She flicked off the outside light as she heard him roar off in the flash car with someone else's initials on the registration plate.

Twelve

Rosie indicated and pulled the car out onto the road. She looked at Naomi and Leona, sitting in the back in their finery. They were quiet. She felt guilty thinking about the preceding hour, certain that her anger and frustration had wafted off her in waves. The girls' long, fine hair had been left to dry after swimming without any attention and it had taken her an age to detangle it.

'Your dad has seen me do this a million times! How hard would it have been to rinse out the chlorine, pop a bit of conditioner in and run a comb through it? Or just tie it up?' she muttered through gritted teeth as she teased out the tangles and tried not to yank at their sensitive scalps.

'You're hurting me!' Leona whined as Rosie set to with the brush, gripping the hair and trying to avoid snagging the knots.

They had both been subdued after their visit to their dad's

the previous evening, a lot more so than she'd anticipated, and she was thankful for it, unsure how she would have coped if they'd burbled on about the marvellous Gerri and her mansion and the view from the pool. She'd also avoided asking the many inappropriate and painful questions that preoccupied her – *Did Daddy kiss her? Did you see where they sleep?* – and had instead settled for a rather neutral, 'Did you have a nice time?' They both nodded casually without lifting their eyes from the TV screen or giving any details.

Rosie had washed, brushed and conditioned Leona's hair, leaving her daughter, at her own insistence, to style it herself. The end result was quite something to behold. She'd gathered one section of hair into a neon scrunchie so that it stuck out at an odd angle and had used some deely boppers with mini disco balls on the end as a headband. It was certainly striking.

Naomi had her grandad's cake on her lap and was holding the plate steady with both hands. It was an iced creation covered in sparkles. Rosie had told the girls to add a few glittery sprinkles, but the combination of an overzealous Leona and a quick nudge from her sister's elbow meant the whole tube now adorned the top in a sparkly summit.

'When do you think Grandad will die?' Naomi asked casually.

'Oh, not for a very, very long time,' Rosie said, using a jolly tone. 'You don't have to worry about that. He's young and healthy. So, what do you think he will make of his cake?' She was keen to change the subject.

Naomi's reply was not what she had expected; her diversion tactic had failed.

'Milly's grandad died and Leah's grandad died and Mrs Williams's dog died and Celia's nanny died.'

Leona took up the reins. 'Moby and Jonathan died, Marshall's mum died and Jo-Jo's grandad died.'

'Okay!' Rosie shouted a little louder than she'd intended, banging the steering wheel for added effect. 'Today is Grandad's birthday, it's a *happy* day and I don't think we need to hear a list of all the people we know who've died. Who wants to hear some 1D?' She fumbled for the CD.

'Did your mummy die?' Leona asked.

They clearly weren't done with the topic. She looked in the mirror at the faces of her girls, their expressions both interested and cautious as they stared at her, waiting for a response.

'She did. Yes.'

'Daddy said that to Gerri,' Naomi said.

Rosie flinched at hearing her daughter say the name of the woman who had ripped their life apart, making her real, bringing her into their world.

'And it made me feel sad, but then I couldn't imagine her and so I thought I didn't mind too much that she'd died, but I thought it might make you sad because she was your mum.'

'It did make me sad and that was very kind of you to think about me in that way. I only found out a little while ago.' She thought back to that horrible, horrible day. 'And I think she probably looked like me.'

Naomi seemed satisfied with this response.

'Mummy?'

'Yes, love?' She looked at her child, fearful of what she might reveal or say next.

'Are you not supposed to talk about dying on people's birthdays?' Naomi looked a little tearful.

'Well, I don't think there are any rules about it. You can talk about anything, anytime you want, but I do think that a birthday should be a happy occasion and so, as a general rule of thumb, talking about something that might make you feel a bit sad or might make other people feel sad might not be the best idea.'

The two little girls exchanged a look.

Someone had tied two blue foil balloons bearing the slogan *Happy Birthday* to the gatepost at Highthorne and they bobbed and strained against their ribbon in the wind. Rosie knew it would only be a matter of time before they made a break for freedom. A quick glance told her the place was Range Rover-free and she breathed a sigh of relief.

The girls unbuckled and shuffled out of the seats with their cake.

'Go steady, don't drop it!' Rosie said, unable to face the tears and theatrics that would ensue if the cake were to get squashed at this final hurdle. She took a deep breath; nerves and fear swirled in her gut.

Kayleigh came rushing out of the front door, her thin hair tucked behind her ears and her mouth poised to speak as she placed her hands on the girls' shoulders. 'Hello, Tipcott family!' she yelled. 'And hello, Rosie!'

Rosie hovered by the car, unable to ignore the ache of embarrassment that washed over her. She got the message loud and clear. *'You are no longer part of this family, you have been replaced.'* She wondered how long Kayleigh had been practising that. Watching as the cake-carrying trio made their way into the house, she knew that she would never forget those words or the way in which they had been delivered. She thought of all the times she had jumped to Kayleigh's defence and felt even more stupid. Her legs shook.

Suddenly something landed on her foot with a splat. Startled, she looked down. A wad of wet loo roll sat on her shoe.

'What on earth…?' She kicked it off and looked up at the bathroom window, out of which leant Kev.

'What are you doing?' she yelled.

'I'm thinking about what to throw at you next. There are surprisingly few missiles at my disposal here.'

His head disappeared back inside, only to emerge seconds later. Drawing his arm back, he launched a small yellow rubber duck that the girls liked to play with in the bath. It hit her arm. She picked it up and tried to lob it back, but her crappy throwing skills meant she barely cleared the car.

'You're still rubbish at throwing,' he observed. 'Do you remember when we'd go to play beach rounders and we had to pick teams and you were always last because no one wanted you on their team, because you couldn't throw or catch? Oh God, you're not crying again, are you?'

Rosie let her shoulders hang forward and her head rest on

187

her chest as the tears came. She felt the loo roll hit the side of her head and looked up sharply.

'That was a gift sent in kindness to dry your tears, not a missile. Don't move. I'm on my way down.'

Rosie gathered up the loo roll and got into the passenger seat of the car. She pulled off a long strip and blew her nose, unable to face going inside just yet. She looked to the left and Kev's face was squashed against the window.

'For God's sake!' She banged the glass.

He chuckled as he walked round and climbed into the driver's seat. 'Hello, ugly-angry-man-faced crier.'

She sobbed shamelessly. 'I know you're trying to cheer me up, but please stop!'

'What's happened?'

Rosie shrugged. 'It was just something Kayleigh said. Maybe I'm being super sensitive.'

'Eeuuw! S-Kayleigh!' He laughed.

'Don't be mean.' She set her mouth in a thin line to stop her own laughter.

'She is scaly – snakey and sneaky...'

'I think she's probably unhappy,' Rosie offered, though even this did little to temper her dislike of the woman.

'I don't think she's as unhappy as you right now, for sure. Because she's inside drinking sparkling wine and you're sitting in the car with a pile of snotty tissue in your lap.' Kev drummed his fingers on his thighs. 'Are you coming inside?'

She shook her head. 'In a bit.'

They were quiet for a couple of seconds.

'Do you want to play think of a person and I've got to guess who you're thinking of and you can only answer yes or no?'

'No, I don't.' She shook her head a second time.

Mo banged on the window. 'What are you two plotting?' she asked as she climbed into the back seat.

'Why do you think we're plotting something?' Kevin laughed.

'Because since you were young, that's what you've always done, with you thinking up the plan and Rosie going along with it.' Mo tutted in mock anger, her affection for the two of them spilling from her. 'Are you not having a good day, darling?' She looked at her daughter-in-law's teary face.

'I'll be okay.' Rosie nodded, feeling embarrassed. This was Keith's special day and she had unwittingly hijacked two of his party guests, who were now sitting in her car.

'Shall I go and get you a cup of tea?' Kev offered.

Rosie nodded at the first useful thing he had said that day.

'I love having him home.' Mo watched him jog into the house.

'I bet.' Rosie smiled.

'Phil's not coming over until this evening. I didn't ask him to stay away, of course, that's just what he's arranged, so please come inside. And you know, love, there will be times – at family gatherings and on other occasions, especially living in a small town like this – when you're going to have to be in the same room as him.'

'I know. And it's not so much being in the room with him,

it's being there with him and her and everyone watching to see how we react. I can't bear to think about it.' Her tears gathered again.

'I will always love you, Rosie. You are the mother of my grandchildren and I think the world of you, you know that. Nothing's changed.'

'I love you too. But I don't think it's true that nothing's changed – for me, anyway. Things aren't the same and they never will be. I not only lost my husband, I lost my place in your family too.'

'I understand that's how you feel, even if it's not true, but what you mustn't do is self-sabotage.' Mo nodded. 'And I guess the big question is this, Rosie: what are you going to do? How are you going to recapture your life?'

Rosie stared at her and shrugged. *What am I going to do?*

Kev reappeared with a mug of tea and handed it to her as he climbed back into the driver's seat.

'Thank you.' She was, as ever, grateful for his kindness.

'That's better – smiling at last!' He threw his hands up in mock celebration.

Keith approached the car and laughed as he opened the back door and clambered in next to his wife.

'Happy birthday, Keith. Did your cake arrive in one piece?'

'It's smashing. Thank you, Rosie, love. Especially the glitter, it's everywhere!' He held up a glitter-smeared palm and as he turned his head she saw the sparkles on his fore-head and in his eyebrow; it really was everywhere.

'Yes, they were a bit liberal with the old glitter pot.' She smiled.

'I tell you what, though, you can keep all my other gifts. This has given me more of a chuckle than anything.' He opened up the card that the girls had made him and read aloud. '*Dear Grandad, happy birthday. Leona and me hope you have a nice day and that you don't die soon. We think you will die soon, but not very soon.*'

He turned the card outwards to face the three astonished faces, keen to show off the crayon-drawn picture of a coffin with a cross on the front and a birthday cake sitting on top of it. They had popped several kisses across the page for good measure.

'Oh my God! Keith!' Rosie hid her face in her hands. At least they hadn't included a list of all the people they knew who had died.

'It's very original,' Kev observed, 'but they may have to rethink their career plan of going to work for Hallmark as verse writers.'

His words made them all laugh and Rosie felt a small weight lift from her. These people, squashed into her little car, were her family.

The week passed in a flash. And in just five short days a change had occurred. Rosie woke feeling different, brighter, as if the fog of desperation was starting to clear, and that clarity enabled her to look forward. Mo's challenging words rang in her head and she began to ask herself the same questions over and over: what *was* the grand plan? How *was* she going to rebuild? This, coupled with Kev's unwillingness to allow her to stew, meant she had walked to work with a spring in her step, cleaned the caravans with gusto and been on good form when she met Mel for a coffee. They banned the 'P' and 'G' words from their conversation and Mel kept telling her how hot she looked. Rosie had rebuffed the comments. She felt as if she'd been dragged through the mire and was only just coming up for air; hot didn't come into it.

The best thing about this new outlook was that the atmosphere at home was less gloomy and Naomi and Leona were more settled as a result.

On Monday she had conducted a spring clean. Getting down on her hands and knees with a bottle of bleach, she did what she was good at, sweeping dirt from every corner, scouring surfaces and polishing glass until their little house was neat, tidy and sparkling. She opened the windows and let the breeze whip around the rooms, sucking out the misery and replacing it with the beginnings of hope.

She still had her moments, though, like when she found a note from Phil scrawled on the back of a receipt and finished with a large X. It was enough to throw her. Her fingers had hovered over the script, scrawled in biro. *Gone to pick up cement, see you about three, so stick the kettle on!* And then the kiss. It was a simple message, written at a time when her life had been just that: simple. She pictured the day, remembered him coming home and her cooking tea for the four of them. They'd watched *EastEnders* and she'd washed the kids' uniforms. Rosie wondered what she'd thought about, unaware that the lovely little life she had was on a timer, counting down to now.

The memory of this seemed to energise her. Seizing the moment, she opened the double wardrobe that ran the length of one wall in their bedroom. Gathering up all the hangers with her husband's clothes on, she folded them into bin liners, along with his stinky old trainers, discarded overalls and other items that had taken root in the bottom of the cupboard. Fabric and objects that she had in the past weeks run her tear-soaked fingers over, inhaling the scent of him, imagining him still present, she now discarded without so much as a flinch. She did the same with the bathroom cabinet, popping his razor blades, spare shower gel and athlete's foot powder into a carrier bag and shoving that in with his clothes. Let Gerri have all his crap.

She found a secret stash of apple-scented candles and moved them down to the sitting room. Phil had always hated the smell, and hadn't understood their emotional significance for Rosie, so she'd only ever used them when he was out, but that hadn't stopped her buying them whenever she saw them on special. She placed two on the windowsill in the sitting room – she would let them soothe her lonely evenings – and cast a lacy counterpane, which Phil had also hated, over the bed. She was reclaiming the space in which she lived and it felt good.

There had been another change too, something that was subtle but empowering: Rosie had stopped crying and was starting to get angry.

The girls were a little skittish, full of excitement and nerves. Tomorrow was the big sleepover.

'Will we sleep in the same room?' Leona asked as they walked to school.

'We'll tell Daddy you want to sleep in the same room and I'm sure he'll sort that out.'

'What if I need you in the night?' She held her mum's hand.

'Then go and find Daddy, or send Nay to find him, and he will bring you home to me straight away, no matter what time it is.'

'What if...' Naomi was clearly thinking on the spot. 'What if we get kidnapped?' She jumped up and down as if delighted by the prospect.

Rosie felt Leona's fingers increase their pressure against her palm. 'That's not going to happen. No one is going to kidnap you, and trust me, if they did, they would bring you back very quickly.' She winked at Leona, who gave a hesitant smile.

'What if Gerri is really an alien and she has put Dad under a magic spell and she's not really human?'

Rosie made out she hadn't heard, obviating the need for a reply. The truth was, she thought this highly possible. She smiled to herself.

They spent Saturday deciding what to pack and what toys

to leave behind. These were big decisions. Rosie and Naomi bartered over how many soft toys it was appropriate to take. She had to admit that her daughter was smart: when the starting point was fifteen stuffed furry things, they both had wiggle room. Six was declared the winning number and Naomi then set about the arduous task of choosing which six she liked best, crying theatrically, kissing and apologising to those she was being forced to abandon for a full eighteen hours. Both girls asked a multitude of questions that told Rosie they were still a little anxious.

'Supposing Gerri hits us with a stick?' Naomi asked as they ate the sandwiches she had prepared for lunch.

'S'posing she makes me eat tomatoes?' Leona scowled. This for her was evidently worse than being hit with a stick.

'I think it highly unlikely that she will hit you with any-thing, let alone a stick, because Daddy wouldn't let her. And he knows you don't like tomatoes, Leo, and he will be there when you're fed, so please don't worry.'

'What are you going to do when we're gone?' Naomi paused from chewing.

'I'm going to have a lovely bath and watch some telly and have a glass of wine!' She smiled, a warm, genuine smile that she didn't have to rehearse.

By the time Phil arrived to pick them up, the girls were in danger of getting over-excited and this usually led to tears or a fight. Rosie answered the door and noted that he was still in his work clothes and looked tired. She didn't waste time on pleasantries but launched straight into instructions.

'I've told them that if they change their mind at any point, even if it's the middle of the night, you'll bring them home.'

'Of course I will.' He nodded on the doorstep.

'And would it be okay if they dropped me a text before they go to sleep?'

'Sure.' He smiled briefly. 'Got your swimming things, girls?'

They screeched 'Yes!' and bounded out of the hallway.

'Phil, I don't want to nag, but could you please brush their hair if they swim – just put a blob of conditioner on it, you know the drill.'

'Sure.' He nodded again. She wasn't convinced by either his response or his intention. 'We thought we'd have brunch tomorrow and bring them back about lunchtime?'

Rosie couldn't help the snort of laughter that escaped her. She had never heard him use the word 'brunch' before, this man who could sniff out a steak pasty at fifty feet, who craved fish and chips in cold weather and who thought that having a dhal side dish with his chicken tikka masala made him a foodie.

She nodded. 'After brunch would be fine.'

Having kissed the girls goodbye, she called Mel.

'Two things. Firstly, can you inform your husband that Phil has just told me he will be dropping the girls back "after brunch". Those were his words, yes, "brunch"!' She paused to allow her friend a good giggle. 'And secondly, I've got a bottle of wine in the fridge and *Mamma Mia* loaded up on the telly, are you in?'

'Brunch!' Mel squealed. 'What next? Quinoa in his packed lunch and a Jack Wills hoodie?' She roared her laughter, apparently incapacitated by the effort of imagining Phil using such a phrase.

Having sung their way through the movie and knocked back the wine, Mel yawned. 'I better get home. I'm knackered. Will you be okay?'

'Of course I will.' Rosie hadn't properly considered how she'd feel sleeping there alone until that point.

'I'm proud of you, you know.' Mel stood up and slipped her arms into the sleeves of her jacket.

'I haven't done anything!' she scoffed, embarrassed by the compliment.

'Yes, you have! You've pulled yourself out of that pit you were sitting in and you are moving on and that takes some balls.'

'Thank you – I think! I'm not out of the woods yet, but I do feel a bit better, stronger.'

'That's my girl.'

'I'll see you in the week.' She liked the feeling of positivity that flowed through her. It might have been wine- and Abba-induced, but she felt good nonetheless.

'You bet.' Mel pecked her friend on the cheek. 'When's Kev off?'

'End of next week. He's stayed on a bit longer – I think Mo's pleased.'

'And you must be pleased too.' Mel avoided Rosie's eye.

'Well, yeah, he's always been my mate and it's nice to have him to talk to. He cheers me up.'

'So I noticed.'

Rosie waved as her friend walked down the street towards home.

'Bye, Rosie Shitstar!' Mel turned and shouted from the end of the road.

Rosie slammed the door, giggling and hoping the neighbours hadn't heard. Her phone buzzed on the sofa. It was a text from Phil. She realised it was nearly eleven, way past the girls' bedtime. *Sorry, forgot to get girls to text. They are asleep and are fine. Very excited – see photo attached.* She scrolled to the attachment and opened up the picture. Her little girls were holding a white ball of fluff with two big black eyes looking up at the camera. They were beaming, delighted and clearly in love with the little puppy they cradled.

'You have got to be bloody kidding me!' Her words echoed in the silence as she sank down onto the sofa, feeling her spark of positivity fizzle away to nothing.

She woke with the vaguest hint of a hangover behind her eyes, which a large mug of coffee almost cured. It wasn't quite brunch, but it would have to do. Jumping up to a knock on the door that came a little earlier than expected, she was happy to find Kev on the doorstep, wearing shorts, an oversized Killers T-shirt and muddy trainers. He was bent double and out of breath.

'I've... run.'

'And you have the nerve to laugh at my sports skills. I might not be able to throw, but I can run without collapsing! Do you want a coffee or should we just go straight to CPR?'

'Very… funny.' He breathed out loudly and straightened up to rest against the doorframe. 'Water and then coffee.'

Rosie tutted and went to put the kettle on.

'Where are the squids?' he huffed, looking round the sitting room.

'Not back from their great adventure, the first sleepover at their dad's.' She pulled a face at him over her shoulder as he took a seat at the table.

'I'm glad that things aren't weird between us because of you know…' He gestured.

It was true. Things were certainly less weird than they had been. She suspected that her improved mental state made her split easier to address. 'Me too. And anyway, we were friends first. In fact, if it wasn't for you, I would never have met him, so in some ways this is all your fault.' She smiled as she reached for the mugs.

'Well, we're even then.' He tapped the tabletop.

'How do you mean?' She turned and gave him a quizzical look.

'Doesn't matter.' He shook his head. 'So, have the girls had a good time?'

'I would say so. Wait until you see this! You won't believe what they've done – talk about trying to win favour.' She grabbed her phone and opened the picture of the puppy.

'Oh, so cute!' He screwed his face up.

'Don't you start. Can you imagine how happy the kids are going to be?'

'Yes, and we don't want that, do we! In fact, that's the last thing we want – happy kids!' He laughed.

'You know what I mean! It's like the ultimate thing, a puppy.' She shook her head. 'Their mansion must seem like a funfair and a shopping mall and a leisure centre all rolled into one, and what can I offer them? A game of Junior Scrabble and some microwave popcorn! And now they've got a puppy! A puppy!'

'Naomi and Leona are not as easily bought as you think. They'll surprise you.'

'Kev, if they ever picked spending time with me over a fluffball pup, I *would* be surprised!'

'I'd love them to see some of the places I live and work. It changes you, you know. That whole desperate acquisition of material things, it fades away. I see kids playing for hours on the shoreline, just digging the sand, swimming, chasing a ball. It's a good life, a simpler life.'

'It sounds lovely, but, sadly, a simpler life isn't one that will earn me money or put food on the table.' She placed the mug in front of him.

'I catch most of my food.' He sat back in the chair and mimed reeling in a fish.

'Do you ever catch chicken nuggets or potato waffles?' She laughed.

'No, but maybe I'm using the wrong bait.' He sipped his

coffee. 'Do you ever think about what you might have done if you hadn't got married and had kids?'

Rosie looked out at the garden. The Japanese maple swayed in the breeze and she pictured Moby and Jonathan in their little shoebox. 'No. I can't remember what it was like before I was a mum.'

'You used to want to be a travel agent, remember? You were really keen, going on about how you'd book tickets and organise itineraries. You did that whole business plan at school once, didn't you? For... what was it called now... Woolacombe Wanderers, wasn't it? What a great name for a travel agent's. And you got an A plus, you jammy cow. I've never forgotten that. And I got a C minus for my effort on how I wanted to be a beach bum when I grew up!' He smirked. 'Not much has changed on that score, anyway.'

She pictured her childhood bedroom; the wall covered in her pictures from all over the world. 'God, you remember everything! I don't think I really knew what being a travel agent was, but the idea of organising holidays, going on holiday, aeroplanes, it all sounded very glamorous to me. Still does, but then I've never been anywhere, have I? I think I'll stick to cleaning caravans, which can be just as glamorous.'

There was the thump of tiny fists on the front door.

'That'll be the squids.' She beamed.

Opening the door was like lifting the lid on a box full of noise. The girls shouted over each other to be heard.

'Mum, you should see him!'

'His name is Truffle.'

'He has a soft little tongue and he licks my hand!'

'I cuddled him under my chin and he kissed me.'

'I love him!'

'I love him so much!'

'I love him more than she does.'

'Okay!' Rosie was firm, her arms in the air. 'I know you're excited and I do want to hear all about Trifle...'

'Truffle!' they both yelled.

'... but you have to calm down and take it in turns to speak. Kev's in the kitchen.'

They both ran along the hall to shower him with facts about the fabulous puppy.

Phil lifted their bags from the boot and carried them to the front door. 'They've gone completely overboard.' He looked up.

'Yes. Who could have called that?'

Phil opened his mouth as if to speak but instead just stared at her. 'I thought it would be a nice thing to do, try and give them something good out of all this.' He kicked the floor. 'Please don't take the gloss off for them, that's not fair.'

'That's me, Mrs Take The Gloss Off!'

'For God's sake, it's a puppy that will stay at our house; it won't affect you at all! You're being petty.'

'Is that right? You just don't get it, do you? You have no idea how I have to deal with the fallout from all of your spontaneous decisions! It's typical. You do it all the time—'

'I do not!'

'But you do. Things like saying you'll be here at midday and then texting me to say it'll actually be two and in those two hours the kids go nuts, having worked themselves up into a frenzy waiting for you. Or like when you tell them you *might* pop in – to them that's an arrangement, and then, when you don't show...' She shook her head, deciding to let it rest. 'And now a dog.'

'I thought it was a good idea.'

'It's a *great* idea! You move out, effectively turn us into a single-parent family, teach them that men can't be relied upon, even their dad, but hey, look on the upside, if you're good enough, you might get a puppy!'

'I can be relied upon.' His eyebrows knitted together. 'I'm not your mum!'

Rosie stepped back as if he had slapped her and shut the door.

'Rosie?' he called, knocking gently. 'Rosie?'

She ignored him, walked down the hall and closed the kitchen door behind her.

Kev, unaware of the exchange, was laughing loudly as the girls took it in turns to regale him with Truffle's exploits.

'You have to come and hear this.' He pulled out the chair to his right.

Rosie sat, digging deep to find her smile.

'Okay, Nay, tell your mum exactly what you just told me.'

Naomi took a deep breath. 'Well, Truffle was running around and we were chasing him and he stopped at the side of the swimming pool and did a poo and Gerri stood in it with no shoes on and she said the fuck word and Daddy shouted at her for saying the fuck word and then Leo did a wee on the side of the pool, it was running down her leg, and so she jumped in the pool and Gerri said it again. And then Daddy said it.'

Kev tried to suppress his hysterics.

'Oh! It's not funny!' Rosie looked daggers at him. 'Why did you wet yourself, Leo? That's not like you. Did you just forget to go?' She ran her hand over her daughter's caramel-coloured hair.

'The loo is far away and I didn't want to walk there on my own and I didn't want to leave Truffle and I started laughing because Gerri trod on his poo and I weed at the same time.'

'Well, we've all done that.' Kev nodded meaningfully in Rosie's direction.

She glared at him, daring him to mention the night in her teens when, while they were sitting on the beach, he had literally reduced her to tears of laughter and as she'd stood up, the inevitable had happened, only there was no swimming pool for her to jump into and the sea hadn't looked that inviting.

'Yes, Uncle Kev's right, we have all done that.' She winked at her youngest. 'And Nay, the F-word is a really horrible word and if you say it, it makes you ugly. There are so many other words you can use, but not that one.'

'Or shitstar,' Naomi reminded her. Kev couldn't help but spray his mouthful of water. 'We're not allowed to say shit-star either.'

Rosie coughed. 'Yes, that one too.'

'Can we let Truffle come here for sleepovers, Mummy? I miss him so much.' Leona's eyes were wide and pleading.

'We'll see.' She looked at Kev. *And so it begins...*

Thirteen

It had been weeks since Kevin left, flying off to his next stop on the world-paradise tour. Rosie missed him, as of course did Keith and Mo. He'd sent the girls a postcard of a deserted beach lapped by turquoise sea, which looked especially inviting now that the weather in North Devon was becoming grottier by the hour, all grey clouds and drizzly wind. The card was stuck to the front of the fridge. On the back it simply said: *Been fishing for chicken nuggets, no luck yet! X*

The girls came and went at weekends, and while Rosie didn't like them being away, the more often it happened, the more used to it she became.

One Saturday she opened the door to her returning children to find Gerri, not Phil, at the door. She felt her face flush as she ran her fingers through the knots in her fringe and wiped her mouth. She felt inadequate, huge and clumsy in the company of this petite, blonde woman whose calves were so slim she could stuff the legs of her jeans into her high-heeled boots. Gerri looked glossy and bright in a way that Rosie knew she never could. She wished she wasn't still in her pyjama bottoms and sweatshirt.

'Sorry to just turn up – Phil's got man flu.' Gerri sighed, raised her hands and let them fall to her sides, as if this state of affairs was far from satisfactory and as if she and Rosie were old friends, mid chat.

'Thanks for bringing them home.' Rosie swallowed as her heart raced.

'It's no bother. Only five minutes.' Gerri pointed up the road, as if Rosie didn't know exactly where she'd come from.

Rosie remembered the last time they'd spoken, pictured herself sliding down the side of Gerri's car, sad and broken and covered in goo. She felt the need to put her side of the story. 'When I saw you before, at Mel and Andy's...'

'Yes.' Geraldine nodded. As if she could have forgotten.

'You thought I'd been sick, but as I told you... it was coleslaw.' She wished she sounded more coherent, smarter.

Gerri furrowed her brow.

'I dropped it, when I saw your car. The coleslaw.' *What are you going on about it for? Stop it, Rosie!*

'Right.' Gerri nodded. 'I was thinking...' She paused. 'As the kids come round to the house a lot, it would make sense if you knew where they were, wouldn't it? And you could pick them up sometimes – I don't expect Phil and I will be available as a taxi service every Saturday morning.' She flashed a wide, social smile.

Rosie gawped at her jibe, temporarily lost for words.

'And of course I'm sure you'd like to know where they are, and that they're safe. Come for coffee, why don't you? Shall we say Wednesday?'

Rosie stared at her, surprised and confused by the invitation. 'I'll, err, have a think about it.'

Gerri nodded and turned to go but changed her mind and headed back towards the front doorstep, from where Rosie continued to stare at her, fascinated and repelled in equal measure.

Gerri continued. 'And, living in this little tiny town, it would be better for everyone if we at least knew each other a bit, don't you think?'

Rosie tried to think of how to respond, but Gerri wasn't finished yet.

'I know the situation is far from ideal, but I'm not horrible or wicked. I'm not the sort of woman that sleeps with married men.'

'I think you'll find that you are.' Rosie didn't know where her confidence had come from, but she was glad it was there.

Gerri looked up at her, as if considering this. 'I mean, I wasn't. I never had until...'

'Until you chose my husband. Lucky me.'

'I didn't *choose* him.'

'Oh God, not you too! I've had enough of that from Phil about the randomness of it all, as though you are two witless, feckless things who have no control over anything. We both know that's not true. Is that how you expect me to believe you live, by accidentally making money, unintentionally building a house, mistakenly taking my husband?'

Gerri stared at her. 'I know you're upset with me—'

'Upset with you?' Rosie rolled her eyes at the understatement and stepped forward into the street. 'You have no idea. Have you ever loved someone so much that you wanted to have their children, loved them so much that you routinely put their needs before your own, willingly sacrificing your own hopes and dreams so they can realise theirs? The sort of love where you lie awake at night, working out how you can make their day better, even if it means getting up an hour earlier every morning to cook them breakfast before they go off to work?'

Gerri shook her head. 'Not until now, no.'

'Well, congratulations. I hope loving him brings you as much joy as it has me!' She spun around and made for the front door.

'I don't want to argue with you.'

Rosie turned to look at her.

'I don't want to argue with anyone,' Gerri continued. 'I want everyone to get along, because that's how we make it best for everyone.'

It's never going to be best for me.

'See you Wednesday for coffee then?' Gerri glimpsed past her into the hallway. Rosie saw the almost imperceptible wrinkle of her nose. She picked a stray hair off her jacket and headed for her Range Rover.

'As I said, I'll think about it.' Rosie closed the door behind her and spied the girls sitting on the stairs with their arms wrapped around each other, listening.

'So, what do you think I should do?' Rosie wriggled to get comfy in the booth and stirred her coffee, looking at her friend for advice.

Mel exhaled loudly. 'It's a tricky one. I don't think I could do it, not without punching her lights out, and I think she's got a nerve asking, but...'

'But what?' She sipped the froth from her latte.

'She's right. It would make it best for everyone if you all got along. It would certainly be best for the girls.'

Rosie scooped her hair into her hands and twisted it into a knot. 'I would like to have a look, it would be good to be able to picture them, and I'd probably worry a bit less.'

'Plus you want to have a nose!' Mel laughed.

'Not really. The idea of seeing where she and my husband sit each night for their tea, and where they sleep...' She shook her head. 'I don't know if I can do it.' 'Do you want me to come with you?' Mel leant forward.

'No! Because you really do only want to go and have a nose.'

'No need, I've already been up.'

Rosie looked up in surprise and Mel froze, as though she had let this slip. She held her mug still, not far from her lips, as she tried to explain. 'I... I didn't say anything to you because I didn't know what to say. They invited me and

Andy up a few weeks ago and you were hanging out with Kev and...' She wiped her forehead. 'I tell you what, I bloody wish everyone *would* get on, this is killing me.'

Rosie tried to dampen the flames of jealousy that flared in her stomach. 'It's okay, Mel. You've already told me that you would choose me, and that's enough. And I know that makes me sound like a six-year-old, but I can't help it. It's important to me to know that I won't lose you.'

'Rosie...' Mel placed her mug on the table, as if this required her full attention. 'That will never change. I will always, always choose you. As if I could have a friend with white carpets! I was scared to move, in case I smudged something.'

Rosie tried to imagine the girls running riot in a house with white carpets and Truffle pooing wherever the fancy took him, and she couldn't. She couldn't picture it at all.

Four days later, Rosie sat in the car, waiting for the tall black wrought-iron gate to slide open, feeling as if her heart was lodged in her throat. She had navigated the narrow lanes of Mortehoe with a rumbly upset tum and a dry mouth, raising her palm to people she knew, including one of Keith and Mo's neighbours, a mum from school, and others she recognised only by sight.

The temptation to turn around and head back down the coastal road to Woolacombe was strong. But having jumped out of the car and pressed the entry button, she knew that the little winking camera had signalled her arrival with its minute green flashing light and it was now too late to do a runner. The gate clanked and then jumped a little, before gliding silently along a rail and disappearing behind the white curved wall that framed the entrance and was shadowed by a dense seven-foot-high privet hedge to ensure total seclusion.

Rosie drove forward slowly in first gear, listening to the pale, weed-free gravel crunch under her wheels. She followed the winding driveway as it swept around in an arc to the left, noting the line of saplings that had yet to mature and were protected in little insulated cages from the harsh sea winds. Beyond them to the right sat a neat football-pitch-sized paddock with a five-bar gate, immaculate hedging and the potential for one hell of a game of rounders, assuming she was picked for a team. To the left, an expanse of land was laid to lawn, close-cropped and leading to a vast marble-floored patio, on which sat the infinity pool. The view beyond was one of the best she had seen and she had lived in the area her whole life. There were no buildings to clutter the scene or spoil the panorama from the cliff edge, just a wide expanse of uninterrupted sea. This was exactly how she imagined it might feel to be on a Greek island or the Majorcan coast: nothing but clear sky, the big sea and the space to breathe.

Sea diamonds sparkled all the way to the horizon as wisps of cloud parted to reveal the brilliant blue of the crisp autumn day. The grounds were as impressive as any she'd seen in pictures of grand hotels: she imagined peacocks roaming and grand parties abuzz with slim, tanned people wearing linen and sipping from fruit-crowded glasses of Pimm's. It was another world and not a world in which she felt comfortable. She held her breath, imagining her daughters at ease there, picturing for the first time the chasm that might open up, placing an insurmountable void between her life and theirs. The thought horrified her.

Rosie parked the car and wondered if she was leaving it in the right spot; not that there was a shortage of space – several juggernauts could manoeuvre freely without having to knock and ask her to move. She looked up at the house. It was certainly imposing but about as far from Downton Abbey as it could be and nothing like she had imagined. There wasn't a Georgian window or a butler in sight. It was a vast, modern, minimalist white box, with grey, metal-framed windows and bi-fold doors along two sides that were clearly designed to open up and connect the house to the grounds when the weather was nice.

Rosie looked towards the voice that called from the entrance.

'Come in, come in!' Gerri waved from the double-width, limed-oak front door at which she stood. Her diminutive stature put Rosie in mind of a child standing in front of a Wendy house.

Rosie trod the gravel, trying to control her nerves and wondering why on earth she had thought this might be a good idea. *I want to go home...*

Gerri ushered her into the high, glass-walled hallway with its dark-grey slate floor. A glass and chrome open-tread staircase climbed to a vast open landing on the right. She tried not to picture her accident-prone little girls slipping and falling on the angled, shiny surfaces, against the glass and metal. There was very little to cushion a fall, unlike in her house, where you were just as likely to land in a pile of laundry or a discarded coat as anything else.

'This is lovely.' Keeping her voice low, she cast her eyes around, noting that there was not a speck of dust or item out of place. It reminded her more of a fancy-pants art gallery than a family home. She felt it best to whisper.

A dog ran towards her, or more accurately, the tiny ball of fluff that was Truffle. He sniffed and yapped as he stood his ground in front of her.

'Bloody dog. Gets under my feet wherever I turn.' Gerri sighed. 'I'm more of a cat person; it's a big deal for me having him around. But Phil was very keen, so…' She smiled.

Rosie didn't recognise this as being the Phil she knew, couldn't picture him being 'very keen' about a dog, just as she couldn't imagine him wandering around these rooms in his plaster-encrusted trousers and dusty hair, or envisage him farting amid all this refinement, after having been out for a few pints with his mates. This raised two thoughts in her mind. The first was that he might be playing a part, presenting an image to Gerri so that he fitted in. Surely he wasn't able to be himself in these lavish surroundings? The Phil she knew was uncomfortable going into a restaurant with tablecloths and instantly pooh-poohed anyone with a double-barrelled surname, and yet this was how he now lived?

The second thought was that she really didn't know him at all, and that the face he had been presenting to her was the fake one, and this idea saddened her beyond words.

She followed Gerri into a vast kitchen, where a multitude of shiny and remarkably similar-looking chrome and silver appliances sat squarely on acres of white granite work surface. There wasn't so much as a crumb on the tops, and the pristine oven and hob still looked brand new. She pictured her own kitchen at this time of the morning, with its chopping board invariably smeared with butter and toast crumbs and a jam-dipped knife resting on the side. The middle of Gerri's kitchen was occupied by a large island with a set of matt-black leather bar stools at one end of it. The whole place felt cool and untouchable.

Rosie looked outside at the rectangular infinity pool; the water seemed to hover on the horizon, as if it was part of the sea.

Gerri was quiet, as if giving her the chance to take it all in, like a saleswoman whose product doesn't need talking up.

'This is so lovely.'

'Yes. It is,' Gerri said. 'Do you want the grand tour?'

'Oh!' Rosie trilled a little laugh, nervous and yet eager, yes, to have a look around. 'Okay.'

'Follow me!' Gerri skipped to the right and along a corridor, with Rosie stepping behind. She let her French-manicured fingers trail along the wall. 'I was thinking of painting this wall a colour but got so flustered by the pressure of it, I just snapped and said go with white. I mean, if it ain't broke...'

Rosie nodded, not sure what, if any response, was expected. All she could think was that if a paint colour decision was the most pressure Gerri had in her life, then she should consider herself very lucky.

Gerri stopped and held out her arm, as if revealing a magic trick.

'Wow!' Rosie was amazed. The fanfare was warranted.

The hall wall had come to an abrupt end and she found herself standing under a vast glass dome sheltering a large rectangular pool. One side wall was glass, affording a view out over the shimmering sea, as far as the eye could see. The end wall was grey slate but veiled by a sheet of water that cascaded from top to bottom in an almost silent waterfall; it looked like dappled glass. Roman steps gave access at one end and were tiled, like the bottom of the pool, in iridescent turquoise glass mosaic. When the light hit and the surface rippled, it was as if the pool was alive. It was magnificent.

'What do you think?' Gerri bent forward, keen to get a reaction.

Rosie shook her head. 'I don't think I've ever seen anything like it.' She pictured the girls sitting on the steps or jumping into the water and she smiled, but this was quickly followed by a lump in her throat as she visualised Phil and Gerri there too, realising that she was the odd piece of jigsaw that didn't quite fit. A day spent here would be infinitely more exciting than a day in a silver-category six-berth caravan, even with chips thrown in. She wished she hadn't come. Far from helping, the images that she would now carry of the people she loved in this incredible place would only torture her further.

'I know it's over the top, but hell, when you've got the vision and the style, and a talented builder on tap...' She raised an amused eyebrow but kept her eyes off Rosie's face.

Rosie inhaled sharply. She couldn't take much more of this.

'And my mantra throughout the design process was light and space. I couldn't live without either – the idea of being cramped or having to look into a shadowy corner... Urgh!' She shivered. 'No thank you.'

Rosie noticed that her singsong tone had slipped and her voice now had a slightly hardened edge to it, making her sound quite bossy.

'Come on!' She trotted across the cool white floor and opened a wide door that led to more stairs. 'This is where the design gets really clever.'

At the top of the stairs was what appeared to be a walkway, with glass on both sides. Rosie hesitated, nervous of the drop onto the hallway below.

'Come on now, Rosie!' Gerri admonished. You're not scared of a little drop, are you? I'll give you a little tip: fortune favours the brave.'

Rosie found herself in a bedroom that was more like a flat. There was so much to take in: Floor-to-ceiling drapes in crushed silver framed yet another glass wall, and the biggest bed she had ever seen sat on a wooden plinth with a similar view to the pool. She wondered what it might feel like not only to wake up looking at it, but also to have so much room in a bed that you could stretch out without banging a wall.

The room had steps down that led to a freestanding copper bath in the middle of the room! There was no way she would ever have felt comfortable bathing in front of someone else. Even Phil.

I want to go home. I want to leave now!

'Are you okay?' Gerri asked.

'I think your house is lovely. I've probably seen enough. I should be getting back.' Rosie's voice was small.

'Oh! We haven't done the guest suites, but I guess they can wait till next time. Back to the kitchen, this way.' Gerri pointed over her head like an enthusiastic tour guide. 'You must stay for a drink?' Gerri asked. 'We still need to discuss pick-up arrangements and there is something else I'd like to talk to you about.'

'Err... just a tea or coffee would be nice, thank you.'

'Well of course a tea or coffee! What did you think, that I sipped champagne all day?' Gerri laughed.

'Coffee then, thanks.'

Gerri collected two plain white mugs from inside a glossy, handleless cupboard. 'Trouble is, when you've built from scratch, you're never quite sure if it's finished, so I keep changing my mind, planning projects, adding things. I'm hoping I get to a point when I just know that it's done and can finally take the tradesmen off speed dial.'

Rosie sniffed at the irony of her words but decided to bite her tongue.

Gerri carried on, seemingly oblivious. 'I've always wanted somewhere I could breathe outside of London and this is it!' She raised her palms to the side of her head and smiled smugly.

'Whereabouts do you live in London?'

'Oh, do you know it?' Gerri whipped around, her eyes bright.

Rosie felt her face colour. 'A bit, not really. I've been a couple of times. We went to Madame Tussauds, although we had to leave before the end because Naomi was scared of David Beckham. And we took the girls up Christmas shopping a couple of years back, mainly to see Father Christmas in Hamleys.' She was embarrassed to be so unfamiliar with the capital city, but also to have mentioned their life before. As usual when she was nervous or anxious, her tongue just ran away with itself. There was no way she'd meant to share all this with the woman who'd split up their family. She was annoyed at how intimidated she felt.

'I'm just off High Street Ken, which is handy for everything. Milk? Sugar?'

'Just milk please.' Rosie thought she might have misheard. *Did she say Kent? That's not London, is it?* She couldn't bring herself to ask.

Gerri picked up the mugs and swept out of the kitchen. 'Come through!'

Rosie trotted behind her, noting the delicate tread of her small bare feet with the scarlet toenails as they padded across the acres of grey slate and pale marble. Eventually they came to a wide, open-plan lounge, where the carpet was indeed white. She made the decision to neck her coffee and go. She'd had enough of the grand tour and had done what she'd set out to do, shown willing, for the girls' sake.

Taking a seat at the opposite end of the sofa, she tentatively took her coffee from Gerri, wary of the white carpet and too ill at ease to adjust her sitting position, which meant she was not far back enough to lean against the huge soft cushion or forward enough to be able to put her feet on the floor. She perched in this half-stance, quite uncomfortable and conscious of her slouch, wondering if Gerri could see the little roll of fat that sat above her bra strap and was visible beneath her jumper.

'So,' Gerri said excitedly, 'thank you so much for coming. I wanted you to see where Naomi and Leona get to play. And Phil too, I guess.' She sipped her drink.

Rosie nodded. She had to admit, it was quite something to think of her children being given free rein here.

'Although it's not all mucking around – some of us have to work. But that's the joy of the internet: I can work absolutely anywhere.'

'Oh, you still work?' In Rosie's head, Gerri spent her days in the pool and her nights rolling around in piles of money.

'Uh-huh.' She nodded. 'I'm seed-funding several projects – app development, telco, fitness, varied stuff, about half of which I fully buy into, but you have to take the gamble, right? That's how you win big. I'm even shoving a bundle into a fast-food franchise. I mean, the idea is abhorrent to me, but fatties have got to eat, right?' She gave a short, unnatural laugh that sounded mean.

Rosie nodded again, wondering if it was because she was tense that she'd only understood about half of what Gerri had said. Gerri snuggled back into her chair, meaning Rosie had to twist her body awkwardly on the wide seat to look at her. 'Do you like your job?' she asked.

'"Like" isn't the word, but... how to phrase it? My work was my life. I'd get by on three hours' sleep, constantly checking stock levels, looking at spreadsheets.' She exhaled, as if even the memory was exhausting. 'You know what it gets like.'

'Not really! I clean caravans. I clean them, I go home and I don't think about them until I pick up that bucket and clean them again. Although I have taken on some extra hours in reception, giving out keys and checking people in. I've been there a while and the people are nice.' She turned to look at Gerri, who stared back with an amused smile playing about her mouth. Her eyes then widened, as if Rosie had said the wrong thing, embarrassing them both.

'Yes, work was everything,' Gerri continued, as if Rosie hadn't spoken, or, more accurately, as if what she'd said was not relevant. 'That was until I built this place. And then I decided I wanted more.' She smirked. 'It was a bit like getting a doll's house – you know, the kind you had when you were young, where you take the front off and there are all these rooms and sweet little chairs and plates and minute beds and pillows.'

'I didn't have one, but I know what you mean.'

'Oh. Well, you'll have to take my word for it.' Gerri rolled her hand in the air. 'So I finished the house and I realised what was missing. I was missing all the little people to put inside it.' She threw a meaningful glance in Rosie's direction. 'You know the ones, Rosie – they stand in the rooms until you move them to another spot, just waiting for you to dip in, pick them up and give them a life.'

Rosie stared at her. Her heart beat a little too fast and she felt the air leave the room. It was as if Gerri was speaking too slowly, sounding slightly slurred in her mind.

Gerri continued. 'There's no point having a fancy toy if half the pieces are missing, don't you think?'

Rosie swallowed and found her voice. 'So you took my little people.'

Gerri's response was speedy and concise. 'What a very strange thing to say!' She placed her free hand on her chest. 'I've only taken one.' Her eyes were wide, animated. She bobbed her head.

Rosie couldn't think how to reply. The words jumbled in her mind, her anger diluted by the fact that she was in this woman's grand house, as if she ought therefore to be on her best behaviour. 'I don't know if you're joking, but it's not funny. What you've done, it's not funny at all.'

'Oh, I'm not laughing.' Gerri's expression changed and she stared at Rosie, whose chest heaved.

'I want you to stay away from my kids,' Rosie managed.

'Don't be ridiculous!' Gerri practically spat the words.

'They are Phil's kids too, and they love coming here. Who's going to be the one to tell them no more swimming, no more Truffle?' She shook her head dismissively. Truffle barked, as if on cue, reminding them both of his presence. 'Although I do get it – to be thrown over by your man is one thing, but to have your kids rather spend time with a dog...' She took a deep breath. 'That must be tough.'

Desperate to leave right away, Rosie shuffled forwards on the deep sofa until her feet found the white carpet beneath her trainers.

'Oh, don't go just yet! I have some news!' Gerri shrieked.

Rosie stood up and looked at the petite woman with the large amount of power. She watched as Gerri placed her manicured hand against the flat waistband of her tight jeans. *Oh no! Please, no, no, no! Not that!* Rosie felt her muscles slip on her bones, felt as if she was falling, unsteady and lightheaded, as yet another wave of sadness threatened to break over her.

'Yep.' Gerri beamed. 'I think Phil's finally going to get the little boy he always wanted.'

'You're pregnant?' she whispered, needing confirmation.

'Isn't it wonderful?'

Rosie turned, stumbling blindly across the lounge area, picturing the pregnancy test that had fallen on the floor at the hospital, how she had cuddled up to Phil that night in bed, lamenting the result and hoping they would get the chance to try again. Through the haze of her distress, she tried to remember where the kitchen was, where she had left her bag, keys and phone. The last thing she wanted was to cry here, in front of her. As she hurried towards the hall, the remains of the coffee slopped in her cup and sloshed onto the white wool carpet. She didn't care; she just wanted to get out of the place.

'Oh, don't worry about the carpet,' Gerri said matter-of-factly, 'that's what cleaning ladies are for!'

Rosie turned to face Gerri, who was now very deliberately tipping the remains of her own coffee cup onto the white carpet. The woman was clearly even more deranged than Rosie had thought. There was no way she was going to let her near the kids again.

'Bear left!' Gerri called in a singsong tone, as if they were playing a game.

Rosie raced into the kitchen and swept her bag from the countertop, placing the mug on the granite surface with such force, she half expected it might crack. Gerri had followed her down the hall.

'Is that why you asked me here, to laugh at me? To hurt me?'

'Oh God, no! Of course not!' Gerri tutted. 'But I did want you to see that you've lost.'

'I don't... I don't understand,' Rosie managed as her tears spilled.

'I dare say.' Gerri toyed with a loose tendril of her long blonde hair. 'You were right, Rosie, I did choose him.'

Rosie took a sharp breath. 'You're bloody mad, you are! And you're nasty. I will never understand how anyone can take pleasure in destroying a family like you did mine.'

'Don't you think I have a right to be happy as well? A right to a family life?' Gerri said, as casually as if they were discussing the weather.

Rosie gripped her bag against her chest. 'I'm telling you now: you stay away from my kids. You fucking stay away from them!' She didn't like the aggression that surged through her, felt sick at the confrontation that was so far out of her comfort zone, but if ever there was a time for anger, this was it.

She heard the faint burble of laughter as she ran out of the front door. She revved the engine and pulled the car forwards to the wide gate. Her limbs were shaking. It seemed like an age before the gate whirred open. As soon as the gap was wide enough, she zoomed to freedom, pulling out onto the lane a little faster and more erratically than she normally would. When she got to the bottom of the hill, she screeched into a layby on the Esplanade and with trembling fingers phoned Mel.

'What's going on?' Mel said immediately when she heard Rosie's sobs. 'You all right, love?'

'Not really.' Rosie tried to catch her breath. 'Oh God, Mel!' She closed her eyes and leant her head on the steering wheel, wondering how to start, where to start.

Mel robbed her of the chance. 'I've just had Gerri on the phone,' she said, 'crying her eyes out. Said you were at the house and you went mental, threw coffee, threatened her, swore at her. She's in a right state.' Mel didn't sound like her usual friendly self. Her tone was odd, a little off; it was the tone she used when referring to Kayleigh. It sounded judgemental. Rosie was shocked.

'Mel, I'm telling you, she's nuts! She was really horrible to me.'

'I thought she'd invited you up to the house to get to know each other, make it easier?'

'She did! That's what she said, but when I got there, she was a bit snooty and weird, felt like she was showing off, really stuck up, and she was going on about seeds and stuff and made me feel like rubbish because I only know Madame Tussauds, and she lives in Kent and that's not even London! And then she told me she was pregnant!' Rosie closed her eyes and cupped her hand over her face; she wanted to hide from the world.

'That's what *she* said, that she told you about the baby and you went ballistic, threw coffee and told her to fuck off. Is that right? Did you?'

'It's kind of right. I did tell her to fuck off,' Rosie admitted. There was something in her friend's response that suddenly struck her. 'Did you *know* she was pregnant?' She was aware of how high pitched her voice had become.

Mel hesitated. 'I only found out a couple of days ago.' Her tone had softened.

'And you didn't think to tell me?'

'I didn't want to upset you.'

'Do you know what, Mel, it's easy to spout all that rubbish about how you would always choose me—'

'I would!'

'Well, it sure doesn't feel like it right now. And anyway, I never expected you to choose. I know that Andy and Phil are mates, but I did expect a bit of loyalty!' She was shouting now.

'Well, I didn't expect you to go and lose it in her house! That's not helpful. And she's pregnant! I know that's hard, Rosie, but it's how it is.'

'You are not listening to me!' Rosie screamed. 'She more or less told me that she had picked Phil, picked out our family to rip apart. She was going on about a doll's house and it felt like she was threatening me. I think she's coming after my kids!' Having to say the words out loud caused her breath to catch. *Oh God, oh my God!*

'I think you're probably just upset, and shocked about the whole baby thing. And I understand why. It's a shock, but—'

Rosie ended the call. She wasn't interested in hearing Mel's reasoning.

She collected the girls from school and walked them home, deep in thought, her eyes darting here and there as she gripped their hands. Woolacombe suddenly felt like a hostile place and she couldn't wait to get the kids home and safe behind their front door. She gave only brief answers to their usual stream of questions, wishing they would be quiet and allow her time to think. She kept looking over her shoulder, half expecting to see a big black Range Rover snaking up behind her.

'Mum, do you think our fish are in heaven?' Naomi asked.

'Maybe.'

'If they are, how can they breathe, because heaven isn't underwater and that's where Moby and Jonathan need to be, otherwise they wouldn't have died when we tipped the mug over?' Leona asked.

'You tipped the mug over,' Naomi reminded her sister.

'You did!' Leona shouted.

'All right, girls. Please, no arguing.' She nipped the fracas that threatened in the bud.

'Do you think Jesus has a fish tank?' Leona asked.

'He might do.' Rosie smiled.

'Because if Jesus put the fish in his fish tank, they'd be special Jesus fish, which would be nice, wouldn't it, Mummy?'

'Yes, it would be nice.'

'Why does the lady next door have such big teeth? They are massive!' Naomi stuck her teeth out over her bottom lip as if to demonstrate.

'I don't know.'

'Have Nanny and Grandad ever been in prison?' Naomi had switched tack.

'No.' Rosie shook her head. 'No, they haven't.'

'If they went to prison, we could live in their house,' Leona added.

'They are not going to prison.'

'What's the smallest crime you can do, so that you only go to prison for an hour or even half an hour, just so you can have a look, but you don't have to stay there?' Naomi was on a roll.

'I don't know.'

'Is it doing a wee in the street, because Leo did a wee in the street?'

'I don't want to go to prison!' Leona started to fret.

'You'd only go for an hour, Leona Shitstar.'

Rosie stopped walking. 'What did you call her?'

'I don't know.' Naomi sucked in her cheeks and stared at her mum without blinking.

'She called me Leona Shitstar.'

'Right. That's it! When we get home, you are both having tea and then going straight to bed. I've had enough today.'

'But she called *me* shitstar – I didn't do anything wrong!' Leona whined.

'You grassed her up and that shows no loyalty and that's a shitty thing to do.'

The two girls exchanged a glance. It was Naomi who was the bravest. 'You said "shitty", are you going to go to bed too?'

'Yes. Yes I am.' She nodded at the girls and marched on.

It was nearly seven o'clock and she could hear their laughter coming through the floor. So much for punishment. Rosie felt out of sorts, replaying not only what Gerri had said to her, but also the way she'd said it. And she was doubly floored by Mel's reaction, to the point where she was now wary of speaking to Mo or anyone else, in case they said or thought the same. She felt lonely. She could no longer confide in Phil, as she had for the last decade, and Kev was thousands of miles away, in the BVI.

The front doorbell rang while she was stacking the dishwasher and her heart leapt at the thought that it might be Gerri or Mel. She needn't have worried. It was Phil.

'Can I come in?'

She could tell by the set of his jaw that this wasn't a courtesy call.

'Gerri is in a bad way,' he began as soon as he stepped into the hallway, obviously keen to get the words out.

She watched how he drew his shoulders in, as if he suddenly found the space in which he'd lived happily for all those years a little cramped now. She walked through to the kitchen and he followed her.

'Please try and keep your voice down. The girls are in bed and I don't want them upset or hyped up.' She tried to keep the shiver from her bones; she was still shaken and on high alert.

'What on earth happened today? Why were you even there?' He paced the floor.

'I thought you'd know. I was there because she invited me. She said it would be best for the girls, best for everyone, if we all got on, and stupidly I thought that was the right thing to do.'

He shook his head, as if that fact alone irritated him. Clearly he didn't like the idea of his two worlds colliding.

Rosie continued. 'She... she made me feel small. The way she spoke to me, Phil, was—'

'Was what?' he interrupted. 'You've just said yourself, she invited you up to the house to try and build bridges.'

Rosie stared at him, the man who with every new rejection hurt her even more. *You're my husband, Phil! How can you even look at me like that?* She took a deep breath and tried to keep a calm head, tried to speak rationally. 'Phil, I need you to listen to me. I need you to trust me.' She cursed the wobble of emotion in her voice. 'We've been married for a very long time...'

He held her gaze.

'... and you have only known this woman for a little while and today I saw a side to her that has frightened me. She honestly sounded nuts!'

'Are you serious?' He squinted. 'When I got home, she was on the bedroom floor. She was sobbing. I couldn't calm her down, and let me tell you, *that* frightened me.'

'She was laughing when I left, sneering at me! And she tipped her own coffee on the—'

'Rosie, stop it! Just stop it!' He sighed. 'She is as house-proud as they come. You expect me to believe she tipped her own coffee onto her own imported, eighteen-grand carpet?'

She stared at him. If he thought she was lying, then they'd turned down another dark road that they'd never travelled before.

'She said she told you about the baby.'

'Ah, yes, the baby. Congratulations!'

'Yes! That's exactly how she said you reacted – nastily, sarcastically – and that then you couldn't stop, you swore at her, threatened her, told her to fucking be careful and to stay away from the girls. Is that true?'

'I did say something like that, yes, but that's not exactly how it happened. She's twisting it! She pushed me into a corner and now no one is hearing what I'm saying. She was threatening, scary.'

'Scary? Have you seen her?' He gave a short burst of laughter, which made Rosie feel big and clumsy.

She crossed her arms over her torso as he carried on berating her.

'I am genuinely surprised by what you've done. Surprised and...' He chose his words carefully. 'Disappointed. She didn't deserve that. She's gone out of the way to make the girls welcome, bought them a bloody dog!'

His words lit the touch paper that saw her fear and frustration erupt. She heard Gerri's words. *To be thrown over by your man is one thing, but to have your kids rather spend time with a dog...'*

'What about what I deserve, Phil? Is anyone considering that? It's like the blows just keep coming. First I lose you, then I have to smile and wave the girls off as and when you feel like taking them, and now, not only is she having a baby, but she was bloody awful to me today. And yet I'm being made to feel like the one in the wrong!' She cursed her distress, wishing she could present a stronger front.

She saw him glance at his wrist before putting his hands on his hips. There was somewhere else he wanted to be. 'Don't let me keep you,' she said angrily.

'Why are you being like this? I didn't mean you to find out about the baby like this. I planned on telling you when the time was right, the next time I saw you.'

'Well don't worry about that. I'm sure I would have heard it eventually, from Mel or Andy or someone else in town like Mrs Blackmore's granddaughter in the Spar.'

'Andy's my mate. What do you suggest, that I just drop him?'

'No, but I am still your wife, whether you like it or not, and I am the mother of your children and you could at least give me the courtesy of not letting me be the last to know about something so important.' She noted the way he was restlessly shifting his weight from foot to foot. 'And even now, you can't wait to be gone. You're so on edge. It's like I don't know you, Phil. As if you have just erased the last twelve years of our lives. Well, the bad news is, I am not going to disappear, no matter how convenient that would be for you.'

He ran his fingers through his hair. 'I didn't plan any of this.'

'Oh God, not that again! And let me tell you, even if *you* didn't, *she* did! She said as much today, said she chose you. And you were so weak and predictable, you didn't exactly make it difficult for her, did you?'

'The way you talk, Rosie, you make me sound callous, but I'm not. I love my kids.'

'Well, good, because you've got another one on the way. Mind you, it should be easy, it's not like you have to worry about lack of finances or lack of space!' She remembered that night, lying against him in their little bed, recalled the feel of his bare chest beneath her cheek, the way she felt like her heart might burst with longing for the baby that wasn't to be.

Phil took a deep breath. 'It's not...'

'It's not what?'

'It's not all perfect. Despite what you think, what you see, it's not all easy.' He looked at her.

'What?' She folded her arms across her chest and stared at him.

'I'm just saying... I am happy, I am. But it's not all perfect. I mean, yes, the house is amazing, but it's not mine, and leaving the kids, dropping them off, is really hard for me. And Gerri, she's... she's a handful. Hard work... you know... and it feels very soon for a baby. I don't know.' He ran his hand over his face. He was chatting to her like they used to, when they were friends, partners in everything, before he left. When they could discuss anything and everything.

She continued to stare at him, absorbing his words, analysing their meaning. Things in the garden high up on the cliff in Mortehoe were apparently far from rosy. This was what she had longed to hear. To be given hope when at her lowest ebb. The number of times she had lain in bed in the early hours, waiting for dawn to break and imagining him saying those words. But it was too late now. The flame had been all but extinguished and Geraldine Farmer was having his baby.

She saw red. 'How dare you? How fucking dare you?'

She took a step towards him. 'It better be bloody perfect! You don't get to do that, you don't get to destroy my life, my family, break my heart, confuse my kids, take my best friend and then stand there and tell me that the grass isn't greener! You are such a prick! How dare you! Why do you think that's okay? Why do you think I give a shit? I don't! Just fuck off! Fuck off back to your three acres and your cold, soulless mansion. Go back and lie in that grand bed that you've made with a view of the sea. And I hope you choke on every morsel of steak, every sip of champagne. I hope every sodding mouthful you put in your deceitful gob is bitter on your tongue.' She pointed towards the front door. 'Get out of my house! Get the fuck out!'

Phil stared at the swearing woman that he didn't recognise. 'Gerri was right, you have lost the bloody plot. And I tell you what, it is very nearly perfect, which is a darn sight better than playing at it and being miserable, like I was for the last few years.'

'Get out!' she screamed, paying no heed to the sound of feet scampering across the floor and down the stairs.

'Daddy!' Naomi yelled and ran at him, throwing her arms around his thighs.

Leona sauntered down the stairs, still not fully awake.

'I heard Mummy shouting.' She looked up into her dad's face as if this might be news to him.

He picked her up and kissed her nose. 'You need to go back to bed, Nay.' He lowered her onto the bottom step and kissed her sister.

'Will you still be here in the morning?' She jumped up and down on the spot.

'No.' He looked at them both. 'But I'll see you very soon, I promise.'

Rosie watched him leave and imagined the conversation he would have with Gerri when he got back. *'I understand completely! She went nuts at me too!'* She smiled weakly at the irony. What was the expression? *Might as well be hung for a sheep as a lamb.*

After tucking the girls into their beds, she made her way back downstairs. Weakened by the dramas of the day, she fell into the sitting room, where she slumped down in the chair that used to be Phil's. Too numb to cry, too tired to sleep, she knew it was going to be a very long night.

Fourteen

Rosie was quiet, as she had been in the weeks following her encounter with Gerri. It was still with a great sense of sadness that she recalled her husband's and best friend's reactions to her account, confident that if it had been them that had come to her with such shocking revelations, she would have supported them.

Phil had seen the girls only twice since, once at Mo and Keith's and once at Arlington Road. She was, in light of recent developments, unwilling to let them go and visit Mortehoe, petrified that Gerri would find a way to influence them against her as well. It didn't bear thinking about.

Mo had called the moment the pregnancy became public knowledge. Rosie had listened to her but found it hard to talk about and harder still to believe the words of solace and reason that her mother-in-law offered.

'I can only imagine what this must feel like for you and

I agree, it is very soon, too soon perhaps. But the fact is, whether we like it or not, that baby is on its way and it will be part of our family, a half-sibling for Nay and Leo. We have to all make the best of it, Rosie. That's the only way. Anything else just isn't fair on that little one.'

Rosie had replaced the receiver quietly, remembering the excitement that had bubbled from them when Naomi, Mo and Keith's first grandchild, was due. No sooner had the pregnancy been confirmed than Keith had started road-testing prams and Mo had started knitting and buying sleepsuits and tiny socks. Rosie used to refer to her unborn baby as 'little one' as well. Carrying a Tipcott child had elevated her within the family and she had loved that. And now her worst nightmare was coming true: she was being replaced. This baby would get equal ranking alongside her daughters, just as she had feared.

The girls were at school and she had finished work for the day. She missed seeing Mel but found her lack of support hard to get over. They hadn't fallen out exactly; they still exchanged the odd text and were civil to each other at the school gate, but that was the extent of it. Rosie had used to enjoy wandering to school as part of her daily routine, catching up with the other mums and dads, but not any more; even that had lost its shine. She noticed how the conversations went suspiciously quiet when she arrived. Being a discarded woman whose husband's mistress was now expecting was big news in a small place like Woolacombe. She would have seen the funny side of the school-gate silences if she'd had Mel to share it with, but Mel was now part of the problem. Gone were the days of nipping in and out of each other's houses and chatting over a jacket spud and a cup of coffee in the café.

It was a blustery old day. The wind whipped along the shoreline and around the Esplanade, carrying with it a fine smattering of sand and salt water that dusted the car park and gathered in a neat strip of paste against the kerbstone. The town centre was deserted, seasonal shops and beach shacks were shuttered and padlocked, and in the midday grey the whole place seemed gloomy. Glancing into the café, she saw Kayleigh's sour face sitting at a table in the window. Rosie decided to make out she hadn't seen her and, fastening her anorak up to her chin, she looked the other way.

She could feel the grit between her teeth as she made her way around the headland. She wanted some bench time.

Pulling up her hood, she took her usual seat at the end and stretched her legs out on the grass. There was no longer any need to hide her pouchy tum as it was now considerably flatter. A storm was building on the horizon. Dark clouds burst over the waves, dumping silver rods of rain straight into the ocean, the droplets hitting the water with such force that they bounced out again, then fell with a pitter-patter. The weather didn't bother her much; there was no make-up to smudge, no coiffed hair to be messed up and no one that would give a fig that her wet lashes had stuck to her cheeks.

The rain swerved like a swarm of bees, changing direction and pushing out to the east, leaving the wind to howl at its sudden change of heart. She let her hood fall onto her shoulders and rubbed her face to rid it of the droplets.

'The calm after the storm,' she whispered.

It was minutes later that a walker in a bright yellow cagoule strolled across the grass.

'I thought it was you!' he called. 'Rosie Tipcott!'

She sat up straight and squinted, recognising the American, Clark, as he got closer. He came and sat on the bench.

'What are you doing here?' she asked, like they were old friends.

'Now there's a welcome!' He laughed.

'Sorry. I guess I'm just surprised to see you.' She stuffed her hands into the side pockets of her anorak.

'I've been walking the Tarka Trail. Well, bits of it.'

'For work?' She wondered if another article was in the offing.

'Actually, no, for me. I never get to spend as much time as I'd like doing things for the simple joy of them, so I thought, why not? And I came back down. My last stop, for real this time, before I fly back at the weekend.'

'Back to straight across from New York and up a bit towards Canada.' She smiled.

'Hey, good memory.' He smiled delightedly and turned to face her. 'So what's been happening in the world of Rosie Tipcott?'

Without warning, though not for the first time, the reality of her situation hit her with sudden, debilitating force and her tears began to fall.

'Oh God, I'm so sorry.' She sniffed, embarrassed.

'Goodness, Rosie! I'm sorry to have asked.' He shook his head, mortified to have been the cause. 'Do you know, I have thought about you often, you and your lovely sunny disposition. I envied your air of peace and contentment.'

'There's nothing very peaceful about me at the moment, I'm afraid.' She wiped her nose on the back of her hand. 'The kids' dad left. My husband, he... he met someone else.' She exhaled and stared out to sea, wondering if it would ever get easier to say those words out loud.

'Oh.' Clark was quiet for a while. 'Well, I am truly sorry to hear that. And I know what it feels like. I was in a similar boat myself not two years ago. It's not pretty.'

'I keep thinking I'm okay, getting better, but as soon as I get used to feeling that way, the next wave comes and knocks me off my feet. It's exhausting.' She thought again about the baby.

'That's how it feels. And it's still that way for me after all this time. It has got easier, but it's not only the sense of loss but the betrayal too, it's a tough combination.'

She nodded. Yes, it was. Too tough sometimes. 'I remember the day we met. When I left you sitting here, I felt sorry for you, thinking how lucky I was to be going home to my perfect life. But it was already broken; I just didn't know it. And that makes me feel so stupid.' She found it surprisingly easy to talk to this man she barely knew.

'Will you stay here?' he asked.

She laughed loudly. 'Yes! Of course. It's where I'm from.'

'I love where I'm from too. Lake Oswego. It's home, but I also knew that if I didn't change my scenery, my routine, I was going to keep running around in circles. I needed to break out, shake things up a bit and it's helped. Travelling has given me a greater perspective on the world and my place in it.'

'You sound like my friend,' she said, thinking of Kev. 'But it's not that easy. It's not like I have a stash of plane tickets and a wad of spare cash, though I wish I did. Plus my kids are young, settled. I'd never uproot them.'

'Well, if you don't mind my saying, that seems rather convenient.'

'What do you mean?' She turned to look at him.

'Using your children as an excuse to stay put.'

'It's not an excuse, it's a fact. They need stability.'

He smiled kindly at her. 'I travel all over the world and meet lots of different people in all kinds of wonderful places, and let me tell you, what kids need most, more than stability, more than laptops, more than anything, is happy parents in a welcoming environment.'

'You make it sound very simple.' She returned his smile.

'It is that simple.' He nodded out towards the ocean.

'Well, I'm working my way towards happiness, I guess, and if I could get there faster, I sure would.'

'Try and find a shortcut. That might help!' He laughed.

'I will.' She smiled.

'Rosie…' He paused. 'Would you like to go and get a drink?' He sat forward on the bench and with his thumb indicated the town behind him.

Woolacombe – where she knew everyone and everyone knew her. She felt a rush of embarrassment course through her body. 'Oh! Oh! I can't. No. But thank you. Yes, but no. Thanks though. I have to go.'

She stood up and hurriedly zipped up her coat, desperate to put space between her and the American, cringing as her stomach bunched at the thought that she might have given him the wrong impression.

Clark stood up too. 'I've overstepped the mark and I apologise. I didn't mean it in any way other than just two rejects getting a glass of something out of the wind. I would never want to offend you.'

'No! Not at all, it's kind of you, I'm just... It's not... I can't see myself as anything other than his wife and that's it really.' She shrugged.

Clark gave her another warm smile. 'You know, Rosie, I have looked in the mirror many a day in the last couple of years and seen the same expression you're wearing staring back at me. It does get easier, trust me. And if you decide you want that change of scenery, look me up – there's only one Clark Dobson in Lake Oswego – and bring the kids. I have a cabin on the shoreline of The Willamette River. It's quite magical. I'd love to host you there, free of charge. I'd consider it a pleasure to show you all around. There's nothing like a winter hike up at Mount Hood, or if it's the summer, take the boat out, catch us a few fish, shoot the breeze. It's very peaceful, a great place to think, get some perspective on life.'

'It sounds lovely,' she said.

'It is, and I mean it, the offer stands.'

Rosie smiled at him, this clever, kind man who had offered her the hand of friendship. It was the biggest compliment she had received in a very long time.

'Goodbye, Clark, and thank you.' She waved at him before walking back down the Esplanade and heading home.

Despite the increasingly foul weather, which was now wrapping the buildings in sheets of rain and spinning mini tornadoes around the lampposts, Rosie walked with a spring in her step. Clark was a writer! He had articles in newspapers and he liked her! She felt grateful and the beginnings of happy. Maybe this was the shortcut he was referring to.

Pushing open her front door, keen to get into the dry, she saw an envelope on the doormat. There was no stamp, it had been hand-delivered, and she instantly recognised Phil's writing from the one word on the envelope: *Rosie*. Without waiting to take off her wet coat, she ripped it open and scanned his words.

I knocked, but you're not home, so I'm writing instead. Whatever has been said and done between the two of us is nothing to do with Nay and Leo. It's not fair, Rosie, for me to be kept away from them because you're angry and upset. You know I always keep them safe, look after them, I always have and I'm asking you to let them come to the house, please. I just want to spend time with them without Mum and Dad being there, or in some café.

We need to move forward and do what's best for all of us, but especially what's best for the girls.

Thanks,

Phil

She laid the sheet of paper on the stairs, took off her soggy coat and hung it on the bannister. *Happy parents in a welcoming environment...* That sounded like wise advice.

Picking up her phone she sent a text. *Read your letter. They can come to the house, but you keep an eye on things. I can't let G be mean to me or about me, that's just not fair. Okay?*

His reply came swiftly. *OK. Thank you.* X

She deleted it instantly.

When the weekend came, the girls were beyond excited. Their enthusiasm for the trip up to Mortehoe was tough for Rosie. She bit her tongue, knowing that any negativity the kids picked up on would only make them feel uncomfortable and she never wanted that.

'I can't wait to see little Truffle!' Leona spun round in a circle with her arms spread wide until she lost her balance and collapsed on the sofa.

'I bet he's missed you,' Rosie managed from the hallway, where she'd placed their rucksacks, packed for an overnight stay.

'Is Gerri going to have the baby this weekend?' Naomi

asked from the sofa, lifting her head from her reading book for the first time that morning.

'Oh no, darling, not for a very long time.'

Gerri was not yet three months, so there was plenty of time for the girls to get used to the idea and, in Rosie's opinion, plenty of time for things still to go wrong. She herself would not have gone public quite so soon, but, conscious that any view she expressed would be seen as a criticism, she kept schtum.

'I hope it's a boy.' Naomi's tone was unusually low-key.

'You do? I would have thought you'd like it to be a girl the same as you and Leo.'

She shook her head. 'No. I like Daddy only being mine and Leo's daddy and I don't mind if he is a dad to a new boy, but I don't want him to get a new girl.'

Rosie dropped down to her knees in front of the sofa. She placed her hands on her little girl's legs and looked at her. 'The thing is, Nay, it doesn't matter what happens between Daddy and me, it doesn't matter if he has a boy or a girl or another three of each, you will always be the oldest, and he could not love you or Leo any more than he does already. You don't have to worry about that.'

'If they have a little girl baby, I don't want them to call it Naomi.' She flicked the page of her reading book back and forth.

Rosie gave a small laugh. 'That won't happen, darling. You will be the only Naomi.'

'But you said Daddy chose my name and he might choose it again.' She looked close to tears.

Leaning forward, she enveloped her daughter in a hug. 'He did choose it, and it's a beautiful name, but that's not really how it works.' She smoothed Naomi's long, silky hair down her back. 'It would be very confusing, wouldn't it? If we'd called you both Naomi?' She laughed.

'Or Leona, you could have called us both that!' her youngest, piped up, standing again, ready to resume her spinning.

There was a knock on the front door and the girls leapt up and sprinted over to it.

'Daddy!'

'Daddy, hello!'

Rosie watched Phil's smile spread as he reached down to hug them both.

'Hi, Rosie.' He looked at her over the girls' heads as they tried to scramble up his front. She lifted her chin in acknowledgement.

'Mum was wondering about Christmas…' he muttered. Rosie swallowed. It was only six weeks away. 'She wanted to make a few plans, I think. I said you'd talk to her.' He looked away, shifty.

She hoped he felt as guilty as he looked. The one time of year they had all always looked forward to would now never be the same again. Just one of the ways that his choice had sent ripples into their lives. 'What are your plans?' she asked.

'Just going to go with the flow and fit around what you and the girls want to do. I mean, we're all ten minutes away from each other, it's not like we can't all get to spend time with everyone.'

She stared at him, taken aback by his relaxed response, wondering if he really did see it as simply a question of logistics. 'I'll go and see Mo.'

'She'd like that.' He smiled and stood upright, shaking off the girls in the process. 'Right, come on you two, I think Truffle is waiting for you.'

'Has he got bigger?' Naomi asked.

'A little bit, I think.'

'Bye, honeys! Be good!' Rosie smiled. 'And don't forget to brush your hair!' she called after them as they raced towards their dad's shiny car.

Rosie slept fitfully, disturbed by bad dreams and invasive thoughts, which always seemed loudest in the hours of darkness. She replayed the way Gerri had smirked at her responses and flitted from room to room, like a game-show hostess showing a distraught loser what they might have won.

It took two cups of coffee at breakfast to shake off the worst of it. She decided to go and see Mo and get the Christmas plans sorted out.

At Highthorne, she just managed to squeeze her car into a small space along the far side of the vans. She knocked and entered and found Keith eating bacon and eggs at the breakfast table.

'Come on in, Rosie, love. Mo won't be a minute. She's just popped a few things up to, erm... To...'

She watched him struggle, unsure how to say 'Mortehoe' or 'Phil's' without actually using the words.

'Tell you what...' He'd obviously decided to go for a diversion tactic. 'You stick the kettle on.'

Rosie nodded and did just that. 'Work busy?' She decided to fill the room with small talk, just like she always had.

'No, not really. But it's not such a problem earning less, now it's just Ross and erm...' Again he stopped suddenly. He placed his cutlery onto the plate, seemingly having lost his appetite. 'I'm sorry, love. Truth is, I'm wary of putting my foot in it. And I don't like being in that position, not one bit.'

'Is Phil not working with you?' She turned to look at her father-in-law, a sweet, hard-working, family man who was incapable of deceit.

'No. He's err... He's doing something different now.' His cheeks flamed.

'Like what?' Rosie wrinkled her nose, trying to think what job Phil, who had left school at sixteen, done a stint in the army and then worked for his dad, might now be doing. And then it struck her. 'Is he working for Gerri?'

Keith looked at the table and nodded. 'I think he might be, yes. I mean, yes. Yes, he is.'

'Doing what?' Again, she was struggling. She knew that Gerri had made her money working in computers and she had no idea how Phil would fit into that world. He couldn't work his phone properly, let alone a computer.

'Oh, you know, driving and collecting things, and I'm not too sure what else. But I guess he'll be happier being inside in the warm and dry and not stuck out on a building site in all weathers. Plus it's probably regular money.'

'But it's Tipcott and Sons! And he's the son! He's always worked with you. I can't imagine him doing anything different.' She stared at him as if she were the only one shocked by the news.

Keith cleared his throat. 'I know. But I guess we're all having to get used to the changes.' He looked close to tears.

'Sorry, Keith, I can tell I've upset you, and I didn't mean to. I wouldn't want to upset you for the world.'

'You haven't, love. It's difficult. All I want is what you want, for my kids to be happy, and sometimes they make choices you find hard or you disagree with, but if they're happy, and that's the goal after all, how can you stop them, and would you want to?'

She thought about Naomi and Leona, happy to be with their dad, swimming in that incredible pool and playing with Truffle. 'I get it.' She nodded.

'I'm back, love!' Mo called as the front door slammed. She continued to shout from the hallway. 'Gerri was as pleased as punch with the little matinee jacket I'd knitted! And the girls were there, which was just lovely, chasing after that little dog. He's a poppet, he is. I've told her we don't know about numbers yet, but Gerri's getting caterers in apparently and has already ordered three big turkeys for Christmas, reckon we could feed an—'

Mo stopped talking as soon as she walked into the kitchen. Rosie stared at her and their eyes locked. Both women were mortified, each wishing they were elsewhere or at the very least could rewind the last few minutes.

'Rosie! Hello, love.' She shrugged her arms from her coat, which she laid on the back of the chair in the corner. 'I've just seen the girls.'

'Yes, I heard.' Rosie's voice was a squeak. She looked at the cluttered surfaces of the kitchen and felt a new level of embarrassment. This wasn't her family, it was Phil's, and she had no place being there, not any more.

'I can't stay, actually.' She picked up her keys. 'I just came to say hi and erm, that's it really.' She smiled and nodded, making her way towards the kitchen door.

'Oh, don't go. Stay and have a cup of tea. Please, Rosie.'

'Actually, I can't. I've promised to go into work, so I'd better get going. I'll see you both soon!' she added with false brightness.

Eager to get away, she practically jogged to her car, which Mo hadn't seen, tucked away behind the vans. Not that this was such a bad thing, not really, she told herself through her tears. At least she had an accurate idea of how things were. She pictured Mo knitting of an evening, pictured the little bundle that would fill the white, lacy wool, and as she did so, her sobs intensified.

Fifteen

The conversation with Doug was still ringing in her ears. Visitor bookings were down and he was reluctantly cutting her hours. 'Truth is, Rosie, I should have done this weeks ago. I've been putting it off, hoping the situation might change, but it hasn't. And I'm sorry. You're not the only one. Mel's been cut right back too.'

She took little consolation from this as she walked down the hill towards the town centre. 'What are you going to do, Rosie girl?' she whispered as she made her way to the school.

'Mum!' Naomi called out to her across the playground, running towards the gate with her hair flying and her coat slipping down her back. 'Mum! Mrs Mortimer says I need to choose my books for next term, but I think I might be at my new school then. I told her, but she wouldn't listen to me!'

Rosie shook her head. 'What are you talking about, Naomi Jo? You aren't going to a new school.' She laughed, trying to get the joke. She rolled her eyes at the gaggle of mums and dads standing within earshot.

'Yes!' Naomi stamped her little foot in frustration. 'The one near Gerri's house with the straw hats!'

'Love, I honestly don't know what you're talking about.'

One or two of the mums halted their own conversations but continued staring ahead, trying to glean any fresh titbits of gossip without looking too obvious.

'Gerri's got the brochure and the lady said we can go after Christmas and they do dancing and *French*!' Naomi's eyes were wide with the possibilities.

'Where's Leo?' Rosie ignored her and stared instead at the throng of children coming out of the school. Her eyes scanned the crowd for her youngest. She wanted to get home quickly. Her pulse raced and her legs felt quite detached from her body.

Mel came alongside her.

'Hey, you.'

Mel smiled, awkwardly. 'Blimey, I'm always late. Don't know where the day goes. Time just vanishes.' She rubbed her palms together, briskly, as if fire-starting.

Rosie couldn't speak to her, knowing that if she did, she just might shout and swear in her urge to know what was going on with Mel's new mate up at Mortehoe, and she would never do that, not in front of the kids or in front of school. Instead, she smiled briefly and tutted in acknowledgement of the fact that the days did indeed disappear; not only the days, but also the weeks, months and years of her life. Everything was being erased, faster than she could handle.

The second the girls had been given a snack and were settled on the sofa, she called Phil.

'Everything okay?' He answered immediately; a call from her was a rarity nowadays.

'I need you to come over now. Right now!'

'What's happened? Are the girls all right?'

'They're fine, but I need you to come right now, Phil. Or I'll come there and we all know that's not a good idea.'

'Be there in fifteen.'

Rosie stood in front of the television and smiled at her children. 'Right, Dad's on his way—'

'Yay!'

'Yes!'

'But here's the thing. We need to have a secret chat about what Father Christmas might be bringing you this year, and we need to do it in peace in the kitchen. So you can see your dad, but only when we're done. Can I trust you to let us have a few minutes chatting with the door shut, without being disturbed?'

'Yes, Mummy.' Leona smiled. 'I want some flashing trainers.'

'Right, they are definitely going on your Santa list.' She winked at her little girl.

'I want a monster truck.'

'You're seven, Naomi. And you can't drive. How would that work?'

'Dunno.' She shrugged, clearly not having given much thought to her request.

Rosie laughed as she backed out of the room and closed the door.

She paced the hall back and forth until he arrived. When he did, she wasted no time on greetings but ushered him into the kitchen, quickly closing the door behind them.

Phil leant on the work surface. He looked clean and well kempt, like a man who drove a flash car for a living and not one who worked on a building site in all weathers. 'What's going on?' he asked agitatedly.

'Couple of things. Firstly, Doug's cut my hours, so I'll need to ask you to help out a bit more with finances for the kids. We don't need much, but I don't want them going without and things are tight as it is.' She hated having to ask, resented the position he'd put her in.

'Of course. I'll sort something out.'

She nodded in response and swallowed; her mouth had gone dry. 'Secondly…' She licked her bottom lip. 'Naomi told her teacher today that she might be going to a new school. She said she'd seen a brochure of girls in hats, or something. What's that all about, Phil?' She leant against the sink and folded her arms across her chest to stop them shaking. She silently prayed that he would just laugh, stare at her quizzically and wonder too where on earth their daughter had got such a notion. But he didn't.

'Oh.' He took a deep breath, looked skywards and rubbed the designer stubble on his chin.

With every second that passed, Rosie felt the fear swell in the pit of her stomach.

'Okay...' He began again. 'Gerri and I are going to be spending more time in the London house.'

'Is it in Kent?' she asked.

He narrowed his eyes and shook his head. His lips curved briefly into the beginnings of a smile, as if she were stupid. 'No, it's in Kensington.'

'Right.' She must have misheard.

'And she mentioned to the girls that there's a very good prep school a short stroll away. It's...' He shook his head as if to convey the wonder of the place while trying to select the most appropriate superlative. 'Amazing! A big old house with a walled garden, and the lessons are something else – ballet, languages, music, science, you name it! All in tiny classes of up to ten kids. Literally, just ten. And Gerri said that she'd be more than happy to pay.'

Rosie stared at him. At first she thought he might be joking, but his enthusiasm for the syllabus soon convinced her otherwise. A small laugh escaped her mouth. 'Is this some kind of joke?' She tittered again, as much through nerves as anything else.

'No. The London house is incredible. Every bedroom has its own bathroom and there's a huge kitchen and a den and you can walk to everything – restaurants, cinema, the Tube, the supermarket.'

She looked at the man that she was having difficulty recognising, a man who now went to restaurants and said 'the

Tube' instead of 'the Underground' like he used to. 'Well, that must make you happy. I know you were getting quite fretful over not living near a supermarket not so long ago.'

He ignored her. 'The point is that the school is only a short stroll away as well.'

'No, Phil.' She cut him short. 'The point is that this school is not a short stroll away. It's in London and my children live with me in Woolacombe, so it's a pointless conversation.' She hoped that would be the end of it, hoped he didn't detect the naked fear in her eyes.

'We are having a baby, Rosie.'

'I had noticed.' Mo's matinee-jacket conversation leapt into her mind.

'And we think it's important that the girls are involved. We don't want them to feel left out or rejected in any way.'

Again she laughed.

Phil continued. 'We think it might be an idea for them to stay with us in London during term time and attend Glencote. They have so much time off, literally six months, so it would be a neat split, and the education they'd get is a once-in-a-lifetime opportunity.'

She stared at him. She could hear the words he was saying, but it was as if he was speaking a foreign language. They made no sense. Rosie cocked her head to one side. 'Are you mad?'

'What?'

'Do you actually think I'd contemplate for one second letting the girls go and live away from me for a week, let alone half the year?' Her anger intensified. 'Have you actually lost the plot?'

'I think it's a good idea. I'm their dad and I want to see them more than the odd weekend.'

'Well, you should have thought about that!'

He sighed, raised his palms and patted the air as if there was an invisible table in front of him. 'I've taken legal advice and we'd have joint custody, which would mean dividing their time equally. It makes sense to give them this opportunity.'

'Legal advice...' she whispered. She could barely afford a cup of coffee in a café any more, let alone legal advice. Her legs began to shake.

He looked at her as though she was being unreasonable. 'I think you need to get over the idea that you can and should punish me because things didn't work out the way you wanted them to. It's selfish. You need to start thinking about what's in the best interests of the girls.'

That's me: selfish...

His words sounded professional, rehearsed.

She held her nerve. 'I only ever think about what is best for them! How dare you! They are the first and last things I consider with every decision I make. And if you think you can bully me, take them away...' Her voice cracked. '... you can't. Because I'm their mum and I won't let you. Do you understand me?'

Phil pulled his keys from his pocket, clearly preparing to leave in the dramatic manner that was now his preference. 'It's not up to you, Rosie. It's the law.' And he was gone.

Rosie sank down into a kitchen chair as the strength left her legs.

'What's for tea, Mum?' Leona asked from the doorway, twirling her long hair around her fingers.

Just the sight of Leo was enough to cause Rosie's tears to pool. The idea of her little girl being away from her was unthinkable.

After dropping the girls at school the next day, Rosie made her way up to Mo and Keith's. It was time to try and make good her last awkward visit and she was also hoping to find an ally. She desperately needed to talk to someone.

Mo was in the yard. Resplendent in wellington boots and Keith's old navy-blue overalls, she was scrubbing chicken poo off the coop frame with a stiff broom. 'I get all the glamorous jobs!' she called as she waved at Rosie. Then she strode over, broom in hand, to hug her daughter-in-law.

'So I see.' Rosie smiled, relieved at the sincerity of the welcome. A small part of her wondered if Gerri would receive a similarly warm greeting and secretly hoped that she wouldn't.

'I'm glad you came over.' Mo released her and took a small step backwards. 'I wanted to say—'

'It's okay, Mo, I understand.' She didn't want to hear the many variants of apology or explanation as to why and how Mo was torn between Phil's old and new life.

'He's my son, Rosie. My boy.' She swiped at the ground

with the brush. 'And I know you understand what that means because you're a mum too.'

Rosie nodded. The message was clear: she'd choose him every time. Ironically, and no matter how much it hurt, she *did* understand. 'Has Phil mentioned to you this whole school thing?'

Mo nodded. 'Yes. Yes he has. They showed me the prospectus.'

Rosie stalled, trying to quell her rising fear. 'I don't... I don't see how it's even up for discussion. It's crazy! As if they'd go and live in *London* for half the year! It's not going to happen.'

Mo sighed and leant on the long brush handle. 'I don't know what to say. But I do know that, despite everything, Phil is a good dad. He always has been and I can see that it would be wrong not to let him have an equal role in their upbringing.'

Rosie stared at her mother-in-law; this was beginning to sound like she supported the absurd suggestion.

Mo continued. 'And if you take all the emotion out of it, it looks like a really wonderful prospect for them. To have a first-class education, all those opportunities that they wouldn't get here.' She shrugged. 'It's food for thought.'

'So you'd be happy, would you, having them living hundreds of miles away, seeing them only occasionally?'

'No. No, I wouldn't. I'd miss them dreadfully, but as I said, I was trying to take the emotion away and look at it practically. And I can see that it would be a great thing for them. I worry about the kids' future.'

'You think I don't?'

'No, I know you do and that's the only reason this feels worth considering. They'd have all the chances that we never did and that's all I'm saying.'

'I can't even think about it, Mo. There is no way on God's earth I am going to be separated from my girls. No way!' She turned down her mouth, jutted out her chin and shook her head to emphasise the point. 'Would you have let Phil and Kev go?'

Mo looked past her towards the coast. 'I can't picture it, no. But then things are different for you two: you're not living together and that changes everything. Phil might have done well in a school like that, and Kev, well, he's so clever, he did well enough, didn't he? But if he'd had those opportunities, those connections, who knows what he could have done?'

Rosie felt her calmness evaporating. 'Well, I can't do it. I won't. I need them with me. I didn't have kids so someone else could tuck them in and cook their tea. I don't want to miss a single second of their growing up and I won't. And that's that.' She squeezed the car keys in her hand until they bit into her palm.

'I understand, Rosie, but as hard as it is, it's not only about what you want. I think the girls would thank you for letting them spend half their time with their dad. It makes it fair and I think an education is the greatest gift you can give.'

Rosie turned to leave. She spoke over her shoulder as she made for the car. 'Trust me, Mo, there is nothing fair about any of this. And, actually, an education is not the greatest thing you can have; a mum is. I should know, I never had either and I know which I'd have preferred.'

Rosie tackled the next few days at maximum speed. She was a human hurricane of activity because she knew that if she were to stop for just a minute, if she were to pay heed to the thoughts and sirens that whirred in her mind, she'd risk going mad. She hiked in and out of town for the smallest of reasons – to post a letter, fetch a pint of milk or take the carrier bags to the recycling bin, all tasks that could just as easily have been done on the way to or from school. When there were no chores left, she began her cleaning routine again, emptying, scouring and reorganising the kitchen cupboards, scrubbing the wainscot in the hallway, even taking an old toothbrush to the insides of the window frames. The only way for her to sleep at night was to be so physically exhausted that her mind had little option but to switch off.

Friday evening arrived quickly. She sat on the sofa, with Naomi on the floor in front of her, and brushed her daughter's hair.

'You're hurting me!' Naomi wailed.

'No, I'm not. And if you let me brush it properly more often, we wouldn't have this rigmarole. Long, thick hair needs looking after or it gets tangly, you know that.' She continued wielding the brush in long strokes, her deft fingers clamped over the roots to minimise any tugging.

Leona turned from in front of the TV and smiled at her sister's discomfort.

'You can smile, Miss Leo, but you're next!' Her littlest daughter stopped smiling.

A little while later, Phil arrived to collect the girls. He hovered on the pavement. Rosie left the front door wide and wondered at his hesitancy. It was only when she took the girls' bags out to him that she saw the shock of blonde hair in the front seat of the Range Rover. Phil's eyes looked from left to right as he blinked rapidly. He was nervous. She guessed he'd told his pregnant girlfriend that he conducted all his family business on the pavement and didn't want to shatter that illusion. The coward.

'I'll bring them back on Sunday at the usual time, okay? Mid afternoon.' He addressed the ground.

Rosie nodded and looked towards Gerri, who stared ahead, determinedly unseeing but clearly not uncaring about what was happening over her shoulder. Phil lifted the tailgate, stashed the two rucksacks in the boot and opened the rear door. Rosie kissed her girls and stood back slightly but was still able to hear Gerri's greeting as her children clambered into the back seat.

'Here are my gorgeous girls! Who wants to have some fun?' she sang.

Rosie shrank back against the wall, unable to wave, unable to move. *They are not your girls! They are not...* She felt worn out. As the hard work of the past week caught up with her and Gerri's words echoed in her ears, her gut twisted in anguish and her tears fell. She had no one to turn to. Not Phil, not Mel, not even Mo. And as for her own mum... With the prospect of losing the girls now becoming scarily real, it was harder than ever to understand Laurel's departure. 'I miss you, Mum. I miss you so much.' She spoke aloud to the smiling mother of her childhood, ignoring the letter of rejection that sat in the chest of drawers in her bedroom.

Later that evening, Rosie sat on the sofa and drank two large glasses of wine. The bottle had been nestling in the cupboard under the sink for an age and tonight it was just what she needed. She didn't bother chilling it but instead just glugged it down, hoping for the desired effect sooner rather than later.

Her phone buzzed. Mo. She closed her eyes and took the call.

'Hey, Mo.' It was hard to disguise her downbeat mood.

'Wrong again.' Kev laughed.

'Kev!' She smiled. 'You need to stop using your mum's phone.'

'And you need to be more pleased to hear from me.'

'I am! Are you home?'

'No. Yet again, I got Mum to send her phone to—'

'I get it. Shut up. You're home. It's good to hear your voice.' She whimpered as she spoke.

'For God's sake, are you *still* crying? How is that even possible? I'm surprised the drains of north Devon aren't overflowing. Who knew the human body could make this much water?'

Rosie sniffed. 'I'm just having a bit of a shit week.'

'Bench time?'

She looked out of the window at the cold November night. 'It's bloody freezing!'

'So?' he shouted. 'What are you, a lightweight? In fact, don't bother answering that. I know the answer.'

'Can't you just come here? I've got wine.' She held up the inch or two that was left sloshing around in the bottle.

'Oh well, if you've got wine! Why didn't you say so?' he gushed sarcastically. 'This is like when Mum and Dad went away and we blew the weekly food budget on marshmallows and vodka and you were sick in dad's coolbox.'

She laughed. 'I haven't drunk vodka or eaten a marshmallow since that day.' She grimaced at the memory.

'I told you you were a lightweight. Shall I come over then?'

She tutted. 'Yes! Come over.' As if there could be any other answer.

Opening the front door minutes later, she stood back to let her friend in. He was dressed for a more tropical climate, in jeans and a thin white T-shirt.

'Aren't you cold?' She shivered in sympathy.

'Yes.' He nodded.

'Your hair's grown.' She noted that, and his deep, dark tan.

'It keeps doing that.' He nodded. 'And you're shrinking! Where are all your curves? I could snap you like a stick!' He pinched her shoulder.

'Ow!' She punched his ribs in retaliation. 'So, how's life in your new location?'

'It's...' He tried to think of the word. '... perfect!'

'So, paradise found?'

'Yes, for now, and that's all you can ask for, isn't it?'

'I guess. It's so good to see you! And you're staying till Christmas?'

'That's the plan.' He looked her up and down. 'You look great. Still a bit sadder than I would have hoped...' He let this hang.

'Well, the good news is, I'm not so sad about Phil any more. I mean, still sad, but I've turned a corner.'

'That's good to hear. The baby news was a bit of a shocker.'

'You think?' She sighed. 'To be honest, I haven't even thought about that for a while. I've got bigger things to fill my head.'

He followed her into the sitting room.

'Urgh, what's that smell?' He sniffed the air.

'They're my scented candles. Apple flavoured – I love them. Phil hated them.'

'Well, there's not much I agree with Phil on, but in this case...' He waved his hand in front of his nose before taking the seat in the middle of the sofa.

Rosie sat at the end and stretched her legs over his lap, the way she used to when they were teenagers, nestling against the wide arm, overjoyed to have her friend to talk to. She handed him the remains of the wine, which he swigged from the bottle.

'Cheers!' She raised her glass. 'I'm sad because I'm afraid

they're going to take the girls away and send them to school in London!'

'Mum mentioned it.'

'What do you think?' She balanced the wine glass on her lap and tied her hair into a knot.

Kev blew out his cheeks. 'I think it's bloody ridiculous. As if they'd want to be away from you, or vice versa. It's just bonkers. I'm not saying anything about them spending time with their dad, I think they should, but I don't see that just because a school is expensive, it makes it good. It's just preposterous.'

She beamed. This time it was tears of gratitude and relief that fell. 'Thank you, Kev. I knew you'd get it. I've been feeling guilty because I don't want to hold them back, I *want* them to have good lives and all the things I didn't have, but at the same time, they're my babies and I want them close to me, you know?'

He nodded. 'Yes, I do know.'

'They're all I've got! As if I'd want them to live anywhere but with me!' She shook her head. 'I love them so much, even being away from them for one night is like torture. I think about them all the time. Even when I close my eyes, I see them. Does that make sense?'

Kev stared at her and placed his free hand on her toes. 'It makes perfect sense, Rosie Watson.'

There was a moment of quiet before he spoke again. 'It's the same for me.'

'What's the same for you?' She sipped her plonk,

confused, wondering if there were little Kevs roaming the planet that she was unaware of.

'That's how I feel about you.' He looked straight at her, speaking without guile.

'What do you mean?' She gave a nervous laugh. With her booze filter in place, she wanted to make sure she had the right end of the stick.

'I came back early from the BVI to see you. No other reason. I think about you all the time and I always have, since I was twelve. Since you first walked home with me and made me laugh.'

Rosie laughed. 'Are you mucking around?'

'No, I'm not.' He spoke in a tone that was unfamiliar to her; earnest and calm, keen to be understood.

She screwed her face up.

He took a deep breath. 'Okay. I'm just going to say it.'

'Say what?'

'I love you, I always have. And no girl at uni, no girl I've met anywhere else in the world has come close. Never has, never will. And I think if you let yourself, you could love me. I know it.'

She stared at him in silence.

'I should have spoken up before, when Phil made his move, but I just wanted you to be happy, that's how much I love you. You being happy is the single most important thing to me, and I thought that he might be the one to make that happen. I wanted you to have a family and all the support you never got from your mum. That's why I went abroad, why I travel. I wasn't about to interfere in your choices, but I sure as hell wasn't prepared to hang around in the wings and watch the performance.'

Rosie thought about how she'd felt seeing Gerri in the car earlier, cosying up to her husband, her daughters. 'I... I don't know what to say.'

This was new territory for them both. They'd always been easy and open with each other, ever since they were kids. But Kev's declaration had introduced a new strangeness.

'I'm married to your brother!'

'I had noticed.'

'Why didn't you ever say something to me?'

Kev gave a short burst of laughter. 'Good God, Rosie! It was obvious to anyone who ever got within ten feet of us. Apart from you, apparently. Everyone knew!'

'Did they?' She thought of Mo, Mel, all of them.

'Phil certainly did.' Kev bit his bottom lip. 'But that was him all over. I think he took you because he knew I loved you. I really believe that. He was a jealous bastard, didn't like that I was the youngest, the one set for uni, the one with a plan. And when he stepped through that door and saw how I looked at you, it must have seemed easy.'

Rosie snatched her legs from his lap, planted her feet on the floor, jumped up and turned to face him.

'How dare you say that, Kev? How can you talk about me as if I was a thing to be taken, owned! How can you cheapen my marriage, my existence like that?' Her face was flushed now, her voice trembling. 'That's my kids' dad you're talking about! How d'you think Nay and Leo would feel, hearing that when they're older? That my whole marriage, my whole family was just some bloody extension of a fight over a toy!'

Kev twisted on the sofa. His voice was quivering too. 'That's not what I'm saying! I don't doubt he loved you when he married you and I know he loves the girls, I *do* know that. But I'm saying that of all the girls in the whole wide world that he could have picked, he chose the one that I loved and that was a shit trick.' He stood up and placed his hand on the top of her arm. 'This isn't how I planned this moment and, believe me, I have thought about it a lot, millions of times. And I'm sorry you're upset, that's the last thing I wanted, obviously, because of the whole crying thing.' He looked up at her. She wasn't laughing; this was not one of those times when his humour could make things better. 'But the fact remains that I love you, Rosie. It's you. You're the one.'

Rosie placed her face in her hands and closed her eyes. 'What is wrong with you boys? Are all the Tipcott men fucking idiots? Have you any idea what you're suggesting, what that would do to Mo and Keith? To Phil?'

'Like his opinion counts now! He's having a baby with another woman, for God's sake! He did what he always does, whether it's the army or working for Dad, or your marriage! He gets fed up, bored, has a change of heart, flips his mind and bails. He bins things. He's always done it and he always will. So I'm sorry, but I don't give a shit what he thinks!'

Rosie shrugged her arm free from his grip. 'Just go, Kev. I really want you to leave.'

'Can't we talk about it?' He stepped back.

'There's nothing to talk about! And the saddest thing is that everyone I thought I could rely on, everything and everyone that's been a constant in my life, is slowly disappearing, one by one. Even you.'

'I'm not going anywhere, ever.'

'Don't you get it? You've changed things, just when I needed it to be like it always was. I'd like you to you leave, please, Kev.' She raised her voice. 'Just leave me alone.'

'All right. All right.' He raised his palms and walked backwards out of the room. 'I can't help loving you, Rosie Watson. Trust me, my life would have been a whole lot easier if I didn't love you. But that's just the way it is. I always have loved you and I always will.'

Rosie turned her back to the door. She listened to him leave, then sank down on the sofa and buried her head under a cushion. Not for the first time, she wanted to disappear.

She woke with a headache woven from wine and confusion. She couldn't recall the last time she'd slept on the sofa. Her neck ached and her eyes were bloodshot. One thing that remained crystal clear in her mind, however, was Kev's revelation. She had always, always loved him, but in the way a best friend loves a best friend. Yes, there had been times in their teens when it had come close to being more, but those moments had always been punctured by some hilarity, split seconds of hesitation that were quickly filled with laughter rather than intimacy. Kev was the boy who chased her with seaweed, who put her on his shoulders and then fell over, head first, into the sand dunes. There had been no tender declarations of love, no thunderbolt moments of epiphany; they were simply the very best of friends. Or they used to be.

The way he had supported her and Phil, slapping his brother on the back at their wedding and jetting off as soon as he was able, had only reinforced her view that his feelings towards her were platonic.

Rosie soaked in a hot bubble bath and ate three slices of toast and jam. She began to feel better and decided to call him; it was the only way to stop any awkwardness between them, nip it in the bud.

Mo answered, her tone unnaturally curt.

'Hey, Mo, it's me!'

'Yes, Rosie.' She almost sighed her response.

Rosie wondered if she'd interrupted something. 'Is this a bad time?'

'No, go ahead.'

'Is Kev there?'

'No. No, he isn't. He's gone. Took the coach this morning. He's flying from Exeter to Amsterdam, then New York and on to wherever.'

Rosie caught the irritation in her tone. 'Is he coming back for Christmas?'

Mo took a deep breath. 'Apparently not.'

'Oh.'

'Yes, oh. I have to go now. Speak soon.' Her mother-in-law ended the call.

Rosie opened her mouth to say goodbye, but the line was already dead. She stared at the phone in her hand.

Grabbing her coat, she left the house, suddenly in need of some fresh air. It was a cold afternoon. The sky was clear and bright blue, the colour of summer, but the wind was definitely a winter wind, brisk and cutting, the kind that made her bones shake beneath her goose-bumped skin. Dipping her head, she walked headlong into it and made her way through the town and up around the Esplanade. One or two cars were parked on the clifftop, their occupants watching the wild, rolling sea from the comfort of their vehicles.

With her bench in sight, she quickened her pace. Reaching it, she sat and stared at the familiar view, the view that greeted her in all seasons and had done for nearly her whole life. She turned to her left, closed her eyes and inhaled the scent of apples.

'So, Mum, it seems you're the only person I've got left to talk to now. Ironic, isn't it!'

She sniffed and stared at the horizon. She still wasn't sure how she felt about Laurel's letter, but she couldn't bring herself to hate her mum, especially not now that everyone else seemed to be dropping like flies.

'It's been a really horrible week. I just can't imagine being without the girls. How could Phil even—'

She stopped, swallowed her sobs and changed tack.

'I just want to go forward now... So far forward that this

is all behind me. You, more than most people, understand that, I know.'

Her mum nodded.

'I'm getting there, Mum. But I can't pretend it's been easy. I used to think six months was the blink of an eye, in the scheme of things. But now I know that it's a lifetime, a sentence. I'm only just coming up for air, learning how to breathe again.'

She took a deep breath as if to emphasise the point.

'I'm sorry that I never met you, not in real life. I think you would have liked me, you know. I think I might have won you over. I hope so. I haven't had a bad life, not at all. But it feels like everything is slipping away. And now Kev; he was my one good thing, my friend, since I was little. I've messed it up. The things he said... I can't think about it, can't consider the possibility that Phil only wanted me because Kev did. The truth is, I don't know what to believe any more. But I do know I'm fed up of feeling this sad.'

It was getting dark as she made her way back to Arlington Road and she noticed that all the lights were on in the house next door and the telltale Mercedes estate was parked outside. The von Trapps were down for the weekend. She felt her tears welling again as she recalled how Naomi had shared her honest opinion on rice cakes, the little devil.

Desperate not to allow herself to dwell on thoughts of possible legal battles ahead and the inconceivable prospect of not having the kids with her three hundred and sixty-five days a year, Rosie lit a couple of apple-scented candles,

switched on the telly and stretched out on the sofa. She reluctantly answered the call from Phil, not wanting to hear his
voice, but was delighted and relieved to hear Leona on the
other end of the phone.

'Mummy, I have teached Truffle a trick!'

'Oh my goodness! What did you teach him?'

'I put my biscuit on the floor...'

Rosie pictured the pale marble surfaces and white carpets
and wondered quite where it might be appropriate to lay
a biscuit.

'I tell him to stay and then I walk over to the biscuit and
pat my legs and call him and he runs up and I give him the
biscuit!' Leo sounded delighted with both herself and Truffle,
and Rosie glowed with the knowledge that her daughter was
bursting to share this incredible feat with her.

'Wow! That's marvellous and really clever of you, Leo.
I love you.'

*As if I would let this precious girl go and live miles away
and go to a posh school where it would be someone else
waiting at the gates for her every afternoon. London! That is
never going to happen. She has taken Phil, but my girls...?
Never.*

'Love you too. I got to go now!' Leo ended the call.

The familiar feelings of love, guilt, pride and jealousy
bubbled inside her. She wondered if it would always be that
way. She loved hearing her daughter so happy, of course, but
that was quickly replaced by a flare of anger at Leo being
in that woman's house. And then came an overwhelming

loneliness at the realisation that she had absolutely no one to discuss it with. She thought again of Kev.

To distract herself, she decided to go and get ready for bed. Then she'd come back down, make herself some cocoa and slob out on the sofa until she couldn't keep her eyes open any more. She left the telly on and the candles burning on the windowsill but decided to draw the curtains in front of them – she couldn't face Mummy von Trapp peering in at her sad and solitary Saturday night.

Wearily, she trod the stairs to her bedroom. After changing into her pyjama bottoms and an oversized T-shirt, she lay down briefly on the bed, gathering her strength to get on with the rest of her evening. She placed her hand on the pillow where Phil had laid his head so many nights and once again gave way to the tears that were never that far from the surface. Within minutes, she had sobbed herself into a fitful doze.

Some time later, something alerted Rosie and she twitched and shuffled on the bed. She pulled the duvet over her and snuggled in for the night. She was drained and sleep was beckoning; so what if it was a bit early. She smiled drowsily as the scent of apples filled her nostrils. The smell was stronger than usual, almost overpowering, and there was a warm orange glow behind her eyelids. She felt snug, as if she was being hugged. *I can see the sun. No, better than that, I can feel the sun.*

She nestled her head into the pillow and suddenly Laurel was standing by her side, calling her name. 'Rosie!' Gently at first and then with more urgency. 'Rosie! Rosie!'

It was amazing and wonderful, and she was filled with joy because this was the first and only time in her whole life that she'd heard her mum's voice. She sounded like her! Their voices were the same and this made her smile, happy to know they shared something.

Rosie felt calm and filled with love, not just for her mum but also for her children and for all those who loved her. She couldn't recall names and faces at that precise moment, everything was blurred and jumbled, but it was enough to have her mum close and to be able to see and hear her.

Knowing Laurel was close made her feel calm, quieted any potential panic and filled her with a sense of peace that had been lacking of late. She could let go. Everything was under control. It would all be fine.

Rosie stayed in this comfortable stupor, sinking deeper and deeper into the mattress while that sun burnt brightly. Shades of orange, red and gold leapt behind her eyelids. It was beautiful and warm and she was at peace.

Sixteen

There was a deep, low hum in the room, like the whir of a machine, just loud enough to annoy. And there was an unusual sensation, unfamiliar to her and one that she couldn't quite identify.

Everything was hazy. She knew she was Rosie but was conscious of little else. Her senses were numbed, her body unresponsive; it was like trying to decipher detail while looking through dense fog.

She opened her eyes a millimetre or two and closed them again immediately. The bright light filtering through her lids caused a pain in her head to flare. Her chest felt sore, her throat more so, and her eyes stung badly, even though they were clamped shut.

'*Where am I?*' she wanted to ask, but instead she emitted an incoherent mumble. Panic rose in her chest as she tried in vain to move her head to the left and right. She swivelled her eyes, taking in the unfamiliar surroundings. She wanted to cry out. Then she heard a voice, soft and soothing. A woman came into view.

'It's okay, Rosie. Don't try and talk. Try to relax.'

She didn't recognise the kindly female voice but took comfort from it nonetheless. At least, wherever she was, she was not alone.

'There's no need to worry. Just relax, pet. Go back to sleep. You're in a safe place. You're in hospital, but you're not badly hurt and you're safe.'

I'm what? In hospital? Why? What happened to me?

And then it hit her: the strange sensation was pain! She was in pain! It was her lungs that hurt the most. She tried to scream, but there was something in her mouth, over her mouth and down her throat. She tried to lift her hand, to gesture, let someone know she needed help, but her arms wouldn't move. Panic threatened to overwhelm her and in that second the hum faded, her muscles relaxed and the pain subsided as she faded back into morphine-induced oblivion.

It was two full days later that Rosie woke up.

The acute spikes of pain had dulled to a general wave of hurting that made her whole body pulse. There was a plastic mask fixed over her nose and mouth. She was able to swallow, but it felt like blood had gathered in her throat and couldn't be dislodged by saliva alone. Her nose and mouth felt raw and even the lightest breath instantly caused a biting sensation of soreness. She was short of puff, inhaling sharply and frequently, each intake rattly.

'Hello, Rosie.' It was a male voice this time.

There was something scratchy on her eyelids that she wanted to rub. Blinking hard, she tried to remove the irritation.

'Are your eyes sore?'

She nodded.

'You've burnt your eyelashes and they're a bit stubby, probably scratchy. I can wipe them for you with some damp cotton wool.'

'Burnt them?' she managed, her voice hoarse, her mouth and throat tender.

'Yes.' The man bent over her, younger than he sounded, maybe thirty, with close-cropped ginger hair and pale skin. He was smiling. 'There was a fire in your house. You were very, very lucky to get out. But don't worry, you weren't badly hurt. The smoke did get to you, though, and a bit of heat. It's damaged your lungs, but you will get better.' He sounded certain and this encouraged her. She trusted him.

'My girls?' Her heart raced. She had no memory of the events leading up to the fire.

'They weren't there. They were with their dad. He's been in a couple of times to sit with you and someone is phoning him right now to say you are awake.'

She tried to shake her head, didn't want Phil to be called, but was more preoccupied with the tears she was crying, which were both painful and cathartic at the same time.

She closed her eyes and tried to picture that night. She couldn't. There was a vague recollection of warmth and... and her mum had been by her side and she had heard her voice! This was her last thought before sleep pulled her under once again.

When she woke, Phil was sitting in the metal chair by her side.

'Hello.' He leant forward, his elbows resting on his knees.

She turned her head to the right and stared at him.

'Girls?' she managed from beneath the oxygen mask.

'They're absolutely fine, worried about you, of course, but I'm taking good care of them.'

She felt her muscles uncoil a little. Her eyes flitted around the room. There were three empty beds, two opposite and one between her and the window in the corner. Each bed was surrounded by a rail from which hung garish green and pink curtains with an abstract pattern. The striplights were suspended on plastic arms, setting them lower in the room than usual.

'You've had a lucky escape. The house didn't fare too well.'

'Oh no!' Her sadness was complete. *My house! Our home! That's all I've got left!*

'Yes, well, we need to talk about that at some time, but not now.' He gave a small nod.

'Can we fix it?' She needed to know, needed that light, no matter how small at the end of the long, dark tunnel.

Phil took a deep breath and rubbed his mouth and chin,

a sign to her that he was stressed. 'It's not insured, Rosie. We're not covered. Not for negligence. Not that that helps right now, but it'll be rebuilt, eventually. Main thing is that you're okay.'

'What... happened?' she croaked.

Phil scratched his eyebrow and licked his lips. 'You must have lit some candles in the sitting room, put them on the windowsill and left them burning when you went up to bed. They caught the curtains – quite quickly, by all accounts. The next-door neighbours saw the flames, luckily, and broke in from the back and got you. Thank God they were there.' He shook his head and placed his thumb and forefinger in his eyes, as if he was either tired, angry or distressed, she couldn't tell which.

It's all my fault! All my fault! Oh God!

'Sore.' She placed her hand to her throat.

He sat up straight. 'You inhaled a lot of hot smoke and it's burnt your throat and around your mouth and nose. And you've got a bit of blistering on your face.' He ran his thumb along his own jawline. 'And on your left arm and shoulder.'

She flexed the gauze-type bandages on her arm. Her skin stung and felt tight.

'But it could have been so much worse. The doctor says you're over the hardest bit and that everything is healing nicely. They were worried about infection setting in, as that can be really dangerous, but you've come through that. You've just got to take it easy and let your body heal.'

'Where?' she rasped.

'What?' He leant closer.

'Where will I go?'

'I spoke to your dad. He's going to collect you when you're well enough and you can go and stay with him.'

I don't want to go there! She wracked her brain for alternatives and found none. 'Nay and Leo?'

'We all have to make economies right now.' He sighed again. 'We have to go back to London so that we can work. Glencote said they could attend temporarily until you're back on your feet. It's the only way I can look after them and earn money at the same time.' He looked at the floor.

Rosie's chest heaved and her tears fell at the prospect, the plan that she was powerless to change. In every sense, she had no voice.

'Even Mel said she thought it was best under the circumstances.'

She hated the way he threw her friend's opinion into the mix to bolster his argument. Letting her know that they were in contact. She pictured Mel gingerly treading the white carpets and sipping wine while Andy winked at their good fortune in having friends with such a pad and Phil played lord of the manor.

'Don't cry.' He sounded curt rather than sympathetic. 'Mum's going to bring them in to see you. They're not going to just disappear. I've already told you that.'

She turned away from him and cried harder, trying to swallow, trying to ignore the unremitting soreness.

Day by day she felt a little better, physically. Her dressings were changed and everyone cooed words of encouragement at how well she was doing. Her rapid breathing had slowed and the cutting pain every time she inhaled had subsided to an ache. Her wheeze was less acute and her chest less rattly.

Mentally, however, she was sinking. Mel had sent a jaunty card with a generic message. Rosie had put it straight in the bin, upset more than angry that her friend hadn't seen fit to visit and had actually thought a card would do instead.

A surprise had arrived in the form of Mummy von Trapp, whose name, it turned out, was Phillippa. She tiptoed cautiously into her ward one afternoon, crying big fat tears as though they'd been close.

'I can't stop thinking about it. I went out to the car to get some bed linen I'd left in the boot and I knew something wasn't right. Then I saw the colour – bright orange, vivid, scary and already throwing out such heat.'

Like the sun, I thought it was the sun...

'I banged on the door, but nothing. Then the fire seemed to flare and it was too hot to get in. I called the fire brigade and it felt like an age until they arrived, even though it wasn't. It was the scariest thing. I ran round to the back and Jack got the ladder and we put it down into your garden from our flat roof at the back, and then up to your bedroom. Jack smashed the window and you were right there on the bed. He thought... he thought you were dead. You weren't moving.' She stopped to blot her tears. 'And just as he was figuring out how to get you out, the fire brigade arrived. They went in from the front top window and they lifted you and handed you to Jack and then another ladder appeared and they got you out.'

'Thank you.' Her words were small, inadequate.

Phillippa patted her forearm. 'I can't stop thinking about what might have been. It's a godsend that the girls were away.'

Rosie nodded. The same thought had been playing in her head day and night. 'What does the house look like?' she rasped.

'The roof's intact, and the outside walls, but when I saw inside...' She hesitated. 'There's quite a bit of damage and I think lots got ruined when they put the fire out, but you have to not worry about that, just concentrate on getting better.'

Rosie nodded again. If only it were that easy. It was her fault they had lost their home, god only knew how they were going to afford the renovations. She couldn't help but picture Gerri's luxurious pad. A small part of her wished Mummy von Trapp hadn't needed to get the bed linen that night and that she had simply been left to disappear. It wouldn't have been so bad.

Today was a big day: her girls were coming to visit. She hoisted herself into a sitting position and practised her smile. It was difficult. The muscles required for grinning were the ones beneath the sorest patches of skin around her nose and mouth.

The noise of their chatter and laughter woke her; it was the sweetest sound she could imagine. The girls fell silent, however, when they arrived at her room. They stood in the open doorway, staring. Each held one of their nan's hands as they studied her, their legs twisting and their fingers in their mouths, embarrassed, unsure.

'Well, am I glad to see you!' She spoke as best she could, but her voice was strained and husky and the effort was painful. Even so, it seemed to do the trick. They slowly came closer, eyeing her suspiciously from top to bottom. She took in their clean clothes and unfamiliar hairstyles. Someone had given them each an elaborate, tight, side braid that fell against one shoulder; it looked complex and professional and certainly wasn't Phil's handiwork. She blotted out the image of Gerri touching their beautiful long hair, chatting over their shoulder into a large mirror.

'Do I look a bit funny?' she asked Leona, who nodded.

'Your face looks funny,' Naomi said. 'You've got scabbies here...' She dotted her finger around her mouth. 'And here.' She did the same around her nose. 'And your eyes are all puffed up, like you've been crying.'

'I have a bit.' She looked at Mo. 'Thank you for bringing them.'

'Oh, Rosie.' Mo's lip trembled and she looked close to tears. She coughed and ushered the girls forward. It was down to her to present a calm and dignified front for the kids. 'I came in before, but you were sleeping. So I sat with you for a while.'

Rosie was happy to know this, pleased that she had bothered.

'Wow, that's an amazing card! Who's it from?' Mo nodded at the enormous one-foot-square picture of a kitten.

'Doug and the girls at the site.'

'That was kind.' Mo paused. 'Kev sends you his best; he's phoned every day. I told him you were on the mend.' She pursed her lips as if to stop herself from thinking about the reason for her son's absence.

Naomi leant on the bed. 'Mummy, look what we got!' She lifted her leg up onto the mattress to showcase her little pale pink Ugg boots.

'Oh!' was all Rosie could manage as a sour taste filled her throat.

'And Daddy said we have to get new clothes and new toys because ours were in the fire.' She stood within touching distance and ran her little fingertips over her mum's bandaged arm.

'Yes. That'll be fun!'

Naomi smiled at the thought and nodded. 'And we've got to get our uniforms for Glencote.' She straightened, as though the place was worthy of a more dignified posture.

Rosie hated the name of the place, even more so hearing it spoken by her child.

Naomi continued with gusto. 'I am getting a skirt and jumper and shirt and shoes and coat and a hat and a swimming costume and special socks!'

'Special socks sound good.' She gave a false smile.

'I feel sad, Mum, that my house has gone.' Tears welled in her eyes.

Rosie held her hand. Her precious girl. 'Of course you do. I understand and I feel the same, but it won't be for long, darling.' She swallowed, struggling for breath. 'We'll get it fixed up in no time and I'll be back on my feet soon. You can help me choose the paint, we can have any colour you fancy!' She tried to sound bright, excited, despite her slow speech and the panic that swirled in her gut when she considered how she was going to be able to afford a tin of paint, let alone a rebuild.

'I want green!' Leona nodded. 'I want everything to be green. Green walls and green carpet and a green chair, so it's like walking in the grass!' She grinned, as though this was the best idea in the world.

'Green will be lovely.' Rosie smiled. A cough built in her chest. She tried to suppress it until she had no choice but to wheeze and cough, leaning forward with a tissue over her nose and mouth, trying to clear her lungs.

'Sorry,' she managed, between bouts of breathlessness.

Leona took a step backwards and once again gripped her nan's hand.

'I think you might cough your guts up,' Naomi observed, half fascinated, half petrified by the display.

'Hope not!' Rosie croaked.

'We made you a card.' Leona stepped forward warily and handed her mum the folded sheet of paper. It was remarkably similar to the one they'd made her a while ago, but this time her head was swathed in bandages and she was in a bed with a big red cross over the top, presumably to indicate the hospital. Her face was still streaked with tears.

'It's lovely.'

Leona opened it up to reveal both their names ringed in a neat chain of Xs.

'The doctor said we weren't to keep you talking for too long.' Mo stepped forward and placed a kiss on her daughter-in-law's forehead. 'I'd better get them back.'

Rosie grabbed her arm. 'Mo! Oh God! What can I do?' she whispered, fighting the urge to shout out, *Stay with me, girls! Don't go to London! Stay here! I need you!*

'You'll be okay. You will.' Mo was firm.

First Naomi and then Leona wrapped her in a tentative hug, but it was obvious she didn't feel or smell like their mum, not really.

'I'll miss you.' Naomi's words were like gold that she would sew into a pocket above her heart and keep safe.

'And I will miss you too, every second of every day, but you know that Daddy and I will always make sure that you are safe and happy.' She paused to catch her breath. 'We will make sure of it because no matter what happens between us, we both love you very much. You don't have to worry.' She tried out a smile of reassurance.

Having waved off her visitors, she sank back onto the pillows, more weakened by the exertion than she could have imagined. She closed her eyes, swamped by the ache of loneliness and doing her best to shut out the dark fear that Mo was wrong and that she would never be okay again.

*

The doctor was pleased with her progress and had told her to expect to be allowed home later in the week. The news buoyed her up a little, although the prospect of going to stay with her dad and Shona hardly filled her with glee.

She had taken her painkillers and was waiting for the effects to kick in. Her days were a cycle of pain and pain relief and she had learnt to look forward to the moment the little pills were handed to her in a tiny pleated paper cup. She sipped the weak tea she'd been given to take away the taste, then looked up to see Gerri standing in front of her. Her first reaction was embarrassment at being so incapacitated in Gerri's presence. She noticed, as she had before, that despite her diminutive stature, Gerri filled the space. The swish of straight, shiny hair, the whiff of expensive-smelling perfume and her confident stance made up for what she lacked in bulk. Rosie considered patting her hair into place and checking her face, but there was no point; no amount of primping could disguise the mess that she was in. And, in truth, she didn't care.

'Oh, look at you! You poor old thing.' Gerri's fake sympathy was grating.

Rosie looked at her and blinked. The hard, stubby eyelashes dug into her lids and made her eyes water, which, ironically offered some relief to her sore, dry eyes.

'I hope you don't mind me coming. I guess I just wanted to say don't worry,' Gerri cooed.

'About what?' Rosie croaked, her voice rasping as it tended to when she hadn't used it for a bit.

'About Naomi and Leona. I can assure you that they will have the *very* best time in London. I know you aren't in a position to do much for them, but even if you were, you'll agree that this really is a fabulous opportunity for them.'

'Please just go,' Rosie managed, looking towards the window, as if she might magic up a view to distract her from this odious woman and her hurtful words.

'Don't be like that. I come in peace!' Her tone was mocking, superior. 'Glencote really is the best school, and they'll be living in my beautiful house, and they'll be with their dad, who loves them. They'll have all they could wish for. To deny them that would be very selfish.'

Rosie turned to look at her. She noted her still enviably flat tummy and her white, white teeth. Her tears fell and her breathing stalled with every sob.

'Don't cry. You're doing the right thing, recognising that we are a family, allowing them to bond with their little brother.' Gerri patted her stomach over her baby-blue jersey. 'Yes, it's a boy! Darling Mo and Keith will visit us a lot, so there'll be familiar faces around. Phil works for me now, as you know, so he'll always be on hand to care for them and to do the school run. It really is for the best. You can see that, can't you, Rosie?' She sighed. 'I mean, what can you offer them right now? You're effectively homeless.'

Rosie felt her face fold in distress. The skin around her mouth pulled, and the painkillers dulled her senses, sending a hazy mist over her world. 'I know,' she whispered. 'I can't offer them anything. Because I haven't got anything.' She closed her eyes, the admission taking the last of her strength.

Gerri turned to leave. 'He'll want a divorce, you know. I can't have my baby's dad being married to someone else. But you knew that was coming, right?'

Later that afternoon, Mel turned up, clearly nervous and feeling guilty about not having come sooner. Their chat was strained, awkward.

'Gerri said she popped in.' Mel's tone suggested she was a mutual friend.

'I don't want her near me!' Rosie replied hoarsely.

'She just wants to help. She's not a bad person.'

When she heard that, Rosie knew there was no point in trying to convince Mel she'd got Gerri all wrong. It was yet another wedge between them and one that might never shift.

'Tyler said the girls said goodbye at school,' Mel continued.

Rosie stared at her friend, wondering if she had the slightest concept of how much this little titbit hurt her.

'I don't want them to go!'

Mel sat forward. 'Course you don't, but you know, honey, they're having a great adventure. They're staying in some incredible places and doing some amazing things and before you know it, they'll be back for the holidays and you'll be wanting a break from all that chatter.'

She shook her head. Not even her friend's lies, intended to placate her, could make the situation seem better. She closed her eyes and feigned sleep until, eventually, Mel tiptoed from the room.

At the end of the week she was discharged.

'We'll get a wheelchair to take you down to reception.' The male nurse gripped the pen and wrote on her chart as she waited for her dad to arrive.

'I don't need one.'

'It's hospital policy. You've been lying down for a long time and even though you're much better, you might be a bit unsteady on your legs and we can't have you falling.'

'I'll manage.' She stared at the card in her hand, the drawing of her and her sad, sad face. *I don't want the girls to think of me like this...*

Her dad entered the room a little sheepishly, unsure of what to say.

'Is this all your luggage, love?' He picked up the carrier bag containing her toiletries, hairbrush, pyjamas and a couple of pairs of pants. She was wearing the jeans and jersey that Mo had picked up for her.

'I haven't got anything else.' Phil had told her he'd managed to salvage a few bits and pieces from Arlington Road. His descriptions had been vague, so all she knew was that her worldly possessions now fitted into two plastic storage boxes and were in the yard up at Mo and Keith's for when she could get back into the house. The one saving grace was that the girls' lives had been documented in photographs which had been distributed to their grandparents, so at least she could make copies. As she visualised the charred remains of their family home – everything from their comfy sofa to their favourite books, all gone – her tears fell again, tracing a familiar route down her cheeks.

'Right.' Roy nodded and picked up the bag for her, quietly and apologetically, as had always been his way.

'We're just waiting on her medication, pain relief, dressings and some emollients for her skin and when we've got that lot from the pharmacy, she's all yours.' The nurse smiled. Her dad nodded his thanks.

I don't want to be all his. I want to turn the clock back to the time when I woke up next to my husband, with my children sleeping down the hall, in my house...

Just as the nurse had anticipated, she was quite shaky on her feet, but she managed to get into the front seat of her dad's car without assistance. 'Can we go and look at the house before we go back to Exeter?' she asked meekly, as if she was once again a young child in her dad's care.

'I don't know if that's a good idea.' He put the key in the ignition.

'Please, Dad.'

He nodded and sighed, then pulled out of the car park and joined the road that would take them to Woolacombe.

When they reached Arlington Road, Rosie stood on the pavement and stared. No imaginings could have prepared her for the sight. As she let her eyes rove across the boarded-up frontage of her family home, she realised just how much she'd loved their house – the very bricks and mortar of it, the hard-earned and carefully chosen furniture and furnishings, the mess of normal family life and all the memories contained within. And now all that remained was a blackened shell.

The smell was invasive and intense, like a bonfire but laced with the toxic stink of everything that had melted inside. She reached out and touched her finger to the blistered wooden doorframe in which their front door used to sit, the door for which she'd had the key, the door she'd walked through with her new babies, the door her husband walked out of.

Carbonised ghosts were everywhere. They had invaded her house and taken up residence on bare surfaces; they were clinging to once pristine paintwork and jumping up walls. She wanted them gone.

Her eyes lingered on the patch of tarmac, now filled by a neighbour's van, where her car had often lurked; that too, damaged in the fire, had been scrapped.

'I want my home back!' she rasped, as loud as her voice would allow.

'I know, love. I know.'

'I've got nothing!' she shouted, hoarsely, caring little who overheard. Her sobs a desperate wail that carried on the wind. 'How has this happened to me? How has everything disappeared, what did I do, wrong? I want my family back! I want my life!' she howled.

As the strength left her legs and her knees buckled, her

dad placed his hand on her back. 'It's time to go now,' he cajoled, trying to guide her towards the car. Part of her wanted to stay; the other part couldn't wait to get away. 'There's nothing we can do here just now, love. We'll get you nice and comfy in Exeter and there'll be a cup of tea waiting. And trust me, you have to believe that good things are around the corner.'

Rosie cried, his words did little to pierce her shell of utter despair.

During the rest of their journey he tried hard to fill the silent interludes. 'Shona's got the spare room ready,' he said.

Rosie could only nod her thanks. The image of the blackened walls and boarded-up windows would haunt her for a long, long time.

'Makes you realise how lucky you were, doesn't it?' he asked softly, as if reading her mind.

'I don't feel very lucky.'

'I know things must feel like the end of the world right now...'

They do, Dad.

'... but they're not. There will come a time when you'll count your blessings. Trust me.'

'I don't understand how I've lost control. I've lost control of everything, my whole life. I've got to start again, but I don't know if I can.'

'Well that's the thing, love. You don't have any choice.' He sighed and gripped the steering wheel in the ten-to-two position, carefully and slowly changing up to fourth gear.

*

Shona waved from the open front door, her tan as dark as ever and set off by hot pink lipstick. 'Oh, Rosie, look at you! Come on in, love, and make yourself at home.'

It was the warmest welcome Shona had ever given her, but Rosie baulked at the tone of it, which made her feel like a rescue puppy. The moment the front door closed behind her, she wanted to leave. She turned her head and stared at the burgundy runner and the back of the door with its polished brass letterbox flap, as if trying to figure out the exit code. But even if she found the confidence to run, she had nowhere to go and no one to run to.

She couldn't help but think of the day six months ago when she'd left the same house, happy to be heading back to Woolacombe with nothing to occupy her thoughts but the letter from Laurel that sat in her bag, its contents waiting to be shared with her husband. She remembered later that night, holding up her palm, as if, like a superhero, she might be able to deflect his words, erase his thoughts, change her fate. *'I've met someone...'*

But it wasn't just someone he had met. It was Geraldine Farmer, the woman who had everything she had ever wanted, apart from the little people to populate her beautiful home. Rosie felt that Geraldine was more than her in every way: prettier, slimmer, richer and cleverer. She had beaten her at every turn. *'I mean, what can you offer them right now?'* The words rang inside her head as she pictured her little girls in their pale pink Uggs.

'Nothing,' she said out loud.

Shona shot Rosie's dad a wide-eyed look. 'Nothing?' She gave a small laugh. 'I said, would you like to go up to your room?' Clearly Rosie had missed her question the first time.

'Yes, please,' she whispered, deciding it would be better to be alone than to sit and watch the two of them try to think of what to say next.

Shona closed the bedroom door behind her and Rosie heard her speedy tread on the stairs. No doubt she was keen to discuss events with her dad. She could sense their whispers floating up through the floorboards and bouncing off the shiny floral wallpaper and built-in white laminate wardrobes: *'What did she say in the car?'* and *'How long is she staying?'*

She sat at the dressing table with its large, oval, white and gold mirror on a stand and swivelled it to see her reflection. Her face was now mottled with little white patches that looked like countries on a map, irregular shapes that sat around her mouth, under her nose and below her left eye. She touched the tip of her finger to them. The doctor had told her they would fade a little; she wondered how much. Not that she cared about her altered appearance, not really. It didn't matter. Her hair was dirty and knotty and she couldn't wait to give it a good wash. She tried to imagine bathing and washing her hair in Roy and Shona's bathroom, among their unfamiliar lotions and towels, thinking how odd it was that he was her dad, her flesh and blood, and yet still in so many ways a stranger.

Lying on the floral bedspread of the single bed, Rosie

looked around the small room in the cold, silent house. Several dolls sat in a row on the windowsill, all wearing Victorian high-necked blouses, full skirts and high-buttoned boots and each either holding a dinky parasol or sporting a large hat with a feather. She found them creepy, and being stared at by unblinking glassy eyes did nothing to change this. A shelf opposite the bed held several large trophies, faux-brass columns topped with dancers that were yet more proof of her dad and Shona's prowess on the dance floor.

She sat up and slid from the bed. Reaching up, she opened the wardrobe doors to find a rack of padded satin hangers bearing elaborate dresses in every garish shade of the rainbow. She let her fingers trail the sequins, net and diamante that sparkled under the light. Then she sank back down on the bed, feeling so lost and alone that she thought her heart might break.

For the next couple of days she kept a low profile, hiding away in the spare room, sneaking to the bathroom and down the stairs to fetch a glass of water, eating alone in silence, trying to be invisible. The monotony was broken when the phone in the hallway rang.

'It's for you!' Shona called, sounding slightly harried, Rosie thought, as if the novelty of having her under their roof had already worn off.

'Thank you,' Rosie whispered as she made her way downstairs.

'Mummy?' Naomi's voice asked a little uncertainly.

'Yes! Yes, my baby, it's me!' She tried hard not to let her distress be heard in her voice.

'Daddy said you were at Grandad Roy's?'

'Yes, I am, just for a little while, until the house gets sorted out and then we can all head home.' She bowed her head, her voice catching and still a bit crackly as she wondered if she was telling the truth. 'How's school?' she managed.

'It's good. My teacher is called Madame Froubert and she is French, from France.'

'Oh wow! That's exciting.'

'But Leo is in a different class, she's in Mr Dobrey's and he is just English.' She huffed, as if this was suboptimal.

'Have you made friends?'

'I've got Melody and Jess and Tilda and Melody is from China.'

'China? Goodness me, Nay, it sounds fantastic!' She closed her eyes, trying to picture a school, a life in which she had no part. 'Are you having a nice time in London?'

Rosie knew every nuance in her child's vocabulary and the pause before she answered spoke volumes. 'Yes, but...'

'But what, Nay?'

'Truffle had to go and live on a farm,' she squeaked.

'He did?'

'Yes, and I miss him too,' she whispered.

'Oh, darling!' She closed her eyes, wishing she were there to hold Naomi tight, kiss her better and make promises.

'I can't even visit him because it's far away and he's not allowed any visitors.' Her voice cracked.

'Don't cry, little Naomi. Don't cry. Truffle will be thinking about you too, so when you miss him, just think about him and picture him and he'll get that message and that will make him feel better as well.'

'You'd take me to his farm, wouldn't you, Mum?' Her voice was barely audible.

'If I could, darling, then I would.'

'I know.' Naomi hesitated. 'I've got to go now. I love you.'

'I love you too.'

Rosie sat holding the phone, oblivious to the tone that indicated the call had ended, hoping for more. How could they give a child a dog, a pet, something to love and then take it away? Who would do that? Kev's words floated into her mind unbidden. *He gets fed up, bored, has a change of heart, flips his mind and bails. He bins things. He's always done it and he always will.*

'Your tea's ready,' her dad called from the kitchen.

'I'm not hungry, thanks Dad.' Naomi's tears were still fresh in her mind.

'I've made you a nice omelette and chips. Come and eat it off a tray with us, in front of the telly.'

It sounded so much like a request from her smiling dad that she nodded and plodded through to the lounge. Shona budged up on the sofa, even though there was plenty of room. She took her place and stared at the television.

'How *are* you feeling?'

It could have been her imagination, but the way Shona asked the question suggested to her that what she really wanted to know was, '*When will you be better? When will you leave?*'

'I'm okay,' was the best she could offer and in truth she didn't want the discussion. She was utterly sick of the spiral of thoughts that swirled in her mind, trying to figure out how she'd been reduced to this shell of a person.

'Tell you what...' Shona shuffled off her seat. 'Why don't I put one of our DVDs on and you can see us in competition.' Without waiting for a reply, she pulled open the drawer in the TV unit and selected a DVD from one of a dozen.

Rosie listened to the little tray whir open and watched as Shona gently placed the disc in the holder. And suddenly, there they were: bodies touching, heads arching away from each other, hands interlocked, grins fixed, hair set and sequins sparkling. Shona's yellow frock swished and swirled with every step, folding around the couple and enveloping them in a froth of baby-duck-coloured tulle.

'That was the regionals two years ago. I'd say we've come on even since then.'

Her dad entered the room bearing two trays. He handed one to Shona and one to her. 'Mind out, the plate's hot.' He smiled.

Rosie stared at the pale omelette and mountain of oven chips and pictured the little girl who'd set a place at the table every night for her mum, a place that remained empty. For the first time she wondered what that must have been like for her dad, cooking to the best of his ability, keeping a routine going, while being reminded daily of the woman who'd left.

'I was just saying…' Shona nodded her head at the screen. 'I think we've come on, since this video was taken.'

Her dad beamed. 'I'd say so. Look at my footwork – shocking.'

'Not shocking, Roy, just not polished.' She smiled at him, then placed a large chip in her mouth. 'We still won though,' she noted with pride, her eyes fixed on the screen, her head moving in time to the music.

Rosie wondered how her life had gone so wrong. Even Roy and Shona, with their obsessive ballroom dancing and shiny shoes, even they had found love and happiness, and she was all alone…

Roy sat down with his own tray and looked aghast at his daughter. 'Oh, Rosie! Oh, love! What is it?'

She hadn't realised she was crying until he pointed it out.

Seventeen

With no one else in the house, Rosie reluctantly rose from her bed and trod the stairs at the sound of the doorbell. It would probably be a delivery that needed signing for or one of their neighbours dropping off the parish magazine. She considered hiding away, but knew that was unfair on both her dad and Shona, but also on whoever was making the delivery. She planned on making as little small talk as possible. It was, however, Keith who stood, a little sheepishly on the doorstep.

'Keith!' Crying seemed to be her natural default and the sight of him set her off.

'Now, now, we'll have less of that, Rosie.' He smiled.

'Come in, come in!' She sniffed and stood back, wishing she had got washed and dressed. 'Let me make you a cup of tea.' She hated the formality of their surroundings, the awkwardness in front of the man who was her father-in-law.

'Thanks, but I'm not stopping love. I'm on me way to Bristol, but I wanted to stop and see you.'

'It's lovely to see you. The girls seem okay? I do speak to them.' This fact, again caused new tears to pool, she pictured the card they had made him for his birthday and her sitting in the car with Kev.

'Well, you mustn't get upset Rosie, Mo sends her love and I wanted to tell you that I've started work on the house, Ross has been helping me. It shan't be quick mind, but we'll get there.'

'But... but I haven't got any money! I don't know what Phil's got, but I don't know how we'll pay you!' she gushed.

'We'll work out a plan, don't worry. Is Roy not in?' He looked past her, down the long, neat, narrow hall.

'No. They must have gone shopping.'

'Give him my best regards. And I mean it, try not to worry, we'll work out the money, somehow. You'll be home before you know it.'

'I... I don't know what to say!' She felt a wave of love for the man who was throwing her this lifeline. 'But thank you.'

Phil had called a couple of times to let her know he was dealing with the house, the insurance company had again denied their claim and it was indeed going to be down to Tipcott and sons to try and get things moving. Christmas was slowing work down, but come the new year, they would crack straight on, as and when they could.

It can't come soon enough! I want my home! I want my girls! She wished silently.

'How are you feeling?' His concern sounded genuine.

'Much better, thank you. Less sore and my skin's healing well.' She didn't confess to the black hole of emptiness that she had tumbled into, the loneliness that threatened to send her mad.

'You sound much better. Less gravelly, less wheezy.'

'Yes.'

He fed her snippets of information about her girls that she stored away, dipping into them in her darker moments, which were not getting any less frequent.

'When are you coming back to Devon?' She closed her eyes and waited for the answer.

'Not till they break up in a few weeks, but you should come and see them, they'd love that.' He lowered his voice conspiratorially.

Rosie nodded, as if he could see her. 'What, get a train up?'

'Yes, it's easy. You just get the train to Paddington and then jump on the District Line. We can meet you at the Tube.'

It was odd to hear him speak with confidence about routes and train lines, telling her to "jump on the District Line" like he'd been doing it his whole life. 'I don't have any money, but I'll try and sort something out.' *I don't even have a purse to put money in. I don't have anything.*

'I can transfer some to your bank account. Shall I do that?'

'I'll have a think and let you know, thank you.' She kept

it polite, it was one thing asking him to help out financially with the girls, but when it was for her? She didn't want to be beholden to him and Gerri in any way. They were both silent and it was awkward.

'Oh, I meant to say, Leo lost a tooth!' he gushed.

'She has? Oh! Was she excited?' In her mind's eye, she replayed the rigmarole she had always gone through, watching them place the tooth under their pillow and then sneaking in in the dead of night, easing her hand under their sleeping head and putting a fifty-pence piece and a note from the tooth fairy in its place, trying not to catch their long curls that tumbled over the edge of the pillow. Then waiting patiently in the morning for the squeals of happiness and excitement. She pictured the destroyed rooms in which she had performed this ritual.

'Not really. It was a bit of a disaster. Gerri kind of let slip that there was no tooth fairy.' He gave a nervous laugh. 'It's not her fault, she's new to this whole parenting thing.'

Rosie didn't know what to say. Her sadness for Leo was edged with dislike for the woman who'd spoilt the joy for her little girl. 'Well, she'll need to get better at it now she's having a baby.'

A few days later, Rosie woke early and lay staring at the window. She now recognised the signs and rhythms of the neighbourhood: the woman next door who stood at the back door every night at ten o'clock calling 'Oscar! Oscar!' over and over until her cat crept home; the sound of the milk float's electric engine that, like Oscar, purred as it roamed the streets in the early hours; the wheeze of the bus's brakes as it pulled into the layby further down the road to collect shoppers with their pull-along trolleys. She was of course grateful to her dad and Shona for having scooped her up in her hour of need, but she still hated being there and couldn't wait to return home.

There was a light rapping on her door. 'Are you awake, love?'

'Yes.' She sat up and tied her hair in a knot at her neck.

Her dad poked his head around the door, uncertain and tentative. They were still awkward with each other; it was difficult, sharing a house for the first time as adults.

'I wanted to give you this.' He handed her an envelope.

'What is it?' She stared at it, turning it over to confirm that it was indeed blank on both sides.

'Open it!'

Rosie poked her finger under the flap and tore it open, revealing a return train ticket to London and a twenty-pound note.

'Oh, Dad!'

'I thought it was about time you got up there, love, and I know those girls will be missing you just as much as you're missing them. The tickets are valid for any weekday, so pick one and I'll drop you at the station.'

She looked up at him. 'That's brilliant. Thank you.'

'You're welcome. I think seeing them will be good for you. It'll either help you settle or stir you into action. Either way, you should go.' He made his way sheepishly out of the room, embarrassed by the love that cocooned them inside the small space.

She smiled after him. The thought of seeing her children filled her with a rare burst of joy.

Rosie anxiously trod the stairs and walked through the barrier of the Tube station, grabbing embarrassingly at her ticket as it disappeared for good at the end of her journey. She found herself in an elegant glass-roofed arcade where shops and cafés clustered around the wide walkway, each with a fancy glass fanlight above its entrance, patterned plasterwork beneath the ceiling and a festive garland of spruce and holly dotted with gold and red baubles. Despite the familiar names of the shops and cafés, which could be found on any high street, the whole place felt very Victorian.

She was nervous, clutching the bag Mo had sent her and pulling the back of her jumper down over her jeans, worried about how she looked. The pixie boots and tight jeans were charity-shop finds, but she was grateful to have something to wear other than the clothes she'd left the hospital in and her pyjamas.

Walking out onto the crowded pavement, she felt overwhelmed by the throng of people coursing towards her. Everyone looked glossy and well dressed, kitted out in branded items, and they all seemed to be talking into or staring at smartphones. She stared up at the high shopfronts with two or three floors of offices or accommodation above them. Someone grabbed her arm. Gasping, she spun round, instantly relieved to find herself staring into Phil's face. She was very happy to see him, unsure what she would have done if he'd neglected to meet her as promised.

There was a split second when she forgot their new circumstances. The way they looked at each other reminded her of when she used to welcome him home after a long day of labouring; it was as if he'd walked into their kitchen and the girls were playing in the sitting room while she prepared his supper. *'Hello, love, how was your day? Cup of tea?'* He smiled at her in the way he had when he'd walked into his parents' kitchen that first day with his army rucksack over his arm and his face and arms tanned, his expression cocky, as if he knew what he wanted and how to get it.

'Look at us, eh?' She smiled at him, glancing over his head at the ornate fascias and rooftops where Christmas lights twinkled. There was bustle all around them: taxis beeped, neon-clothed cyclists whizzed by and couriers on motorbikes weaved in and out of the traffic with their engines revving. It was chaos, but with his hand on her arm, she felt quite calm.

'You look really well, much better.' He leant in towards her so he could be heard above the din.

She could smell his natural scent, as familiar to her as her own, and to be this close hit her like a punch to the gut. Stepping back from his grasp, she placed her hand over the scars around her mouth, the skin pale and shiny against her lips. 'I am a lot better. Getting there.'

'I thought we could go and pick up the car and then go and get the kids from school. How does that sound?'

'Is... Will Gerri...' She stumbled on the words.

'No, she's away for the night. Paris, on business.' He said this matter-of-factly, as if nipping off to Paris was a normal thing; maybe it was in the new world he now inhabited, but to her it was just another reminder of how glamorous Gerri was and how she fell well short of the mark.

She felt her shoulders unbunch with relief at the knowledge that she wouldn't have to encounter her. The thought of having to suffer more derogatory comments and mocking nastiness had filled her with a cold dread, although she'd decided before she set off that if that was what it took to see her girls, then she would do it.

She followed Phil along the pavement, stopping every few yards to say sorry to the people she bumped into and to allow them to cross her path, which they did without offering thanks or even acknowledging her. She had yet to master the purposeful stride that Phil had perfected. They turned immediately left into Wrights Lane, where concrete and glass-fronted offices stood opposite a row of red-brick mansion blocks. The doors had shiny brass plates and a concierge hovering in front of them; he was wearing a green hat and matching greatcoat, with gold braid on the peak of his cap and his epaulettes.

'How's your dad?' Phil asked, almost over his shoulder, as he walked slightly ahead.

'Good. The same. You know.' She hated that she had

nothing to say, nothing to offer. 'I've spoken to your mum too. She sent me this bag.' She held it up, but he ignored her.

'These flats are upwards of a million.' He pointed to the boxy, modern apartments to his right.

'I'll settle for our little house in Woolacombe any time.' She knew how provincial she sounded, but it was the truth.

He smiled briefly. 'Dad says he's making a bit of progress. He and Ross have started ripping out the timber that's been damaged, took a good couple of skips away and more to come, he reckons.'

'I can't wait,' she whispered. 'I'm so grateful, him and Ross will do a cracking job, I know it.'

Phil laughed. 'Yep. If Kayleigh doesn't slow them down, coming up for a moan and a good old nose.'

Rosie looked at the floor, not wanting to laugh with him, not wanting to be reminded of the old life that she had lost. 'I'm worried about how it's being paid for…' she let this hang, wondering how she would face the dilemma if it were his girlfriend's money that was putting her little house back together.

'He's getting materials at cost of course and they're working for free when they have time off. I think he and mum have covered some of it personally and we need to work something out for the rest.'

'That's amazing.' She felt quite choked.

They followed the road as it curved round. She liked the London street sign, the distinctive black lettering on a white enamel background that read *Marloes Road*, with the borough, *W8*, in red beneath. They strolled on. She was finding the short trek quite exhausting, having been confined to her dad's spare bedroom for so long and with her lungs not yet working at full capacity, but her eagerness to see the girls fuelled her out-of-condition muscles.

'This is us!' He stood back as if to admire for the first time the five-storeyed terraced house with its white columns and tiny roof garden above the front door, whose uniform bay trees in oversized zinc containers were just visible from the street. A wide path of black and white tiles led to the front door, which was flanked by another pair of bay trees in identical pots. Black, wrought-iron, arrow-tipped railings encased a front courtyard and basement, matching the rest of the street.

The three middle floors each had a square bay window set in carved stone, painted white and fronted by a smaller zinc windowbox full of pretty pink flowers and trailing ivy. Rosie let her eyes travel the full height of the building, wondering what lay behind each window, particularly the smaller dormer in the attic, which had its own mini balcony. She noted that every window had a roman blind that was pulled to the exact same height.

'Wow!' It was hard not to be impressed. 'It's like the Mary Poppins house.'

'Fourteen million quid's worth!' He nodded.

'I don't know about working for Gerri, you sure you're not an estate agent, Phil? You seem quite obsessed with house prices around here.'

He ignored her jibe. 'Do you want to look round?'

She remembered the grand tour Gerri had given her, the way the images had filled her brain for months. It had proved to be torture and she didn't need more of that, especially now she didn't have a home of her own.

'Not really.' She wrinkled her nose at him. 'If you don't mind.'

'Sure.'

She could sense his disappointment at being denied the chance to impress, but that was just too bloody bad.

'Car's just along here.' He gestured down the street.

She followed him past houses that were all remarkably similar.

'Most of these are flats,' he said. 'There are only four houses in the street.'

She found the pride he took in all this quite astonishing, as if he'd had a role in the acquisition of the property and hadn't simply committed adultery with the woman whose name happened to be on the deeds.

The familiar shiny Range Rover sat in the street in a residents' parking bay. She pictured the side of it dripping with coleslaw. Phil pressed a button and it lit up like a Christmas tree. It was her first time in the car that she had both spied on and hidden from on more than one occasion. The girls were right; it was indeed high up, like sitting on a throne.

'Comfy?' Phil asked as she clipped the seatbelt into place.

'Don't think I'd be able to park it.'

'Rosie, I've seen you trying to park your old banger and I would have to agree.' He winked at her, again like they were on a jaunt together, happy. It made her feel uneasy, as if behaving this way together was illicit and they might get thrown out at any moment.

'Are you happy, Phil?' She felt bold asking.

He stared ahead and breathed in. 'I'm living in the best city in the world, in a mansion—'

'Yes, you said. Fourteen million.' She couldn't help herself.

He continued. 'Work is easy, I've got money in my pocket and my summer will be spent somewhere hot, probably a private villa with a swim-up pool. What's there not to be happy about? I'm living the life.' He started the engine.

Rosie placed her bag on her lap and wondered if he realised that not only had he failed to mention his daughters, his girlfriend or their impending new arrival, but also that he hadn't answered her question.

He threw the car around tight corners and down narrow residential streets with ease. She got the sense that he did so for her benefit, keen to show that not only could he handle the powerful engine, but also that he could navigate the streets of Kensington and Chelsea as if it was second nature. Eventually they pulled up outside a playground on an ordinary residential street. If you didn't know it was a school, Rosie thought, you might easily have missed it. It was quite unlike the girls' school at home, where signs, the staff car park, the football pitch and numerous sprawling, low-rise, felt-roofed buildings left you in no doubt.

There was a square of tarmac with high mesh fencing reaching up to the sky; it reminded her of a cage. She thought again of the wide sloping field that their school had at its disposal and the vast expanse of beach on which they could run; this felt rather claustrophobic in comparison. Or maybe she was just trying to find the negatives.

'I'll go get them.' He smiled, jumped down and walked through a side gate, into which he had to punch an entry code. She watched with her nose pressed to the tinted window as he joined a line of other mums, dads and, judging by their age, demeanour and the way they bunched together, a host of nannies and au pairs. She felt a little sad for Phil; he looked out of place among the tweed-jacketed, bearded hipsters in their skinny jeans and aged-leather lace-up boots and the uber-skinny, blonde mummies who reminded of her of Mummy von Trapp. She smiled at the thought of her: Phillippa, the woman who had saved her life.

The front door of the large, higgledy-piggledy Victorian villa opened and out walked an upright woman with a serious face, who was a lot younger than her clothes and stance would suggest. She was wearing a soft, lavender-coloured wool suit and her hair was in a loose chignon. She stood to one side and a stream of little girls in identical hats and coats stepped in front of her. One by one, they shook her hand and then walked slowly with their head held high towards the person collecting them.

Rosie laughed involuntarily as she compared this to the mass evacuation that happened when the bell rang at their school. She pictured the kids running, arms raised and hands clutching cardboard still wet with paint, lunchboxes and daps dangling from their fingers as they hollered at their mums and dads: *'Did you bring me something to eat?'* She thought of Mel for the first time in a long time and felt an incredible sense of longing for all that was familiar to her.

The girls continued to exit like a little trail of straw-boater-wearing ants. And then there was Naomi! Her beautiful girl was in her sights and she was real, no longer just the child of her dreams whom she had missed every day and every night. Here she was, only a few feet away!

Rosie opened her mouth and cried silently, overwhelmed by the sight of her child. Her body pulsed with the need to hold her. She undid her seatbelt and opened the heavy door. Climbing down from the seat, she hovered on the pavement by the car, waiting impatiently.

Minutes later, Leona emerged, looking so grown-up and tiny all at once, doing her best to walk slowly and shaking hands solemnly with the lady in the doorway.

It was only when the girls took their dad's hands and made their way across the playground towards the security gate that Rosie realised what was so different about them. *Oh no! For the love of God! No!* Someone had cut off their hair.

Her heart raced with nerves as her girls drew closer. *Don't be ridiculous! You're their mum!* she reminded herself, but still her insides churned. The trio walked across the square of tarmac and through the gate and there they were!

Naomi broke into a run the second she saw her. 'Mummy!' she screamed, literally screamed, at the top of her voice.

The entire playground looked in their direction – not that Rosie cared or even noticed. She was intent only on grabbing that child and holding her close. Naomi fell into her, burying her face in her mum's neck as she cried.

'Ssshhh... It's okay, my little one. I've got you.'

'My mummy,' she breathed, as if just to be able to say the word was a blessed relief.

They stayed there for some minutes, with Rosie kneeling on the grey London pavement, holding her little Devon maid tightly in her arms while they both gave in to the tears that flowed.

'I missed you so much!' Rosie whispered.

Naomi held her tightly, almost as if she were afraid to let her go.

Rosie ran her fingers up her daughter's back and felt the ends of the blunt bob that sat beneath her chin. She would talk to Phil about it later; this was not the time for anything other than reconnecting.

Leona stood by her dad's side, burying her face in his jeans and stealing glimpses of her mum.

'It's okay, Leo,' she cooed, over Naomi's shoulder. 'It's only me! I look a bit different, don't I?' She smiled, swiping at her tears with the flat of her fingers.

Leona nodded and turned her face back into her dad's leg.

Naomi unhooked her arms from around her mum's neck and placed them on either side of her face.

'They got rid of Truffle. They sent him to a farm.' She spoke with such maturity and sadness, it was almost unbearable. 'But Melody said they probably gave him an injection that killed him, that's what happened to her dog who was old. And Tilda said that might be true and I asked Daddy and he said I was being stupid, but he did that looking-at-the-wall thing he does when he's telling me a fib, like "Oh, sure, you can have a party" or like when I asked him if he could get One Direction to babysit for us. Do you know what I mean, Mum?' Naomi kept her face inches from Rosie's, as if only this proximity would suffice.

'Yes.' She knew exactly what she meant. 'But I don't think Daddy would do that. I really don't.' Again, she prayed this was the truth.

Naomi nodded, clearly hoping so too. 'You've got pinky-white funny bits on your face.' She stuck the end of her index finger against the splotches near Rosie's mouth and below her eye where the skin was shiny, taut and a little puckered in the centre.

'I know.'

'You look like...' Naomi looked upwards, considering how best to describe her mum's face. 'You look like a patchy cow, but a baby cow whose skin is not brown and white but pink and white and a bit wrinkly.'

'Thank you.' She kissed her child, relieved and happy that Naomi had rationalised the way she looked now and wasn't afraid to touch the affected areas.

Leona continued to hide. Rosie winked at her when she peeked from the side of her dad's leg. In response, Leona closed her eyes. *Little Ostrich! Give her a bit of time, Rosie. It's okay.*

Phil opened the back door and the girls climbed in. 'Who fancies pizza?' he asked.

'Me! Me! Me!' Naomi shouted, bouncing up and down on the seat.

Leona buried her chin in her chest and kept her gaze pointing downwards.

Phil started the engine and indicated.

'They've had their hair cut.' Rosie spoke through gritted teeth.

'Gerri said Daddy didn't have time to do our hair in the morning and it was easier to get it cut off, so we did.'

Rosie turned to the girls and smiled to show that it was fine, not wanting to alarm them or fight with their dad in front of them.

'It feels weird, Mum. I can't do bunches and when I shake my head I can't feel it on my back.'

'You look lovely. You both do. Very grown-up.' She knew it would be hard to explain to anyone other than the mother of a little girl just how important their hair had been. She swallowed the sorrow, not wanting to taint any of their precious time together.

'Who fancies Venicci's?' Phil shouted.

'Me!' Naomi yelled and even Leona managed to raise a half-smile.

Rosie felt a spike of alienation, which persisted as they parked and then walked along a cobbled street at the back of High Street Kensington towards the little Italian restaurant that the girls were clearly familiar with. Naomi held her hand tightly, telling her how she could count to ten in French and going on to do just that, loudly. She stared at her daughter, who looked so much older without the tumble of baby curls around her face. Leona, too, looked more pointed, less rounded, as though she had grown up. Rosie didn't like it one bit.

'I'm sitting next to Mummy!' Naomi shouted and pulled out one of two high-backed chairs.

Leona climbed onto the one opposite her mum. Rosie could feel her staring at her, but when she looked towards her, Leona closed her eyes.

A charming, portly, curly-haired man in a V-necked cashmere sweater and white shirt swooped over and slapped Phil on the back. 'What's going on here? You've traded in Miss Farmer already? I'll tell her, you know!' He laughed, winking at the girls to show it was all in jest, no harm done.

Rosie again felt her cheeks flush at the fact that she was an interloper. She pictured the four of them visiting the place with such regularity that her kids knew where to sit and the owner felt comfortable coming over to make physical contact with her husband.

'Can I have garlic bread and some Coke and a Hawaiian pizza. Please,' Naomi said without looking at a menu. She beamed at the man.

'Of course, bella. And for you, shy little one?' He looked towards Leona.

'She'll take the same.' Phil smiled at his new friend.

Rosie registered the fact that she felt unable to answer for Leo, so quickly had she slipped from her role as primary carer. It didn't matter how many times she told herself that it was temporary, the sense of loss was still acute.

Opening the menu, she stared not at the food on offer but at the prices. Twenty-four ninety-nine, eighteen pounds, forty-three pounds a bottle... She considered the fourteen pounds in her purse, the remains of the money her dad had given her, looked up at the girls' neat, short hair and then at Phil, the man to whom she was married, and her sadness threatened to crush her. This was a world that was unfamiliar to her and the thought that followed almost knocked the breath from her. *They are leaving me behind and I can't catch up even if I want to. I have a life of omelette and chips, eaten on my lap, of charity-shop bags and an uncertain future. I thought loving you was enough, but maybe it isn't, maybe I was wrong.*

'Rosie?' Phil prompted.

She looked up to see all four faces turned towards her. The man was holding the others' menus aloft, waiting.

'Sorry. Just a coffee, please.'

'Have pizza, Mummy!' Naomi urged.

'I'm not hungry, darling,' she lied, 'but a nice coffee would be great.' She handed the tall menu back to the man and placed her hands in her lap.

'It was lovely to talk to you on the phone, Leo. And a little birdie told me that you lost a tooth?' She bent her head low and caught her daughter's eye.

Leona opened her mouth to show her mum the gap where her tooth used to be.

'Wow! That's so grown-up. Did you have to tie it to a piece of string and then a door handle and get someone to slam the door? That's what we used to say was the best way to get your teeth to fall out, but we didn't really do it.'

'It came out in my apple.' Her response was almost inaudible.

'Goodness me, you could have swallowed it!' She gasped.

'Mum...' Naomi swivelled on her seat. 'Gerri said that it was you that put the money under my pillow and not the tooth fairy, is that true?'

Both girls were staring at her now, waiting for her response.

'Well, sometimes there are things mummies and daddies do to make things exciting. You know, like when we used to build a tent in the lounge and eat our picnic in it. Or when we had pirate day and we could only use our pirate names.'

'Aye aye, Captain Tipcott!' Naomi showed she hadn't forgotten.

'Well, I guess it was a bit like that. We all pretended and it made us happy.'

Leona continued to stare at her mum. 'They sent Truffle away.' And then her tears fell, like droplets of glass sliding down her perfect skin.

'Don't cry, Leo. Don't cry, little one.'

Rosie reached for her hand, but instead of taking it, Leona climbed down from her seat and walked round the table. Lifting her youngest child up onto her lap, Rosie held her fast, inhaling her scent and committing the feel of her to memory once again.

'Oh, not this again.' Phil sighed. 'We've been over it so many times. It wasn't fair on him. We travel and we're out of the house all day and in the summer we'll be away for months.'

The girls ignored him, as if this justification had not only worn thin but did little to ease their loss.

Rosie spoke over Leona's head. 'I think what is unfair is letting them fall in love with a pet, giving them the thing they had always wanted and then sending him away at a time when things were already new and uncertain for them.'

'Well, thank you for that helpful insight. *I* think what's unfair is talking about things in front of them that you know nothing about.'

She shrank back in the seat.

'Gerri shouted at Daddy and he took Truffle to the farm.' Naomi filled in some of the gaps.

Rosie watched as Phil rubbed his palm over his face. He didn't look at all like a man who was living the life.

Saying goodbye to them at Paddington was harder than she could possibly have imagined. She held them tightly and whispered reassurances, as much for her benefit as theirs.

'As soon as we can go home and the house is fixed, we'll make it lovely and we can celebrate by going for a long walk on the beach.'

Naomi looked downcast as she held her one last time. 'I'm sorry, Mummy,' she whispered.

'What are you sorry for?'

Naomi swallowed. 'Because I talk too much and I am never quiet and I don't give you a minute to think.'

The words she spoke were not her own and Rosie felt her heart constrict. 'No! No, darling! You listen to me. Your noise, your chat and the way you laugh, those are the things I miss most. Don't ever stop being you. I love you just the way you are, noise and all, and when we all get home, I want you to make as much noise as you can! Do you understand me?'

Naomi nodded. 'I love you, Mummy.'

'I love you too.'

'I miss you, Mum.' Leona joined in.

'I miss you too.'

Standing on the concourse watching her children walk in the opposite direction left her distraught. She climbed onto the train and cared little that her tear-stained face and noisy sobs drew the stares and comments of her fellow commuters. They didn't matter. Nothing did.

Arriving at Exeter St David's, she found her dad standing in the ticket hall, rocking on his soft-soled shoes, his pale blue car coat zipped up under his chin as he waited for her on the other side of the ticket barrier. A group of carollers in bright scarves, gloves and hats, wrapped up against the evening chill, stood in a circle and were midway through 'Hark! The Herald Angels Sing'. The sound they made was beautiful, angelic, and Rosie found it quite unbearable.

She stumbled towards her dad and uncharacteristically fell into his arms and clung to him, all self-consciousness gone. She needed her dad and, this time, he was there for her.

Eighteen

Rosie had taken to her bed. Like the ladies of the Victorian era who simply retired upstairs with an undiagnosed malaise, refused visitors and spent their days prostrate with nothing but their thoughts for company, she lay there day after day, in deep reflection. Only this was no fictitious disorder; she was full of sadness that weighed her down mentally and physically. Her main preoccupation was wishing that time would go faster, faster.

Christmas was a miserable affair. Hearing the girls' excited chatter down the line, as they described the vast Christmas tree in the grand hallway and a busy morning with Nanny Mo and Grandad Keith, the cooking of pancakes with bacon, and the rich haul of booty that Santa had delivered, was horrible. Not that she wasn't delighted for her girls to be the proud owners of iPads, furry ear muffs and trainers with wheels in the base; it was more that their gifts emphasised both her inability to provide for them and her loneliness as she pictured the family that used to be hers gathered round the abundantly decorated tree of her imagination.

Mo had whispered her festive refrain a little awkwardly, obviously within earshot of Gerri and embarrassed by the absence of her daughter-in-law. Rosie had politely declined the offer of staying at Highthorne while Gerri, Phil and the girls were down for two days, knowing it was more than she could cope with. She now refused to leave the bedroom. Not even Shona's offer of a bowlful of sherry trifle and first dip into the Quality Street tub was enough to tempt her.

Her dad spent the weeks ferrying cups of tea and slices of toast up and down the stairs. If think-positive clichés and self-help quotes could heal, she'd have been leaping about with joy after day two. The only glimmer of hope came in the form of a message from Phil informing her that Keith had spent another couple of days at Arlington Road; still the thought that the materials needed to be paid for gnawed away in her stomach.

She knew that even once the house was habitable again, she could not compete with iPads and Uggs? It felt hopeless. A year ago she would have pooh-poohed the materialism and said that the only things that mattered for her kids were her warm embrace and her unconditional love. Now, though, Leona's initial reluctance to come to her and Naomi's tears of apology replayed in her mind like a broken record and each time she went over it her spirits sank a little lower.

Her dad knocked gingerly on the door and entered the room. 'Morning, Rosie. It's a lovely bright day and you need to get up and get outside. There are plenty worse off than you.'

She glanced at him from the pillow, as if this reminder of how very fortunate she was could make the slightest bit of difference. *I don't want to talk to you. I don't want to talk to anyone. I want to go to sleep and never wake up. I want to disappear, like Laurel. I want to run away.*

He pulled the curtains and opened the window, letting the fresh breeze in and some of the sad, stale air out.

'I've made you a doctor's appointment. So, in your own time, get yourself together and I'll run you down there,' he said matter-of-factly, giving her no choice.

'I don't want to,' she managed.

'I know. But it's not only about what you want, love. It's about what you need. I'm your dad and this is what we're going to do.' He sounded uncharacteristically assertive.

Her eyes followed him as he left the room. She didn't have the energy to argue with him.

The doctor was young, busy and distracted. He tapped his pen impatiently against his leg as he spoke; it was like his own private metronome pacing out his day.

'I see that physically you are healing well. Lung function improved, skin less sore.'

'Yes.' She nodded, instinctively placing her fingertips on her face where the skin was damaged.

'They will of course fade more in time. You were very

lucky.' He now used the pen as a pointer, directing it towards her.

So I've been told, again and again, but I don't feel very lucky.

'Do you think you're depressed?' His eyes darted from the computer screen and back to her.

'I might be.' This half-admission felt more realistic.

'Have you had any suicidal thoughts?'

Her fingers fidgeted in her lap. 'I sometimes think I would like to disappear.'

'And do you ever think about *how* you might disappear?' His tone was more impatient than sympathetic.

She shook her head. It would be hard to explain that the level of thought required to plan her disappearance was currently beyond her.

'I'd like to start you on anti-depressants, but you have to understand that they are not a quick fix: you won't take them today and jump out of bed feeling happy tomorrow. They are a long-term strategy that will help in time. When you're in the routine of taking them, we can monitor how they're working, how you're feeling and either change the medication or increase or lower the dosage. It's not an exact science. But it will help you feel better in the long run, take the edge off, give you some equilibrium.' Without waiting for a response, he reached for his prescription pad.

'I don't want to.' She spoke clearly.

'You don't want to take tablets?' He held his pen mid flourish.

'I don't want to get better,' she clarified. 'I don't want the world to think I'm happy or coping, because I'm not. I want to be broken like this because it's how I feel, like everything is pointless, because it is. Without my kids, my family, my home, everything is pointless.'

The young, impatient doctor stopped tapping and looked at the photograph on his desk of a young woman holding a toddler, both of them smiling into the camera. He was quiet, as if deep in thought.

Her dad drove her back to the house in silence broken only by his occasional disappointed sigh. It seemed he too had been hoping she would be popping happy pills on the return journey. As she stared out of the window, she sensed him casting surreptitious glances at her.

Shona rushed to the front door to meet them, alerted the moment her dad ratcheted the handbrake into place. 'How did you get on?' she asked eagerly.

Rosie stared at her. Shona's tone made her feel like a bag of rubbish that someone had forgotten to take out and was starting to stink. She lingered in the hallway. 'I think the trouble is, I don't want to feel better. It's something to focus on until I get my kids back and we can go home. A reminder, if you like.'

Shona looked from Rosie to her dad and back again. 'But that's not healthy, Rosie! Not at all. I know you've been through a lot, but you were always so full of sparkle – you lit up the room! You'd be a wonderful dancer.' She twisted the scarf at her neck. 'You can't just give up, you have to fight!

You have to get up and get out and go and grab life, no matter what that life looks like. You have to make the most of it!'

'Shona, please!' her dad interjected meekly. 'It sounds like you're pushing her and that might not be what she needs right now. We need to coax not push – that's what families do.'

'But that's just it, I'm not her mother, I'm her friend.'

No, you're not my mother. That was Laurel and she didn't want me either.

'And I'm sorry, Roy, but it's time she pulled herself together and moved forward. For her own good!' Shona looked close to tears. 'Look at her!' She gestured. 'How does letting her mope around help anything?'

Rosie felt numb. She turned to look at her dad. 'I'll go get my things.'

'No, Rosie. This is my house.' This last point he directed at Shona. 'You go when you're ready.'

'That wasn't what I meant!' Shona shouted, her fists clenched.

The next two weeks felt like years. Rosie continued to hide away in the bedroom, restricting her visits downstairs and her walks around the block to when Shona was out on an errand or the two of them had gone to dance practice. She tried to be as quiet as she could; all she wanted was for this living nightmare to end.

'Phone call, Rosie!' her dad called up the stairs one morning.

She brightened, longing to hear her babies' voices; it was the one thing that fortified her. Swallowing her nerves, she left the bedroom, still fearful of having to interact with Shona.

'Thank you,' she whispered to her dad, taking the phone between her palms and watching as he crept into the sitting room and shut the door firmly behind him, giving her privacy of sorts.

Pushing the phone into her ear, she struggled to make out the noise on the other end. 'Hello?'

It was a few seconds before she realised she was listening to the sound of crying.

'Rosie,' Phil sobbed, 'I've fucked up.'

'What? Are the girls okay?' Her heart leapt at the thought that they might be hurt in some way. His lack of response sent her pulse racing. 'Phil!' she shouted. 'Are the girls okay?'

Her dad turned up the volume on the television in the adjoining room.

'They're fine. Fine. But it's over. We're coming home.'

The car tootled along the A377. Her possessions sat at her feet in a Bag for Life.

'Bet you're feeling nervous.'

She looked at her dad. 'I am a bit. Excited too, though.'

'Of course.' He nodded at the road ahead. 'Shona's not a bad person. She just gets wound up and I suppose a bit jealous.'

She shrugged, finding it hard to discuss Shona or her behaviour. But her dad clearly wanted to get it off his chest.

'Thing is, Rosie, I've never had anyone care about me enough to be jealous.'

'I don't think jealousy is the way to express love, Dad. I think…' Kev's words floated into her head. *I just wanted you to be happy, that's how much I love you. You being happy is the single most important thing to me.* She took a deep breath. 'I think it's about freedom to make choices and knowing that no matter what those choices are, that person will still be there.'

'Are you saying you're going to forgive Phil?'

'I honestly don't know. I can't think about it too much. If that makes sense.'

'It does, love. Sometimes you just have to keep a lid on, keep the wheels turning.' He glanced across at her. 'Are you going to be okay?'

'I don't know. I hope so.' She gave him a brief smile.

'I think you'll go back to him,' he said.

She sighed and twisted the thin gold band on the third finger of her left hand.

'And I don't want to interfere, but I will say this: don't be in any rush, girl. Remember what you've been through. I'm not saying fight with him, life's too short not to forgive, but don't make a decision in haste. It's too important, for you all.'

'I won't ever forget what I've been through, Dad, and I suppose I've learnt that there are no guarantees, ever, about anything. Even if you think something is forever, it probably isn't.'

'Your mum...' He coughed. 'She had many faults, but she always listened to that little voice of instinct. She followed her heart and that takes some courage, even if it hurts others along the way.'

'Yeah, Phil followed his heart and look where that got him.'

'I guess what I'm saying is, Shona's right, even if she's not very good at expressing it. Don't be afraid to grab the future that's right for you. You deserve happiness.'

'Would you have taken Laurel back if she'd pitched up years later, wanting to pick up where she left off?'

He looked over his shoulder, as if checking that they were alone. 'In a heartbeat, at first,' he whispered. 'But then, years later? No. I never stopped loving her, but I stopped trusting her and that's far harder to live with.'

'I just want the girls back and I want them to be happy and I can't really see beyond that.' Rosie smiled at the prospect. 'But thank you, Dad, for saying that, and thank you for being there when I needed you most.'

'I don't know if that's true, Rosie. I think you needed me a lot more than I realised when you were growing up.'

'You can only ever do your best, Dad, and you did.'

He nodded and kept his eyes on the road; they were a little misty.

The *Welcome to Woolacombe* sign had never looked so vibrant. Rosie sat up and looked out as they drove up and over the hill. And there it was, her town! With the sea beyond and the long, wide beach that held so many memories.

'Don't you ever miss living here?' She turned to her dad.

'No. When I picture that time in my life, I can only see sadness. Even coming here now reminds me of all that. But visiting is okay.'

'The girls would like to see more of you, you know. When we're settled, please come down, and bring Shona too, of course.'

'She's a funny old fish, but she means well, you know.' He cleared his throat.

'I know, Dad.'

'She never had children, and she was an only child, so she's not that good around people, really. But oh, Rosie, when she gets on that floor...' He paused. 'Her face changes! It's like she's lit from within. I could dance with her all night, if only my creaky knees would allow.'

'She makes you happy.' Rosie smiled. She was glad for her dad. He deserved to find joy.

'She does. She's kind too, and she loves you.'

Rosie nodded, awkward at the topic. Roy continued, 'she might not always know how to show it, but she does. Do you know she won a few grand last year, dancing?'

She shook her head. 'I didn't know that.'

'Yep, we thought about taking a cruise, rumbaing under the stars!'

'Sounds lovely, Dad.' She smiled, picturing just that.

Roy took a deep breath. 'Yep. But instead, she has transferred it into Keith's account, for materials, for the house. And then when you get sorted, you can pay her back, bit by bit, whatever suits. We're in no rush for that cruise, got everything we need at home really.'

'Dad!' Her hand flew to her mouth. 'I don't know what to say! I can't believe it! Tell her thank you!' she managed, her voice thick with emotion.

'You give her a ring, tell her yourself.' He nodded.

'I will,' she sniffed, 'I will.' She was quite overcome.

As the car pulled into Mo and Keith's driveway, she felt exhausted at the prospect of what lay behind the door. *Just focus on the kids, that's your job, that's all you have to do...* It saddened her that regardless of what happened next, things between her and Mo had been changed forever. She could close her eyes now and recall Mo's singsong tone: *'Well, Gerri was as pleased as punch with the little matinee jacket I'd knitted!'*

'I won't come in, if that's okay?'

'Of course, Dad. Thank you for bringing me home – or back, anyway. I don't know where home is, really. Not while I still can't live in Arlington Road.' She smiled at him, trying to lighten her nerves.

'Well, there's a big old world out there, Rosie, and you can make a home anywhere you choose.'

She reached across and kissed her dad goodbye.

As she stood at the front door, she could hear the girls' shouts and laughter coming from within. It was the sound of chaos and it made her spirits soar. She knocked lightly.

Kayleigh answered the door and Rosie immediately felt her heart sink.

'All right, Rosie?' Kayleigh had two high spots of colour on each cheek. She was clearly happy to be observing the drama unfolding at Highthorne.

Rosie nodded and looked down the hallway, already seeking out her children.

'It's all kicking off!' Kayleigh pulled a face and hunched her narrow shoulders, as if the whole episode was highly amusing. She leant forward conspiratorially. 'Is it true that Kev fancies you? Ross was talking about something Keith said?'

Her casual, gossipy tone made Rosie see red. 'I'm not sure, Kay, but you'd better watch out, eh? Phil, then Kev, that only leaves Ross.' She winked and pushed past her, heading for the kitchen.

Kayleigh was left uncharacteristically speechless.

Phil was sitting at the table and Mo, as usual, was busying around the sink.

'Mummy!'

'Mum!'

Both girls ran at her, jumped on her and wrapped their arms around her. She beamed as she held them. To feel their bodies so close, to know that they were back in Devon was pure bliss.

'Has my hair grown?' Naomi turned round, tipped her head back as far as it would go, then touched the point on her back where her hair now reached, a good six inches further down than normal.

'It sure has!' She smiled.

'Did that fire go out into the garden, Mum?' Leona had apparently lost her shyness, for which Rosie was hugely grateful.

'I haven't been back there, but I think it did a little bit. Why, darling?' She crouched down until she was Leona's height.

'Because I'm worried that it might have cooked Moby and Jonathan, like when we do fish barbecues.'

Rosie shook her head. 'Don't you worry, that didn't happen. They're quite safe in their little shoebox.'

'They're still dead though.' Naomi clearly thought this might be a useful thing to point out to her sister.

'Yep.' Rosie nodded. 'They're still dead.'

'Tell you what, girls,' Mo interjected, 'why don't you give Grandad a hand in the yard. He's having a good old sort-out and I know he could do with some help.'

'Okay, Nan!' Naomi yelled and raced out of the kitchen with her little sister following in her wake.

'Cup of tea, love?' Mo asked, as if this was just another normal day.

'Yes, please.' She took a seat opposite Phil. He looked dreadful: unshaven and with greasy hair and bloodshot eyes from lack of sleep. But that wasn't what struck her most. He looked beaten.

'I'll be off,' Kayleigh called from the hallway, obviously having seen and heard enough.

'Righto, Kayleigh, see you soon!' Mo shouted in reply.

'How are you?' Rosie laid her forearms on the kitchen table and clasped her hands. Vengeance was far from her mind; despite the dark thoughts that had plagued her over recent months, she took no pleasure in seeing the father of her children in such a state.

Phil shook his head and licked his dry lips. 'She changed her mind.' He jutted out his jaw and blinked, trying to stop the tears that threatened. 'I did everything she asked, everything she wanted. But she was just playing with me.'

With us... 'I'm sorry to hear that.' She meant it.

'Here you go.' Mo placed the mug of tea in front of her daughter-in-law and put her hand on her shoulder before slipping from the room.

'What about the baby? How's that going to work?' She tried to imagine how this situation would pan out, pictured him rushing up and down the motorway at weekends and wondered how it might affect the girls, having a half-brother that they saw infrequently, and with money already tight, she wondered how they would cope if Gerri wanted him to contribute.

He gave a small laugh. 'There is no baby.' He shook his head again and this time the tears found their release.

'What?' She squinted. 'What do you mean?' It made no sense.

'She made the whole thing up. She was never pregnant.' His voice cracked.

'Good God! But...' She stared at him, lost for words. 'I don't believe it.'

'Well, it's true. She's a fucking nutcase.'

There was a pause while they both considered this. Both heard Rosie's words of warning months earlier, but this offered scant comfort now.

'I should have listened to you, Rosie.'

She didn't say anything. It didn't seem to matter so much now. The damage was done.

He cried openly; his swagger and poise had been left in W8 outside that fourteen-million-pound Mary Poppins house. 'I'm so sorry!' He held her gaze. 'I fucked everything up. Everything. I let my dad down, you, the girls. I'm so sorry!'

She stared at him, this broken man. There was a time when to see him cry would have crushed her. The man she loved. And there had been innumerable nights when to hear his apology was all she longed for. But now?

He reached forward and took both of her hands in his. The physical contact surprised her. She felt her cheeks blush. But what swirled in her stomach wasn't close to happiness; she wasn't sure it was even love, not any more.

'I will spend the rest of my life making it up to you, Rosie. I swear to God. I will be the best dad and husband in the world, I promise you.' He sniffed, wiped his nose and eyes with the back of his hand and reached again for her hands.

She gazed at him. Words tumbled in her mind, unsettled by the sentiment of the moment. She felt numb, confused. It was all way too much to take in and respond to in such a short space of time.

'Phil, I'm not sure if—'

The back door opened. Rosie sat up straight and stared at the space, a smile of anticipation forming on her lips, as if she was expecting someone to waltz through the back door and change the course of her life. But it was the girls and their grandad coming in from the yard. She winked at them, trying to hide the edge of surprise.

Phil spoke loudly and with confidence. 'Daddy is coming home, kids. We're going to go back to our little house when it's finished and you can put your feet on the furniture and you can make as much noise as you like and you can eat in any room you choose!'

His announcement shocked her, but his words also came as a surprise, giving an insight into the rules and regulations of Marloes Road.

'Can we get Truffle back?'

'Can we, Dad, please?'

The girls stared at him hopefully. This seemingly more important to them than his declaration that they would all be moving home together.

'We can't. He can't leave that farm we sent him to.' He looked at Rosie and she considered for the first time that maybe Melody and Tilda had been right. The idea horrified her.

The four of them took up residence in Mo and Keith's spare room. Rosie and the girls were squashed into the double bed, with Phil on a camp bed in the corner, and this arrangement suited her just fine. She tried not to look too far ahead and was content to fall asleep every night with the familiar sea breeze wafting through the window and her daughters right alongside her. Being with them was her cure for everything.

Her despair had lifted and her outlook was, if not sunny, then improved. She and Phil were polite to each other, more formal than they had ever been, while he struggled to come to terms with the way his life had been turned upside down and she tried to analyse his apology and intentions.

They dropped the girls at school together, both choosing not to comment on Mel's enthusiastic wave from her car, and went to visit the house. The charred wood had been replaced and parts of the upstairs floor too. Keith had started the rewiring and new windows had been fitted. Ross and Phil had nearly finished plastering and the smooth walls were nearly ready for them to decorate with all that green paint.

'It's a new beginning, Rosie.' He took her hand and squeezed it tightly.

She looked up at the place that had been her home for all those years. 'It's funny, Phil, it wasn't me that wanted a new beginning. I was happy.'

'I know.' He nodded and swallowed, still uncomfortable at having this conversation. 'And if I could turn back time, I swear—'

'But you can't,' she said. 'You can't turn back time. You can only work with the now and with what you know, the facts. And what *I* know is that you left me, left us.'

'But—'

'No, just let me talk, Phil. I had it all. I was content, but you changed that. You made me look at my life, made me question everything and I realised that you were a different person to the one I married.'

'I want to go back to being that person.' He looked her in the eye. 'I do.'

'But that's the thing. I'm a different person now too. And I don't know if I can go back or even if I want to. I need some time.'

'Don't talk like that, Rosie, please! We can figure it out. You can have all the time you need, but please, I need you. I'm not going to rush you. I made a mistake and I'm just asking for the chance...'

She spoke slowly. 'You should know, more than most, that those words don't mean anything when there's been a change of heart.'

As she walked away from the house towards the seafront, she took no joy from the sound of his crying, which echoed down the street.

Ten weeks later and the house was finally ready. The girls were ecstatic, excitedly planning the garish colour scheme for their bedroom. Rosie smiled at them over the kitchen table.

Mel was busy organising the housewarming. Rosie had received several texts along the lines of: *Oi! Shitstar! Are you serving coleslaw at this do or are you just going to tip it over your head?* They had made her laugh. Things would never be the same between them, but they were talking and trying and that was enough, for now.

'You've still got a couple of boxes of bits and bobs in the

yard, love,' Mo reminded her. 'Stuff they salvaged from the house.'

'I'll have a look through.' She sipped her coffee.

While Phil took the girls to school, she gingerly unpacked the boxes and picked through the contents. The smell was the first thing that struck her. Everything stank of bonfires. It turned her stomach to think how differently things might have ended. It was mainly rubbish: some make-up, a couple of books, the odd bit of clothing and some crockery. She decided to throw it all away. Digging deeper into the box, beneath some underwear that had been inside her chest of drawers, she pulled out a blank, white envelope. She held it against her chest, then carefully lifted the flap and removed the single, precious sheet. She read the words slowly.

I wanted more than to be known as my husband's wife. I wanted a life for me. I wanted to be me. I know you thought that a baby might make everything okay, but it didn't. Not even a bit. I knew if I came home with you both, I'd be trapped, possibly forever. It's best for you both that I went when I did, a chance for everyone to have the life that was meant for them. You included. This is kindest.

Rosie couldn't even begin to conceive of abandoning her children the way Laurel had abandoned her, but she was beginning to understand what her mum meant about everyone needing the chance to have the life that was meant for them. Raising the note to her mouth, she kissed it before putting it back in the envelope and tucking it into her charity-shop handbag.

Her phone buzzed. A text from Mo.

Bench time?

Rosie read and reread the message, then raced into the kitchen, where her mother-in-law was washing up mugs in the sink. 'Where's your phone?' she asked.

Mo turned to her. She spoke slowly, deliberately. 'I lent it to someone.'

Rosie raised her shaking hand to her mouth and began to cry.

'This is no time for tears.' Mo walked over to her and put her arms around her. 'You have to be strong, my girl.'

'I was so upset, Mo, when you knitted that jacket for Gerri. I thought she'd replaced me and losing you was just as hard as losing everything else. I thought you were mad at me.'

Mo released her from her grip and stood back, facing her. 'I was mad at you! But not because of Phil. He can make his own bed. As much as I love him and, God knows, I do, he's a grown man, a spoilt one at that. He needs to learn, he needs to step up to the plate and be the best dad he can, that's all that matters.' She took a deep breath. 'No, my love, I was mad at you on Kev's behalf. That boy has worshipped you since you were young and I wanted you to wake up and see that, not hurt him more! When he came back here and told me he had to leave again, miss Christmas...' She shook her head at the memory. 'I will never forget his face, and I couldn't get over the bloody stupid waste of it all!'

'Oh, Mo!'

'Don't "Oh, Mo" me!' She threw her car keys at her. 'Get off to that bench and start your next chapter, Rosie, my girl.'

Rosie jumped in the little Renault and sped along the lane until the Esplanade was in her sights. She parked haphazardly and ran up the grassy incline until her bench came into view. Suddenly self-conscious, she raked her fingers through her hair and wiped her cheeks and mouth. She walked slowly to the seat, where he was sitting with his legs stretched out, crossed at the ankles. His long, blonde, sun-kissed hair and his tan made his teeth and eyes look bright.

'You see, that's the thing about your one,' he began, still looking out to sea. 'Sometimes you have to fight for them. Sometimes you have to fight and wait, hoping and trusting that one day all the planets will align and it will be like a moment of realisation when everything falls into place and they finally realise that you are their one too.' He stood up and took a step towards her until they were only inches apart.

'Why should I believe you?' she whispered.

'You shouldn't. You should believe your own instinct – trust it. You know it's you and me. Kev and Rosie, Rosie and Kev. You *know* it.'

'I do,' she admitted, and it felt good.

'I will always fight for you, Rosie Watson. Always. I have no choice; you are my one.' He smiled, took her in his arms and drew her towards him. 'Oh God, no! Not the ugly crying thing again! We really need to work on that.' He pulled away and kissed her gently on the mouth.

'I look horrible now.' She touched her scars.

'You could never look horrible to me. I love you,' he whispered, in a way that sounded as if he'd been saying it for years.

'I love you too,' she managed through her tears.

'Don't cry! I've got you now and I'm not going to let you go. Not ever again.'

Epilogue

She lay on the folded vintage quilts that lined the bottom of the boat, letting the rocking motion gently soothe her. The green/blue water was quite hypnotic. Fish jumped and splashed, breaking the surface and sending tiny ripples that gently rocked the flat bottomed fishing boat. It was so peaceful. This was possibly her favourite time of the day, as the sun began losing its heat in the late-afternoon shadow. She closed her eyes in a semi-doze, completely lost to the paradise in which she found herself. She ran her fingers over the warm, broad mahogany deck and smiled at the sound of a ring pull being released on a cold tin of beer.

He blocked the sun, as he bent over and kissed her forehead. 'Are you sleeping?' he asked, wary of disturbing her.

'No, just thinking, dozing.' She stretched her arms over her head, her t-shirt rising up to reveal her flat, tanned tum.

'Good, because we've got fish to prepare. They aren't

going to cook themselves, you know. And it looks like the barbecue is just about ready.' He shielded his eyes and squinted at the pebble-strewn bank forty feet away, where a thin wisp of smoke rose from the charcoal pit they had prepared.

'Just five more minutes. It's so peaceful,' she whispered. Her hand held the cold tin against her stomach.

Kev gathered up her long hair and coiled it around his hand. 'I've always loved your hair.'

'You've always loved all of me.' She opened one eye and peered at the man who had always been there for her.

'That's true, Rosie Watson, I have. By the way, Mrs Mackenzie called. She wanted to know if you've organised their boat trip?'

'Yep, all done, and their flights home. I'm efficient, you know! And I think I deserve at least one day off!'

The online travel agency, Woolacombe-Willamette was going from strength to strength. She and Clark had a thriving clientele; indeed she sent many people to holiday in the glorious cabin that they were staying in, situated among the tall trees on the wide bend of the Willamette river and he in turn sent walkers and surfers to Woolacombe where they could choose from charming B&B's, snazzy hotels and the new, fabulous 'glamping' experience that she had talked Doug into. It was bringing in a small fortune! She had identified a niche market of people who yearned to go travelling but weren't interested in the mass tourist experience. She knew all the small details that would assuage their nerves and give them confidence; little things, like identifying someone locally who spoke their language, instructions on how to phone home and the best place for a cup of tea. Their business was thriving, which meant she had been able to pay Shona and Keith and Mo back. It had felt good.

'Are you going to miss this?' she asked, raising her palm at the dense variegated forest that edged the broad river, the glorious big sky where a variety of multi-coloured Finches darted and the majestic Mount Hood stood grandly on the horizon. In just two weeks they would be back in the rat race.

'Are you kidding me? I rather like the position of Senior Lecturer in Marine Biology. I think it suits me!'

'Exeter Uni is lucky to have you.'

'And the best thing is, I get to come home to you every night. And I get to set up my train set, get all my vinyl out, put my pictures on the walls. I can't wait!' He smiled.

The novelty of their new home, a shiny modern flat on the sea front with a glorious terrace, didn't seem to be waning. Soon after they had bought it, Rosie had arrived home to a letter, lying on the welcome mat:

Dear Rosie,

This is a hard letter to write. My name is Jo. I live near Salisbury with my husband Martin, a soldier, and two step children, Peg and Max. My mum passed away a little while ago and I have just discovered that we might be related. I hope this isn't too much of a shock, but I think we may be sisters! My mum's name was Laurel. A rather glorious name I always thought...

Rosie had replied, cautiously at first, but gradually gaining confidence as her new half-sister proved to be a funny, warm woman who was just as happy as Rosie was to take their new-found relationship slowly. They still had not met in person, but the plan was to get fish and chips together soon after Rosie returned from her honeymoon.

Rosie smiled at her man.

'You're right – going home from here won't be too bad will it? We get to go to spend the weekends on Woolacombe beach.'

'We can go snogging in the sand dunes!' He waggled his eyebrows.

'Snogging? What are we fourteen?' she laughed; secretly delighted that he viewed her in this way.

'We can double-date with Phil and Mrs Blackmore's granddaughter!' he joked.

'Don't! I still can't get over it – she's at least ten years younger than him. But as long as she makes him happy.' Rosie bore no malice towards her ex-husband and was genuine in her desire for his happiness.

'She does, for now. But I wouldn't go buying a new hat just yet.' Kev winked.

Suddenly, the peace was shattered.

'Mum! Mum! Kev!' The yell came from the entrance to the cabin.

'What is it?' Rosie sat up.

Naomi scrambled to the shoreline, hopping up and down in her swimming costume. 'Leo has put a little pebble up her nose and I can't get it down.'

Kev jumped up. 'She's what?'

'She's put the pebble up her nose!' she screeched.

'What pebble, Nay?' Rosie asked calmly.

'The cute, little round one we found on the bank. It's up her right nostril, which is her nose hole.' She clarified this for Kev's benefit, in case he was unaware.

'I know I'm going to regret asking, but what is up her left nose hole?' Rosie held her breath and tied her hair into a knot at the base of her neck.

'Nothing, Mum, we're not stupid!' She tutted. 'She's sitting under the table.'

'Of course she is.'

Kev snorted his laughter and raised his eyebrows at his girls.

Rosie adjusted her shorts and climbed overboard into the shallow water. Naomi rushed forward.

'Don't worry, we've got it all under control. It's all going to be fine.' She looked back at her man, and smiled, as her daughter grabbed her hand and led her through the water.